Alys Larsson

Denise McGahan

ANSTICE

Press

Published in the United Kingdom by Anstice Press in 2022

Paperback ISBN: 978-1-7396591-3-4
eBook ISBN: 978-1-7396591-2-7

For John, Harry, Niamh and Charlie.

'Until 45 I can play a woman in love. After 55 I can play grandmothers. But between those ten years, it is difficult for an actress.'

Ingrid Bergman

Chapter 1

Socks

Winter

Alys had lost track of time again. She shifted, and her bottom dragged along the bottom of the bath, making a sound like a tuba. The water had turned cold. She knew she ought to get out, but couldn't think of anything she wanted to get out for. She hooked her toes around the old hot tap, but it was too stiff to budge. Instead, the cold tap started to drip solemnly, like a bell tolling for lost souls, for the passing of time.

The opening of the tap was an oval shape with a slight dent in its side, making it look like an ear. She listened for a while to the plock of each drop hitting the surface of the water, then she absently inserted her right big toe into the ear-tap.

She let her head slip further underwater until she could hear her own heartbeat and the whale song of her body's movements, her leg slightly lifted and pointed like a ballet dancer in third position. Her thoughts drifted back to the morning, and she felt again that slap of humiliation that had followed her home and driven her to run a bath. No matter how furiously she had scrubbed her skin, she was still tarred with the shame of it.

The day had started harmlessly. She had taken the morning off to get her IUD refitted. The doctor, a brisk Scottish woman, had brought with her a young medical student who, she'd informed Alys, would be observing the procedure. Alys had quelled a flutter of alarm at the sight of the nervous young man who could not meet her eye. She had not been given the option of saying, 'I'd rather not,' and in any case, she hadn't wanted to hurt his feelings.

Behind the curtain, she shed her trousers and knickers, arranged herself on the table and spread a paper sheet over her bare stomach. The gentle slope of her raised knees rose up like twin peaks and she tried to settle herself, feeling absurdly like a virgin on her wedding night. Too late, she realised that she had left her socks on and she was caught up in a panicked tussle trying to take them off—or should she leave them on?—when the curtain swooshed back to reveal the doctor snapping on a pair of floury gloves and the medical student holding a tray carrying what looked like a lollipop stick and a shoehorn.

'You go up to the top end please, Ed. I'm just going to ask you a few questions before we get started, Mrs Larsson.' Her voice rose when she spoke to Alys, as if she were a little deaf.

Ed sidled alongside her with a nervous smile. He kept his eyes on Alys's forehead as he learned that she had not had sex with her husband in the last seven days (when was the last time?), and that she had not had sex with anyone other than her husband recently. The question surprised her. How many women confessed to having had sex with men other than their husbands?

Ed's skin was pasty and moist, as if he had been wearing stage make-up under the lights for too long. The side of his nose was slick with grease and Alys resisted an urge to blot it with the corner of her paper protector. If he was to learn anything, he should be standing down by her socks with the doctor, but the grease on his nose kept her silent.

'Put your feet together and drop your knees open when you're ready,' the doctor chirruped, negotiating the entrance to Alys with the lollipop stick. Alys tried not to imagine the view that would greet the doctor as she ratcheted her open —a vast cantilevered cathedral. No, more likely the open cavity of a chicken carcass. 'Ah yes, I can see the strings,' came a muffled voice.

There was a sharp slick of pain and the thing was away from her. It was displayed to them on a silver salver. She was delivered of a wishbone, her blood splattered on it. She felt more naked showing Ed that blood than she did with her legs spread in front of the doctor.

'I'll just get your new one ready,' the doctor said.

Alys suddenly started and closed her knees together. 'No.'

'I beg your pardon?'

'No, thank you. That's enough. I don't want it.'

The doctor looked down at her from the long length of the table.

'You do realise, Mrs Larsson, there's still a risk of getting pregnant, even at your age?'

'And with your non-existent sex life' hung between them.

Alys shook her head. 'It would be a waste.'

The doctor sighed and tore the curtain across with barely concealed irritation.

As she dragged on her clothes, Alys could hear the doctor showing Ed in closer detail the thing that had been lodged inside her for five years with her blood on it. He asked quietly about the speculum he should use and the doctor proffered the lollipop stick and dissuaded him of the shoehorn. She whispered something, and Alys knew that she was talking about her.

When she got back in her car and fastened her seat belt, her hands were shaking. She placed them on the steering wheel and rested her forehead on her trembling fingers. She couldn't say what had upset her so, only that she been left feeling dirty, ashamed of herself—ashamed of her age, her sagging body, the absurdity of her—those socks—yes, that was it. It was the socks. She was a joke. An old embarrassment. Undesirable, thrown away. Even at your age... Tears didn't come, just a tightness in her chest, and after a few minutes she rallied herself and drove home. She made herself a sweet tea and ran the bath and, after the furious scrubbing had finally subsided, she resigned herself to the water and tuned out.

It was at this point that she realised that her toe joint was firmly wedged in the tap. It had begun to ache and her foot was cramping. She felt a frisson of alarm. A wiggle of her leg confirmed that she was well and truly stuck and sent a small tidal wave of water lapping over the side of the bath. The fronds of her pubic hair waved from side to side in the choppy water: *Au secours!*

When her husband Jack returned home two hours later, he had to break down the door. Alys was stiff with cold, trying to curb the juddering that shook through her in case it set off the cramp in her leg again.

'Why did you lock the bloody door?' He loomed over her prone form, his hands on his hips.

She tried to stretch a flannel over herself, but couldn't decide whether she'd rather cover her breasts or her distressed pubic hair.

'What were you doing in the bath in the middle of the afternoon, anyway? Why didn't you go to work? Are you sick? Oh, for Christ's sake, Al. It's a bit late for modesty. I've seen it all before.'

She opted for the breasts. She had forgotten to call work.

'I was thinking.' Her voice surprised her when it came out. It was shaky and small. 'I think better in the bath.'

'Well, you obviously didn't think about extricating yourself, did you? Why didn't you use the soap and work your toe out?'

'I can't reach it from where I am.'

He eyed the solid ham of her thigh and the swell of her stomach that domed out between her and the soap. She shifted the flannel lower.

He knelt in a puddle of water, swore, adjusted his position, and then cradled the heel of her foot in his hand. Her stomach tightened. With his other fingers, he worked the soap in between the ear-tap and her toe. His warm fingertips were unexpectedly tender as he held the curve of her ankle, gently manipulating her foot to free her. All too soon, her toe slipped out of the tap and her numb leg crashed back into the water, splashing him and he was up on his feet, rubbing his glasses with his shirt and grimacing myopically at her. 'You'd better dry yourself off.'

Chapter 2

Borderlands

Later, standing in front of the open fridge door, Alys found that she could not warm up, nor could she come to a decision about what to cook for dinner. The shrink-wrapped, plastic trays of meat reminded her of a morgue.

She'd once read an article about a man whose job it was to manage a body farm. Unclaimed corpses were transferred to the 100-acre enclosure and left in various conditions—open ground, boggy ditches—so that rates of decomposition could be observed. They had terrible problems with stray cats and dogs who managed to break into the compound and eat the evidence. The dogs were alright, the man said, they'd chew on a knuckle or an elbow but the cats... the cats were something else. They feasted on the soft parts, the eyelids and lips. She perused the pallid flab of a quartet of chicken breasts and closed the door.

She served salad to a set of raised eyebrows. She might as well have slapped her husband with a wet fish.

'I see you haven't had time to cook because you've been

busy thinking.' Jack forked a piece of lettuce into the side of his mouth and chewed savagely.

'To be honest, I thought salad might make a nice change.' She shrugged. 'Having to prepare dinner every night is... sometimes I run out of inspiration.'

'Yeah, I got that. Nothing says, "I can't be arsed" quite like a salad.' Jack had spent the last hour trying to rehang the bathroom door. He was not in the mood for a cold supper. Pushing his plate aside, he snatched the bottle of wine and his glass and headed to his study.

Alys set down her fork. She was too cold for salad. She should have made a stew or a soup. She scraped the salad into a bowl – it would do for tomorrow, no sense wasting it. Her joints ached when she stood up. Every part of her was chilled to the bone, except for her foot where those warm fingers had curled around her heel.

Her gaze drifted over the kitchen. Subdued lighting illuminated shelves lined with jars and crocks of coloured pulses, nuts, and handmade spice mixes. She found the array of earthy pigments comforting. In one corner teetered a stack of well-worn cookbooks, one of her little library clusters around the house. In another, a clattering of carefully tended herbs jostled for attention. In her eyes, it was a welcoming space, or as welcoming as this house allowed for. Wincing as her right foot took her weight, she limped to the sink. A hot supper might make amends. She would make his favourite.

This was the first house they had lived in together, and in the heady months after their honeymoon, it quickly became apparent that Jack and Alys had entirely different ideas of what a perfect home should look like. Jack favoured minimalism, sleek lines, state-of-the-art technology and 'design-led spaces'. Alys wasn't sure that her particular style had a name, but it involved a homely clutter of good things; treasures that told their story and held memories. 'Life is too rich not to have drawers,' she had argued. In the end, when compromise still amused them, they decided to apportion rooms to each other. She had the kitchen, a spare bedroom for her craft room, and the garden. He took the living room, the dining room for client entertaining, and the library-cum-study, although he never read for pleasure and the expensive bookcases he'd bought at auction had arrived filled with antique volumes he never touched. Alys resented the annexation of the library, but resigned herself to finding dark corners to house her own book collection.

They split the master bedroom down the middle, like those houses that are built on the borderline between countries—in their case, Italy and Austria. Alys's side had unwieldy totem poles of unread paperbacks and piles of clothes that were not quite ready for the wash, small trinkets collected from her rambles, and handmade items; perfume bottles, fresh flowers, photos, and her collection of small wooden boxes. The stark emptiness of Jack's side of the room was a barren wasteland. He had taken over another room as his dressing room. On the rare occasion that she threw a vacuum cleaner around it, Alys sometimes pried open the wardrobes to peek at the rows of expensive identical suits lined up like robotic avatars. She tried to imagine him walking to Chambers with his briefcase in hand, one of those sleeves bent at the elbow to hold his phone to his ear.

Absentmindedly swigging from a bottle of ale, she whisked up a cheese sauce, sharing some of the ale with the pan as she went. She made a Welsh rarebit, nursing it under the grill until it was dark and bubbling. Melted cheese oozed as she cut the bread on the diagonal and arranged it on a plate with a garnish of watercress she had plucked from the salad.

Careful not to let the toast slide from the plate, she knocked hesitantly on the study door. He had his head down over a file, the wine bottle empty at his feet, and he looked up distractedly as she skirted the room and edged across to him.

'Sorry.' She slipped the plate onto his desk, taking care not to touch any of his papers.

He slumped back in his chair and rubbed at his eyes under his glasses.

'Why do you always apologise when I'm the one being a shit, Alys?'

He motioned her to sit and passed her his glass. She perched on one of the uncomfortable chairs that lined his study and took a sip of wine, unsure of how to answer the question. She bit back another apology.

He sighed. 'I'm sorry I was an arse. It's been a tough day and Lincoln's been on my back all week. I've got a mountain of work to get through before this hearing on Friday. I wasn't banking on having to break into my own bathroom tonight on top of everything. It just tipped me over the edge.'

'I should have made you something more substantial. Sorry. It's just that so often you eat out at lunch and don't want to eat in the evening.' She had lost count of how many nights she had cooked for them, left dinner warming, waited for him before she ate, only to find that he had already eaten.

'No, this is perfect, thank you.'

He devoured the Welsh rarebit in large gulps. She watched as his bottom lip grew slick with grease. He wiped his mouth, leaving a snail trail across the back of his hand.

'So what happened to you today? Why didn't you make it into work?'

She hadn't told him about her appointment. It felt like something that should be done behind closed doors, or tent flaps, between women with kohl-rimmed eyes. Besides, she hadn't wanted to bring all that up again. 'I didn't feel well.'

He nodded, his eyes still on his plate. She wasn't sure if he'd heard her.

Framed photos flanked the smooth walnut desk, a present from Jack's father on their marriage. There was a photo of a young Jack covered in mud and blood being held aloft on the shoulders of his running team. Beside it rested a group portrait of the Larsson family, taken on Jack and Alys's wedding day, of Jack, his three brothers, Linus, Otto and Eric and his parents, a solemn looking Hannah and Tom. On the other side of the desk, a picture of Lincoln, Jack's instructing solicitor and 'business partner' caught her eye. Jack and Lincoln were standing with their arms around each other outside Nobu, celebrating their first win. If the proper order were being observed, someone as beautiful and successful as Jack would never be mismatched with someone as plain as Alys. She didn't deserve him. Sometimes, she feared that she would wake to find herself alone, and she had only imagined this man with his crisp cotton shirt and his broad shoulders.

A few Christmases ago, she had given him her own photo to add to the collection. It was a beautiful picture of Alys sitting on Jack's lap and laughing into his neck, taken on holiday in Antigua where Lincoln had persuaded them to join him on a last-minute getaway. It wasn't the best photo of either of them, but they looked happy and relaxed, and it had made her smile. She had never seen it again, and couldn't bring herself to ask what he had done with it.

'So, what case are you working on?' she ventured.

'The stalker on sexual assault charges.'

'Did he do it?'

He looked amused. 'Does it matter?'

She pondered this for a moment. 'It does to me.'

'And that's why you'd never make a barrister.' He ruffled her hair, and she thought of the grease on the back of his hand and the grease on the side of Ed's nose, and had to concentrate very hard on not pulling away.

'Actually, I could eat another of those.' Jack reached absently for the plate as his eyes went back to the page.

He didn't look up when she placed a second sandwich on the desk beside him and retreated backwards, as if taking her leave of a visiting dignitary. She stopped when she got to the door to watch him at his work. Alys liked to catch him unawares. She liked to watch her beautiful husband and marvel that he belonged with her, that no one else in the world was his wife.

Chapter 3

Miss Marple

'Alys. You'll be late,' Jack bellowed from the shower.

'Up! I'm up!' When the bathroom door flew open, Alys jumped out of bed and began to rummage through her clothes as if she'd been waiting for him to finish. She kept out of his way as he went through his morning routine, only going downstairs when she heard the front door slam.

Half an hour later, she emerged from the garage, having successfully inched her bicycle past the sleek flank of the sports car that Jack had bought her last Christmas to replace the one he'd bought her the year before. She tried to ignore it whenever possible.

Her preferred mode of transport was her beloved bicycle, Miss Marple. Jack could never fathom her affection for her, but Alys had won her in a raffle when she was fifteen and had basked in that good fortune ever since. Miss Marple took her along the village green, which marked the end of the better part of town. They sped up past The Rising Sun pub with its bright yellow door and thatched roof, towards the high street where Alys worked. From here, she could just make out The Granary at the edge of the old copse on the outskirts of the village. The original farmhouse had long since burnt down, but the remaining outbuilding was home to Alys's favourite place in the world, the village bookshop. The thought of the bookshop's owner, Enid Frew, brought a smile to her face as she reached Seagull Publishing and turned down the side of the building to the small carpark behind it. Hers was the only bicycle ever to grace the bike rack in the carpark. She locked Miss Marple to the railings and absently gave her pat as she passed into the building through the back entrance. This always gave her pause, a brief stutter in the fabric of time, for in a strange twist of fate Seagull Publishing had taken over the building that once housed her father's gift shop, and Alys could not help the flood of memory whenever she stepped over the threshold. In other times, this entrance would have led to the stockroom, full of hideous carriage clocks in the shape of owls and pearlised figurines in crinoline dresses. Now the stockroom was a large cloak room and stationery cupboard. All signs of her father's shop had been expunged, erased, as if Ian Faulkener had never existed. She was still thinking about whether she minded this when she reached her desk.

As befitted a junior proof-reader, Alys's desk languished in a corner with no access to natural light, and on the edge of the thoroughfare between the kitchen and the main floor. It was set at an angle so that it could fit in the corner, which meant that people were forever banging into it, sending her manuscripts flying and creating paper storms that Alys was left to clear up. She had briefly tried to keep that half of her desk clear, forcing her to work even further into the corner, but this had the unforeseen consequence of creating a natural way station where people could continue conversations started in the kitchen. Some colleagues even had the temerity to perch on her desk as they chatted, blocking out what little light there was. Alys had taken to wearing noise-cancelling earphones so that she could concentrate on her manuscripts, which made her at once inaccessible and isolated. She had had the same job and the same desk since she joined. It had never occurred to her to request a transfer.

She fended off Jack's queries about career advancement whenever they came up. He occasionally threatened to 'have words' with Tim Parish, the managing director. These idle threats never materialised into anything more than the odd glower in Tim's direction at the annual Staff and Family Christmas Drinks. Alys suspected that Jack secretly preferred things to remain as they were. How would they have coped if both had high-powered, demanding careers? She had been content to take the back step in preparation for her role as a hands-on mother. When that time had passed, she reasoned that she had never been the ambitious type, anyway. Besides, she liked the work she did. She knew what to do and what was expected of her. She was left in peace, which suited her fine.

There was an unusual amount of chatter emanating from the kitchen that morning, and Alys had to squeeze into the tiny space to make her morning coffee.

'You're cutting it fine.' Candace, Tim's secretary, was furiously stirring a low-cal hot chocolate whilst making Tim's usual, a Lapsang souchong, with her left hand.

'I'm sorry?' Alys lent over the smoke-scented steam from the tea and noted that once again her cup had been left to languish in the washing-up bowl with what looked like baked-on oxtail soup around its rim. The mug had been a present from her best friend, Douglas, and had a large sprawling 'Alys' etched on the side to deter people from taking it. She poured some hot water into the bowl and began to sponge off the grime.

'Big day, today! Don't pretend you didn't remember, Alys!' Candace reminded her of a secretary bird. She was tall, with long skinny legs that went all the way up to her groin without touching each other. Her nose was long and hooked, and she had close-set dark eyes with very long false eyelashes. This was Alys's private joke to herself, because Candace meant well and was sensitive about the nose.

Alys shook her head and reached for the tea towel, taking a cautious sniff at her mug. It smelled like gravy. She would have to keep it on her desk from now on. People would think she was petty, but there it was.

'Honestly! I sometimes think it's like you live in your books and not in the real world. You're so funny.' Candace's laugh was disconcerting. It set her head jerking as if she were furiously pecking at seeds.

'Today is the day that our new finance director joins the team,' she trilled. 'And it's our Team Wellbeing Day, which starts in the boardroom in ten minutes. The facilitator's already here. You'll only just have time for your coffee.'

Alys groaned. Tim had perched on Alys's desk at closing time the Friday before to ask her to be the new woman's 'buddy' for her first week. Tim was a passionate advocate of skip-level engagement at Seagull as part of its flat hierarchy. He attributed Seagull's success to the strength of the relationships across the organisation and was relentless in his efforts to pair unlikely combinations of staff to man his pet projects. The Team Wellbeing Day was the hideous brainchild of the sales and marketing director and the cleaner. It was unclear why Tim had given Alys the task of buddying with the new finance woman, whose name Alys could neither pronounce nor spell. Alys did not consider herself particularly friendly, and since most of her colleagues had long since given up on her, she knew that the finance woman would soon come to appreciate that Alys was not best placed to induct her. It would take less than an hour, Alys estimated, for her to realise that she had been saddled with the least popular girl at school, the nerd in the corner.

Chapter 4

Joy

'Welcome to our Team Wellbeing Day!' Tim slapped his hands together and rubbed them heartily, as if to suggest that whatever was coming was going to be wholesome and fun. The entire staff at Seagull Publishing had been squeezed into the largest of the meeting rooms and were still trying to settle themselves in chairs placed too closely together as Tim began his opening speech. 'I've spared no expense and we're very lucky to have a wellbeing expert and facilitator, Nathalie Borthwick, with us today to show us the ropes with this wellbeing malarkey.' His smile faltered and his Adam's apple worked up and down. 'I'd like your full attention for what promises to be a very valuable experience. I'm sure it will be of huge benefit to us.' He flailed a long, bony arm—all elbow and fingers—towards Nathalie and strode purposely to a seat at the back of the room. Within seconds, he was on his phone, texting furiously.

In stark contrast to the casual dishevelment of her audience, Nathalie was wearing a royal blue dress, tight as a stocking, and black stilettos. Her hairline started towards the crown of her head and her hair fell in stiff, black folds over her shoulders. Someone muttered behind Alys, 'She looks like a Klingon going to a wedding.'

'Welcome. Good morning. How are you all?' Nathalie cast an unblinking stare across the room and smiled widely. Alys stole a look at her colleagues and tried to view them as Nathalie Borthwick might. The sales and marketing director, Valerie, was sitting on the edge of her seat, fizzing with enthusiasm and readiness. She was wearing a top in the exact same shade of blue as Nathalie, as if she had called in advance to ask what she'd be wearing. A quick glimpse at Margaret, the cleaner, slumped in her chair with her arms folded, confirmed Alys's suspicion that this had not been a wholly collaborative effort. The three editors, Michael, Joe and Elsa sat huddled in one corner in a fug of alarm and scepticism. The proof-reader, Edgar, looked annoyed to be pulled away from his work pile. His personal hygiene left a lot to be desired, and so he sat in a clearing, people manoeuvring their seats to sit upwind of him. Candace had trained her eyes on Nathalie's face, but was rummaging in her oversized bag, trying to retrieve what might have been a dried mango slice from a freezer bag without the plastic rustling. She looked like a mime artist. The noise was deafening. Nathalie gazed at Candace until the rustling stopped, and then she smiled again.

'Let's all set down our bags and phones, our literal and figurative baggage, and take a deep breath in and then drop our shoulders.'

Alys could not take her eyes off Nathalie. The woman had not blinked since she'd taken to the floor. She must be Klingon. Her mind began to wander. In the background, she caught the phrase 'your best self' and 'optimal flourishing' and then let herself slip away to a Star Trek episode that explored the rather vigorous protocol that governed Klingon courtship rituals.

Suddenly, the door flew open, banging the wall behind, and the new finance woman bustled in. She was late on her first day, but offered no apology. She was dressed as if she were about to go skiing, buffered against the cold in an aqua puffa jacket.

'Good morning. You're very welcome...?' Nathalie said urbanely.

'Mairéad Doran.'

Ah. Alys silently rolled the pronunciation over her lips.

The woman ignored the glare of Nathalie's smile and cast an eye around the room. Without breaking stride, she made a beeline for Alys and sat down heavily next to her, her coat puffing out over Alys's arm. 'You need a journal,' Alys whispered, motioning over to one seat along. 'Right.' Mairéad hauled herself and her bag over to the next seat. She took some time to settle, oblivious to the group's stares. Her huge bag gaped open, revealing a sheaf of papers and a half-squeezed tube of hydrocortisone. Alys glanced sideways and took in auburn hair scraped back in a short, thin ponytail. It looked not greasy, but sticky. A kirby grip had been scraped up the side of her head, exposing a slice of naked scalp.

A huge, red stain spread across her face and into the hair at her nape. It was raised as if someone had laid a map of the world across her. It looked tight and sore. Over her cheeks, a network of tiny red veins fanned out and joined the stain, like tributaries. She wore thick, brown framed glasses, but took these off to read the journal, grimacing as she squinted, baring lips to show small teeth that slanted inwards.

'Mairéad, the team have just finished answering the check-in questions at the front of their journal, on page three. You might want to take a moment to note your own responses.'

Without looking at Nathalie, Mairéad flipped pages and her fingers reached out and made a pincering movement in mid-air. Caught off-guard, Alys placed her own biro into her hand and shrank back as Mairéad scrawled a comment and handed her the pen. Surreptitiously wiping it across her sleeve, Alys kept her eyes down, reluctant to meet that gaze head on. She noticed Mairéad's feet—tiny, doll-like.

Alys glanced at the questions. 'What did she hope to get out of the day?' *To get through it as quickly as possible*, she thought and wrote 'Balance'. What baggage would she have to leave at the door in order to be fully present? *My life.* 'My emails.' They were encouraged to discuss their responses in small groups and then share back themes in the main room. Almost immediately, Mairéad took control of their group, as self-appointed spokeswoman for the remainder who had already settled into a collective slump of acquiescence and lethargy. She had a clipped authoritative voice that carried with it expectation and disapproval. Having stuttered through her own responses, Alys was fascinated by her. How could someone who bore that face, that voice, be so forthright, so confident, so sure of herself? She must have been an only child. To elderly parents. The woman didn't even know their names, and yet she had effortlessly assumed a leadership role. The team seemed equally mesmerised by her, caught between repulsion and awe, their eyes drawn against their will to her face, straining each time she opened the cavernous bag to see what it contained.

At lunch, they went across the road to the local cafe, where a table had been reserved for them. Tim and Nathalie took up a small table across the room from them, where a platter of sandwiches had been set out. In a side-whisper, Candace explained that they had to buy their own lunches, because Nathalie Borthwick had cost a 'bloody fortune' and there was nothing left in the kitty for the rest of them. Alys thought ruefully of her packed lunch under her desk. Ahead of her in the queue, Mairéad squinted furiously over her glasses as she sifted through her change, nosing through the coins in her palm. The boy on the till wore a pained expression as he looked down at the top of her sticky head. Alys felt a wave of pity for her and knew instinctively that this would not be welcome to Mairéad. Watching her, Alys understood that Mairéad wasn't oblivious to people's reactions. Her refusal to acknowledge the furrowed brows and wrinkled noses was her way of shutting out their distaste. Alys admired her self-containment and how the woman inhabited an island of her own making. Still, she couldn't bring herself to talk to her when they settle back into their chairs. She busied herself with rereading the journal, making small notes in the margin, experiencing a flicker of satisfaction on finding a spelling mistake in Nathalie's text. She wanted to go home.

As the day wore on, the scratching started. First Mairéad's neck began to bother her and she resorted to the tube in the bag, slathering a thick layer of cream into her hair line and massaging it furiously, not quite a scratch, but strong enough to punish. Then the hand-rubbing started. Desperate to itch, but perhaps abiding by some childhood edict, Mairéad wrung her hands over and over again until

Alys had to shift in her seat to move her out of her line of vision and yet still, she could barely pay attention to Nathalie, her ear picking up the rasping of tortured skin.

Too late, she realised that Nathalie had asked her a question. Tim was looking expectantly at her.

'I'm sorry?'

'That's ok. Alys, is it?' Alys's name badge had rotated upside down and when Nathalie tilted her head to read it, her hair stayed where it was. 'I was just asking the group what brings you joy? We are sharing our examples of when we last felt joyful.'

'I... I'm not sure what you mean.' There was a titter in the room. The rasping beside her ceased.

'Which part is unclear?' Nathalie's smile was brittle. It was evident that she had been aware of how little Alys had attended to in her session. Alys felt an old tug of shame. Caught day-dreaming again.

When she opened her mouth, she heard herself confess, 'I don't know what you mean by "joy".'

Someone said 'Christ!' and the room exploded into laughter.

'I mean, do you mean, like happiness?' She cut across them. 'When do I feel happy? Or do you mean something bigger than that? Because joy to me feels like it ought to be the peak, something that transports you. You know, the most you can feel. More than an everyday sort of experience.'

'When did you last feel alive?' Nathalie countered.

Alive? Alys held her breath. There was a rushing in her ears and the skin on her face prickled. The room fell silent. Time stretched between them. After an interminable silence, Nathalie gave a small nod and released Alys like a pent-up sigh. The conversation moved on and Alys did what she always did when faced with something unpleasant that she didn't want to confront. She imagined herself as a small bird and flew up into a tree. She didn't hear another word.

When the day mercifully drew to a close, Mairéad packed up her journal, shouldered on her aqua coat, and walked to the exit without a glance behind, ignoring Tim who was trying to catch her. At the door, she turned to fix that stare on Alys. She called across the heads of the whole team, 'Alys. Coffee. Tomorrow. First thing.'

Chapter 5

Small Things

Alys was still wondering at Mairéad's assurance as she took a kitchen knife to the stalactites that grew inexplicably from the ceiling of her freezer later that evening. Jack would be home late and she was trying to liberate a meal for herself. How did someone like Mairéad become so self-assured?

She carried a cup of tea up to her craft room, turned on the lamps and lit a candle, then settled into her armchair by the window. This was her sanctuary. The smallest room in the house, smaller even than Jack's dressing room, it was full of Alys's craft projects. The walls were lined with long shelves that housed skeins and balls of multi-coloured wool, linen and silk, arranged in colourways in a giant rainbow arcing across the wall. There were books on crafts, pots of utensils—crochet hooks, rug hooks, seam rippers, a small dish of thimbles, a pincushion in the shape of an opera singer, whose skirts were covered in needles and whose open mouth could have been screaming rather than singing. But the altarpiece of the whole room was a small table under the window beside Alys's battered armchair. Here were displayed Alys's works of art: a collection of tiny items, hand-crafted from found things or precious collectibles. To Alys, they were small objects of beauty. She had made angels, owls, acorns, a throne—much like her own chair but twisted from the cork wire from the champagne she had drunk on her wedding night. Beside the owls, there were foxes and hares, a tiny swallow, a badger. Each object had taken Alys days to perfect. Inspired by things she found in the park or in vintage shops, she found satisfaction in making them as true to life and as complex as their tiny size would allow. The most difficult of them had at times given her headaches, swollen fingers, and eyestrain. She couldn't have said why she made them.

She picked up her latest project—a birthday present for her best friend, Douglas. She had always loved the story he told about how he got his name. His mother had named him Douglas for Douglas Fairbanks, the actor. His father had agreed because he thought she was thinking of Douglas Bader, the British flying ace that he had idolised when he was growing up. Alys's Douglas, liked to say that he was fond of his name because though old-fashioned, it reminded him of how two highly incompatible people had managed to stay married by wilfully ignoring their differences.

She was making a tiny Douglas; the second of two mini-Douglas's, although the real Douglas wouldn't turn fifty-one until September, so she had seven months to finish them. She was working on Douglas-as-Douglas-Fairbanks. She had stitched the face to look like the actor, but had kept her Douglas's large brown eyes, and these gazed steadily out at her from under bushy black eyebrows in that trusting way they always did. Douglas-as-Douglas-Bader, was standing perkily towards the back of the table, wearing his flying jacket with its high collar and sporting a pipe. His left hand was held out to the side. Alys would make him a plane out of a Portuguese sardine tin she'd been hoarding, and his hand would eventually rest on its side, but that would have to wait until Douglas-as-Douglas-Fairbanks was finished.

It was quiet in her room and she sipped her tea, and from time to time sang a short burst of an old song she remembered Enid singing to her once. She picked up each of her tiny objects and turned them in her hands, as if greeting an old friend.

'This gives me joy,' she told a miniature bear she had fashioned out of a scrap from an old yellow coat of Jack's. 'What do you think, Yellowstone Bear? Does that make me a weirdo?'

'No, but talking to them does.'

Alys jumped in her chair and tea sloshed over the side of her cup.

'Jack!'

Jack was resting up against the doorframe, his face a mixture of amusement and strain.

'I didn't hear you come in. How long have you been standing there?' *Had he heard her singing?*

'Long enough. Tough day?'

'How did you guess?'

'You always come up here to commune with your little friends when something's troubling you.'

Alys considered this. She carefully set Yellowstone Bear down alongside Douglas-as-Douglas Bader so that the flailing left hand reached across the bear's shoulder, then she rose and ushered Jack out of her room. It was a private joy, this compulsion she had to make tiny things, just as her singing was, and it embarrassed her whenever he brought it up in conversation as if she had been caught eating bath sponge, or tearing out small clumps of her own hair.

'How was your day?'

He waved a weary hand over his head. She followed him down into the kitchen and put the tray back in the freezer.

'I didn't expect you home until later.'

'I decided I'd had enough for the day. Linc was up for a big session, but I wanted a quiet night with you.'

'Are you ok?' she asked, tamping down a frisson of concern.

'God, has it come to this? Do I need an excuse to spend an evening with my wife these days?' He feigned a look of indignation.

She flushed. He was right. Since when did he need an ulterior motive to come home on time? He pulled her towards him and dropped a light, forgiving kiss on her temple.

'I'm fine, Al. Just conscious I've been a bit irritable recently. All work and no play makes Jack a dull boy. I shouldn't take it out on you. I thought I'd put on some music, pour us a glass of wine and work my magic with some pasta.'

'How lovely.' A tremulous hope fluttered up in her. When had he last cooked for them?

'Why don't you go and have a bath? I'll bring a glass up to you. Don't lock the door this time...'

She ran hot water and as an afterthought added her favourite sandalwood bath oil. A moment later, music began to filter through the speaker in the far corner of the bathroom, and Jack appeared with a glass of chilled white wine.

'Take your time.' He disappeared back to the kitchen.

She sank gingerly into the steaming water and let herself unfold. She hadn't seen this version of Jack in a long time. It was like the sun's heat on her upturned face. Whatever had caused this change in mood was none of her business, she told herself. She wouldn't press him. She would just go with the flow and see where it took them. She shaved her legs as a precaution. Reluctant to keep him waiting, she was only partially dry when she slipped on a silk dressing gown, peeling its thin fabric off her damp skin as she went down to join him.

'Good timing.' He glanced up briefly, before expertly turning a large forkful of linguini onto a plate. He took the preparation of his signature dish—a mixture of capers, anchovies, lemon and garlic—very seriously, and Alys left him to his final ministrations and set off to the dining room where candles had been lit and the table laid.

When he settled into place opposite her, his body was loose, his eyes twinkled behind his glasses. She basked in his good humour.

'This smells delicious.' Alys smiled. 'Although, obviously, I'd have preferred a salad.'

'Obviously.'

She hadn't realised how hungry she was and had to stop herself from gobbling it.

'Tell me, what's afoot at Seagull these days?' he asked.

She did not mention Mairéad. She wasn't sure how to explain the woman, and besides he would be cruel as he always was in the face of physical imperfection, and she wanted to spare Mairéad any more of that for one day. She told him about the workshop instead.

'This woman asked what brought me joy.'

'Did you tell them you like hanging out in Wonderland with your tiny friends?' he asked, pointing his fork upwards to her room.

'Very funny. I couldn't think of an answer. She put me

on the spot and my mind went blank. What would you have said?'

'I'd have told her to mind her own business,' Jack said firmly. 'I'm not sure joyful is an actual thing, is it? Jesus, sometimes I feel like I'm getting old when I hear shit like that. It's psychobabble for morons, isn't it?'

Alys laughed. 'Are you calling me a moron?'

Jack shook his head. 'You're probably the only normal one there, and that's saying something. Seriously, when did everyone get so fucking lame? You don't imagine Cornish miners asking themselves that, do you? They just got on with it. Put food on the table.'

Jack paused for a moment, his fork in midair, and then relented. 'When Linc and I got the keys to the office for the first time, that felt sweet. When I drove my first Lexus out of the forecourt. Beating my brothers at, well, anything. Your cooking—that always makes me feel happy. A new shirt, fresh out of the tissue paper. Is that what you mean?'

'I think she was trying to get us to say what mattered to us. I sort of zoned out after a while,' Alys confessed.

'I bet you drove her crazy. Imagine asking Alys Larsson what she most desires in life and expecting a straight answer. Priceless!' He laughed, not unkindly.

Alys tried to think of what the opposite of a straight answer was. Perhaps she should have aimed for that. She had dripped a little oil on the front of her dressing gown and was beginning to feel a chill. She had forgotten how much cooler this room was than the rest of the house.

'She asked when we last felt alive.'

She regretted the words as soon as she'd uttered them. She had ruined the atmosphere and now Jack was frowning, as if an unpleasant thought had disturbed him. 'Who asks that sort of question, for fuck's sake? What's it got to do with them? It's a workplace, not a counselling centre.' His voice echoed in the stark chamber of the dining room.

'There's no need to get upset.' She reached a hand across to him. 'I'm sorry I brought it up. I thought you'd think it funny.'

His smile did nothing to reassure her.

'The facilitator looked like a Klingon.' She threw Nathalie Borthwick under the bus, a last Hail Mary to restore the mood.

He gave a snort, but finished his meal in silence. Alys knew from experience that he was embroiled in imagining cross-examining Nathalie Borthwick on the stand. She noticed that he didn't have an answer to the question either.

Chapter 6

Puff Pastry

When Alys pulled up outside Seagull Publishing the following morning, Mairéad was climbing stiffly out of an ancient, dark blue Mini Clubman. The stain on her face didn't look as shocking this morning. She hadn't thought Mairéad had noticed her—she had begun rummaging through the same giant bag—until she called out to her, 'Good morning, Alys.'

'Oh, good morning.' She busied herself with her bike lock. 'I like your car.'

Mairéad had located a tube of cream and pocketed it before glancing back towards the Mini. 'That's Crispin,' she said. 'I've had him for years. I like your bike.'

'This is Miss Marple,' Alys faltered.

'Of course it is.' Mairéad seemed nonplussed. 'I thought we'd go for coffee in the Café. I don't much like the office. Too many ear-wiggers.' She took Alys's elbow and steered her down the laneway and across to the café. She chose a table at the back, which met with her approval and ordered a flat white with an extra shot and a Danish pastry. Alys once again felt that strange magnetism that had drawn her to Mairéad the day before and ordered the same.

They didn't speak until their order had arrived. Mairéad tore into her cinnamon swirl, then spoke through a mouthful of pastry.

'Do you know what my nick-name was at my last job?'

Alys took a bite of her own and shook her head.

'Puff pastry. Not to my face, of course. They wouldn't have dared to do that.' Mairéad smiled, revealing small flakes of pastry that stuck to her front teeth.

Alys looked away.

'That's terribly cruel,' she replied.

'People can be. Do you know what your colleagues call you behind your back?' Mairéad asked.

Alys looked blankly at her.

Mairéad sat back and studied her.

'I thought not.'

Alys wiped her mouth carefully. She wasn't sure if she was expected to ask, but was almost certain that she didn't want to know.

'I–I don't know if Tim mentioned it, but I'm supposed to be your 'buddy' for your first week.'

'My what?'

'Your buddy. It's a thing Seagull does, pairs up a new joiner with an experienced hire so that they can show you the ropes, introduce you to people, help you get the lay of the land, that sort of thing. Of course, I'm not sure you need it.'

Mairéad looked amused. 'No, I think we'll leave it at that, if you don't mind. I think I've got the lay of the land already. How did you find yesterday?'

Alys busied herself picking off the icing from her swirl.

'Oh, you know. Not really my cup of tea, all that.'

'I rather gathered that. Have you been with Seagull long?'

'Yes. It was my first proper job. It feels like a lifetime when I think about it like that.'

'And yet, life slips past so quickly, doesn't it, when we're not paying attention to it?'

Alys glanced up at her, but the expression on Mairéad's face was bland.

'Did you grow up wanting to be a proofreader?'

'Oh, goodness, no,' Alys spluttered.

In her youth, Alys had thought that she would grow up to be a writer. She was named after her father's mother. Grandmother Alys had an orchard at the bottom of her garden and wrote poetry, and little Alys was always proud of sharing a name with a poet who was as tall as her grandmother, with shoulders like coat hangers and who smelt of fresh air and moss. Sometimes, on bad days, Alys wished that her mother would be sent away on a long trip, and that her gran with her sharp, grey eyes and long bones would step in to claim little Alys as her own. In Alys's imagination, her mother would write from some far-off place, like Gibraltar, to bestow her blessing on them, and her grandmother would remove Alys from school so that they could spend their days eating apples and writing. It seemed only natural that she would lead a life like her grandmother's—tranquil and solitary and peppered with good food. That life hadn't panned out. When her grandmother died during Alys's first year at university, the words died with her. Alys began clowning around, then sleeping around, acting the party girl to distract herself from admitting that she had given up on herself.

'I never had a clue what I wanted to be,' she said in a tone she hoped carried finality. Mairéad had a way of asking questions in a casual manner that, all the same, left Alys feeling as if she were sitting the interview of her life.

'Are you married?'

This was safe ground and she breathed out. 'Yes, to Jack. He's a barrister.'

'Where did you meet?'

'University.'

She had met Jack at a party. In the first few years of their marriage, he loved to tell the story of how they had met. He had been bored and had decided to call it a night when Alys burst into the room backwards. She was wearing a salmon-pink fifties style dress, with bare arms and legs and black stilettos, and her devil-may-care attitude had mesmerised him. He saw her as a free spirit, with a wild laugh and a fearlessness unlike any woman he had known. It was love at first sight.

In Alys's telling of it to herself, she recalled how he had pursued her with a single-mindedness that disturbed and flattered her in equal measure. Once, in the early hours, bleary with too many martinis and drowsy with love-making, she confessed her dream of being a writer, but neglected to mention that she no longer wrote. It mattered little to Jack. He had a plan for his life, and that felt such a relief for Alys who did not. Jack liked to say that they were 'both on the same page'. Alys did not admit even to herself that she had felt emptied out, and had willingly allowed

Jack to fill the space. She thought of Jack as her fresh start and a chance to rewrite herself. Her wildness, that recklessness that had so inspired Jack at first, had in fact been despair.

'Children?'

'No.'

'Why not?'

Alys blinked. No one asked her that. Still, there was that casual directness that made it difficult for her to take offence.

'We decided not to. We were busy with our careers.'

Mairéad raised an eyebrow and Alys blushed at the thought of her 'career', wedged in the corner desk, doing the same mundane job she had been doing for the past 28 years.

'It seemed for the best.' She closed the subject. 'Are you married?'

'Never. No children, either. I have a tortoise called Maurice, who goes about as fast as Crispin. That's about all of the responsibility I want.'

They ate in silence until Alys asked, 'Where were you before here?'

'London. I was FD for Marshall McKenzie. Seagull acquired them tail end of last year?'

'How come you decided to work at Seagull? Isn't Marshall McKenzie still in operation?'

'I had a run-in with the boss. I blew the whistle on him for assaulting juniors and when the acquisition went through, Seagull declined to honour his contract. He decided to spend his retirement posting shitty letters through my letterbox and menacing at me from the bottom of my garden. That sort of thing. Oh, I wasn't frightened of him, but when this position came up, I decided it was time for a change.' She smiled, and Alys was relieved to see that the pastry flakes had disappeared.

'What's Tim like? He seems a bit of an arse.'

Alys shrugged. 'He's not as bad as his dad was. His heart is in the right place, I suppose.'

Mairéad nodded, as if filing this news. 'Did you grow up in the village?'

'Is it that obvious?'

'Yes.'

Alys smiled. 'Born and raised here. My father actually owned the building Seagull is in now. I hadn't intended to come back here after Uni, but I met my husband and he loved the place, so here we are. I sometimes think I'll never get away! What about you? Did you always plan to go into finance?'

'God, no.' Mairéad snorted. 'I wanted to be a forensic scientist, but I failed chemistry. I could have resat the exam, but I had a fling with an actual forensic scientist who told me that his work was better labelled Smell-o-vision. Everything he worked with smelled—blood, shit, semen...'

Alys set down her pastry.

'I have a very sensitive nose,' Mairéad went on. 'I did a u-turn and got into finance. It's not all lost. I write crime-fiction in my spare time. It scratches the itch as it were.'

Alys winced, but Mairéad appeared not to notice. Her attention had been drawn to Tim who was making his way towards them in awkward bonhomie.

'Oh, for the love of God,' Mairéad said. 'He's relentless, isn't he? Like a giant puppy. I'd better talk to him.'

Alys took this as her cue.

She was almost at the door when Tim called after her, 'Hey Alys! Have you figured out what brings you joy yet?'

Mairéad's eyes locked on to hers. *Arse.*

'Small things, Tim. It's the little things that count for me,' Alys replied.

Chapter 7

The Oddball League

Weather permitting, Alys liked to spend her lunchtimes in the park with her best friend since childhood, Douglas Weatherley. She was relieved that Mairéad had no need of her buddying. Douglas would not have appreciated the disruption. He liked things to follow a predictable path, fond of quoting his mother, 'The right things done in the right way'. Douglas took her saintly aphorisms to heart and was the most fastidious man Alys had ever come across.

When she arrived at their bench, he was feeding crumbs to pigeons, engaged in a fruitless attempt to get them to fight fairly. Over six feet tall, he had his father's thick, dark hair and large round eyes, and his earnestness made Alys smile. He glanced up at her, shook the last of the crumbs out of the paper bag, and shooed away the pigeons. 'That's your lot, you greedy hallions. You'll have to get lost now my bird is here.'

'Sorry I'm late. I got held up with the new finance director.'

She threw an arm around him, breathing in his scent of

cedar wood and old books, and he lifted his face for her kiss and hugged her briefly.

'Bit of a dragon?' he asked.

'Actually, no.' Alys considered Mairéad for a moment. 'She's a bit scary, I suppose. No. Wrong word. Formidable. Candace craps herself every time she hears her coming.'

'Are you scared of her?'

'I think she's interesting. Definitely odd.'

'One of us then?'

'I think so. Perhaps not as odd as you.'

Douglas was a director at the local funeral parlour, Rushton and Weatherley, at the other end of the village. Arthur Rushton, a sparse man in his late seventies, managed the books and left Douglas to take care of front of house, running what he euphemistically liked to call 'the customer experience'. Working with cadavers was just one of the reasons Douglas topped the Oddball League.

She reached into her bag for her sandwich and passed it to Douglas, who swapped it for his own sandwich. It was a habit of theirs to make sandwiches that they would never eat themselves.

'How's work today?' She bit into corned beef and piccalilli. Douglas always made strange combinations for her, and she mournfully eyed her own coronation chicken sandwich, rapidly disappearing between his lips.

'I've been preparing Mrs Slecumbe for her big day next week.'

'Was she the lady that used to run the tobacconists?'

Douglas shook his head and chewed his sandwich slowly, waiting until he'd finished his mouthful before replying. 'No. That's the elder Mrs Slecumbe. That woman is as fit as a fiddle. There's something odd about her, too. I wouldn't be surprised if she never dies—she must be nearly

100. This is her daughter-in-law, the younger. They never saw eye-to-eye. Old Mrs Slecumbe probably did her in.' He waggled his eyebrows suggestively.

'What are you seeing Mrs Slecumbe the Younger off in?'

'A very nice Aquascutum two-piece in emerald green, circa 1960.'

'Classy. Pearls?'

'Gold studs.' He shrugged. 'Old Slecumbe has probably been through her jewellery box already. There wasn't a lot to choose from.'

Douglas always took great care in selecting the final outfit for his clients. He had an impeccable eye and had been known to source clothes for clients whose own wardrobes he deemed lacking.

'Any children?'

'One. A son. Won't be in attendance.'

'Sad.'

They finished their sandwiches in companionable silence. Alys kicked her feet out in front of her when the pigeons returned looking for crusts.

'How's Jack?' Douglas never failed to ask after Jack, despite the unspoken animosity between them. Jack dubbed Douglas, 'Alys's shadow' behind his back and Alys noted that Douglas always looked slightly over Jack's head rather than directly at him—a tactic he had used when confronted with someone he didn't like for as long as Alys had known him.

Douglas and Alys met at Maltings Primary School when they were nine and eight. He had appeared that first day towards the end of the summer term. His mother dressed him in a handmade version of the school uniform. The fabric was thicker, fustier, and the blue was slightly lighter than the standard navy—more of a peacock blue. He was wearing wrong-coloured socks, and his mother had insisted on sandals. It was his painful shyness and the sock-sandal combination that made him a target for the school bullies who, like a shoal of piranhas scenting blood in the water, made a circle around him and began their usual antics, pushing him and plucking at his uniform. Alys watched from a distance and noticed the way Douglas kept his unwavering gaze just above their hairline, as if he were imagining himself elsewhere; somewhere safer, more enjoyable. She loved him there and then, with his strange home-cut bowl hair, his round brown eyes and his lips so pinky-red, they might have been painted. There was something innocent and pure about him. He looked like a picture of a 1940s schoolboy from the well-thumbed 'War in our Time' book in the school library.

She took a run at the group and launching herself in the air she kicked out sideways, taking the largest of them, Russell Planchett —who would go on to jump off a railway bridge aged 19—out at the knee. Douglas saw this fierce little girl, a head shorter than him, standing with her hands on her hips, taking up position between him and his oppressors. 'You start on him, you get me too,' she said simply. That was the way it was.

In exchange for protection, Douglas showed Alys the world. The natural world. They would skirt the perimeter of the playing fields, where the grass got rough and patchy and the hedgerows started, and he would point out cow parsley and vetch and cleavers, which she spent joyful breaktimes slapping on the unwitting backs of their tormentors. They dug for worms and giant black centipedes that made her skin creep. Once, when Russell tore off the lower branches of a small sapling, Douglas cried. He was a gentle boy, capable of deep love and appreciation. Alys had never experienced such inspiration in all her days. Douglas had never known such admiration. They were inseparable.

The only ripple in their friendship had been Alys's relationship with Jack. When she first went away to university, she wrote to Douglas every Sunday in an effort to keep him with her. Her letters were full of the student life that Douglas had missed out on. She described the stuck-up, unfriendly students and vague, eccentric tutors. She divulged the lurid details of the wild nights when she never made it to bed, but stayed up to watch the sun rise over the Downs. She told him of the local brew—a cider that made her go temporarily blind and her calamitous and short-lived performance as a waitress. In return, Douglas would send his own clipped missives, often with a five-pound note pleated like an origami swan to swell her meagre funds. He knew that the Faulkeners would not have made provision for Alys. By the time she reached her third year, her letters had dried up. She couldn't tell him of her loss of faith in herself when he had so much in her. How could she have explained her failure? He religiously kept up his side of the correspondence, so she would feel obliged to send him an occasional short thank you note. Douglas had always suspected the post office workers of having an x-ray machine to seek out cash in envelopes, and would have worried unnecessarily without her acknowledgement of receipt.

Only once, in her third year, did she write him a longer letter, explaining that she was coming home for a brief visit and would love to see him if he wasn't busy. She hesitated, but then decided against telling him that she would not be coming alone. Douglas met them at the train station, dressed in a paisley waistcoat, and overwhelmed by a last-minute and ill-conceived purchase of an unruly bunch of dahlias. Neither Jack nor Alys had a spare hand to take them, so Douglas had to carry them all the way to The Rising Sun where Alys had reserved a double room.

Later that night, unable to sleep, her heartbeat keeping time with Jack's sonorous breathing, Alys's eyes returned to the dahlias on her bedside table. In the distraction created by the conjunction of Jack and the village, Alys had forgotten to ask reception for a vase and the dahlias had ended up an afterthought, crammed, top heavy and teetering, in a toothbrush glass. Something gnawed at her. She felt discordant, as if her allegiance had been split between her old life and the new life she planned with Jack. She had been embarrassed for Douglas in his strange formal attire. What had he been thinking? He had offered no comment when faced with Alys's lover, and she had tried not to look at the pained dismay on his face, catching instead the smirk on Jack's. His unpleasantness struck a flicker of concern, which Alys quickly smothered.

Douglas had taken on a double shift the following day and couldn't meet them for lunch, as Alys had hoped. That brief interlude, in her mind always complicated by the dahlias, which an exasperated Jack eventually dumped unceremoniously in a bin, was the last she saw of Douglas until she returned as Jack's fiancée. In all their years of friendship, they had never broached the subject of why Alys stopped writing. Douglas's discretion in this matter was another example of how far superior he was to her, Alys decided. She never saw the paisley waistcoat again.

She didn't want to talk about Jack now. She wanted to eat her sandwich in peace and kick pigeons.

'Oh, you know Jack. Busy, caught up in a tricky case, stressed out. The usual.' She felt disloyal, talking about his grumpiness. She suspected that Douglas took a circumspect pleasure in any marital difficulties she shared with him.

She frowned, remembering Jack's gruffness as he left the house that morning. He was in court again today with the stalker. She had forgotten to wish him luck, not that Jack believed in luck—it was all down to brains and brawn. She had also committed the cardinal sin of being less than excited at the news that Lincoln and Kate were having a Valentine's Day party the following Saturday. 'Aren't we a little old for Valentine's?' she'd asked, having difficulty in remembering the last time they had celebrated it. He had accused of her being anti-social.

It was cold sitting still, and she tucked herself into the side of Douglas.

'Are you going to Lincoln's party?' she asked.

'No. I'm planning on battening down the hatches with a good thriller. You?'

'Apparently so.'

'What will you wear?'

'I'll think of something.'

Douglas raised an eyebrow. They both knew that she wouldn't.

'Would you like to borrow Mrs Slecombe's twin-set?'

Chapter 8

Old Dog

The following day, a Saturday, Alys rose early, climbed on Miss Marple with a slice of toast wedged sideways in her mouth, and cycled to the lower end of town and the St Francis Animal Shelter. She heard the barking long before she rounded the last corner and caught a glimpse of the low-rise ramshackle collection of kennels that housed the shelter's guests, or 'inmates' as Alys affectionately called them. Alys volunteered one Saturday in every month. Her duties involved cleaning out the kennels and feeding the inmates. She sped through these tasks so that she could spend longer on her most important job—the cuddling. There was never enough time in the day for the cuddling, Alys found. She wasn't sure who needed it more, her or the dogs. She squeaked to a halt outside the reception area, leaned her bike against the front wall, and slipped around to the back where the kennels began. The shelter's manager, Anna, a ruddy woman in her early thirties, was pulverising a tube of semi-frozen tripe with a sledgehammer for the inmates' breakfast, her ponytail swinging with every strike, but she broke off with a smile when she saw Alys appear. She reached out for a hug, and Alys held her breath and leaned over the tripe.

'Morning, Alys. I'm glad to see you. Dave's got a cold, so you're my only spare pair of hands today and we're full. A few new additions in the top kennels. Do you want to start there?'

'Will do. See you at tea break.' She went to the shed and collected her cleaning kit, a shovel and a wheelbarrow, and headed up to the top of the hill behind the shelter. Outside the first kennel, she lifted a couple of rope leads from a rusty nail on the wall, and let herself into the caged corridor that ran the length of the shed. They were full, alright. She greeted a few old-timers, 'Darius, Titan, Hedley—you're looking well this month,' and let them out into the exercise yard behind. At the far end of the kennel, she stopped and peered into the last cage. A small dachshund with a round tummy was hunched in the far corner. Alys could just make out a pair of wary brown eyes in the dark. 'Hello, stranger.' The dog stared back at her. She checked the front of the cage. Anna often put a note about newcomers on the door. This one read, 'Bitch. c. 7 yrs. Thrown from a moving car. Shy with humans and other dogs.' Alys let out a soft sigh. She wobbled the bolt on the cage door until it screeched open, slipped into the cage, securing the door behind her. She kept her voice low as she crouched down.

'It's ok, darling. You're safe now,' she whispered. The dog watched her anxiously as Alys shifted to find a dry spot to sit down on. 'I'll not hurt you. Do you want to come and say hello?' Nothing. Alys carried on talking, not looking at the dog directly, her voice gentle and reassuring. Gradually, she edged a little closer, the dog watching her every movement, but not retreating. When she was close enough, she slowly reached out a hand. A small black nose dropped to sniff it. Alys waited before stretching a little further and seeking out the soft down under the dog's chin. All the time she kept talking and gentling the dog. When tea break came and went, Anna found them cuddled up together, Alys singing a lullaby, the dog tucked under her arm.

'I'll work late,' Alys promised.

'This one looks like she belongs with you,' Anna chuckled.

Alys shook her head regretfully. 'Who would want to hurt such a sweet creature?'

'Bad eggs. That's why we need good eggs like you and your superior cuddling skills.'

Alys gently set the little dog down and slowly got to her feet. The dog looked expectantly at her. 'I'll come and see you again,' Alys promised, although given her pedigree, it was unlikely the dog would still be there when Alys returned.

'It looks like she's taken to you too,' Anna pressed. 'Couldn't you persuade Jack?'

'Unlikely. Besides, she needs a family. Not fair with both of us out all day.'

She set about her work quickly, occasionally stopping by to check in on the far kennel. At the end of the day, she fed a small treat through the bars and poked a finger through after it. 'You need a new name,' she whispered. 'You look like a Margo.' A small pink tongue flickered over her fingertip and disappeared.

She was still thinking about Margo when she returned home and headed for the shower. Jack always complained how badly she smelled after a day at the kennels. There was no way she'd persuade him that they needed a shy dachshund with a round tummy. As much as she wished for a home for her, she couldn't help hoping that Anna would hold on to her, just so that Alys could see her one more time.

Chapter 9

Funny Valentine

It was the night of the party. Alys was lying on her bed, still wrapped in a towel. Her body felt as if it was melting into the bed frame. She imagined the little blue line drawn to outline where a corpse once lay, then her mind wandered off and presented her with a clear image of Edvard Munch's The Scream. She'd read somewhere that Munch had painted it after an episode with friends when he had been overcome by an 'unspeakable tiredness'.

'Maybe that's what's wrong with me,' she said out loud. 'I'm unspeakably tired. I can't speak of it because people would say I had nothing to be tired about.' She would have to keep the screaming on the inside where it was soundproof. The thought of being ready for the taxi that would be arriving shortly was beyond bearing. Jack was banging around in the bathroom. She needed to get up before he found her there. Slowly, she rolled on to her left, hauled herself to her feet, and opened her wardrobe doors. A real woman would have decided what to wear before this point. She had nothing to wear. Women tended to say that a lot, when what they really meant was a) people hadn't already seen them in, b) they felt special in or c) they didn't feel fat in. Alys meant it in the literal sense, as in d) she had nothing other than old denim, fleeces or frumpy shirts in her wardrobe. There was a time when she only ever wore dresses. Beautiful heels and hip-skimming dresses in soft fabric. She couldn't remember why she stopped wearing them. She couldn't even remember throwing them out. Perhaps Jack had.

The only thing she had that might fit the bill was a strange tangerine silk outfit bought at TK Maxx in their Christmas Clearance. She had bought it for the feel of it and barely noticed it on in the fitting room. At least it was new. She could surprise Jack. She'd barely seen him all week, and when their ships passed over breakfast, he was monosyllabic and distracted. He'd woken up in better spirits this morning—the prospect of partying with Lincoln always had that effect on him, and she found herself unexpectedly grateful for the invitation and its interruption to the grim pattern their days had taken.

She pulled the silk sheath over her head. Her hair was still wet at the back, but she couldn't help that now. She stabbed the mascara wand at her lashes, and some gloss on her lips, and examined her face. She looked strained. Her eyes looked red, not as if she'd been crying, but as if she hadn't slept in days.

Jack strode in and did a double take.

'Wow! Is that new?'

'Yes, sort of. Is it ok?'

'It's certainly different. The cab's here.'

They spent the first five minutes of the journey in silence, then he shifted his body around to face her, and it was not appreciation she saw in his eyes but bemusement.

'What do you call that sort of an outfit? It's not a dress,

is it? Bit short for a dress.' Alys had not thought to classify it before. She had supposed it a dress, but her knickers were visible now that she was seated. Her inner thighs looked huge, like a batch of loaves that had slumped together as they were rising.

'Umm, I think it's called a tunic.'

'Aren't you meant to wear trousers or tights with it?'

It hadn't occurred to Alys that it might be a long top.

'It's a bit shapeless, isn't it?' His mouth turned down. 'Did it come with a belt?'

Alys glanced down. 'No. It didn't come with a belt. It's meant to be this shape. It's very soft.' In the silence that followed, Alys blurted. 'It is a bit of a tent, isn't it?'

Jack sniggered. 'You look like Gandhi.'

She was moments away from a party she didn't want to go to and looked like Gandhi—a fat one. She looked out of the window and felt her eyes smart. She wanted to ask the taxi to turn around, but it was too late. They turned into Lincoln's driveway. Tiny tea lights had been set out along the gravel path, and every light in the house was on. It looked like a small country estate.

Jack rang the bell and turned to cast a final eye over his wife. 'Is your hair still wet?'

The door opened and Kate stood silhouetted in the doorway with her arms spread wide, effortlessly chic in a navy trouser suit, with large gold hoops at her ears and a thin gold bangle on her wrist.

'Jack! How lovely to see you! And Alys! You're looking very ethnic tonight—how wonderful! Come on in. You're the first here. Goodness, is that the time? You are the early birds, aren't you? Lincoln is still upstairs putting his make up on, and I've a few last-minute instructions for the catering staff, so why don't you go through to the bar and help yourself to drinks. I won't be a tick.'

Jack turned to Alys. 'Go through to the bar! I fucking love these people,' he whispered. Alys tucked herself into his slipstream and made her way across the living room, where she ordered two margaritas from a surprised waiter, who was still setting up, and downed them in one. Why were they so early? Jack had insisted on booking a taxi for seven when the invitation had clearly been for eight o'clock. He couldn't wait to get out of their house, as if he couldn't bear it to be just the two of them. If she hadn't known better, she would have thought he was avoiding her.

She sat alone at the bar as Jack took his drink on a tour of Lincoln's living room, examining his treasures. There was a sculpture of a pair of quail resting on a large coffee table book, their faces peering over the edge of the console. A beautiful gold floor lamp graced one corner of the room, illuminating a single red silk amaryllis bloom in a petrol-blue glass vase. On the wall opposite there was a large wall hanging made of long white feathers and felted tufts of wool. 'It looks beautiful,' Alys whispered to herself. It was Lincoln's house. Kate had moved in three years before, but had changed nothing of the décor. She tried to imagine what it would be like to be Kate, living in a house that was both beautiful and homely.

Jack stood for a while, sipping his drink and running his hand backwards and forwards across the textiles until another couple arrived, and he turned into them and began a loud and noisy conversation with the husband about Formula 1. It was as if a lightbulb turned on in him and he became a performer. Alys stayed with the waiter, who spoke not a word, but regularly replaced her drink, sliding its replacement before her with a discrete flourish.

It wasn't until her fourth, or maybe her fifth, margarita that Alys became aware that her limbs had melted and her vision had softened sufficiently for her to blank out the stares that her tunic had been attracting from the other guests. She knew most of them, but they had been looking at her as if she was something they had never encountered before. She had perched on the bar stool until she remembered her knickers, and so had to stand at the bar, her back to the guests. Her legs were already aching, but she couldn't see how she'd be able to sit for the rest of the evening. Perhaps she could lounge somewhere, lie down on one of Lincoln's velvet chaise longues, with a cushion over her crotch.

She was about to go and sit in the guest room for an unspecified amount of time—she often did this when Lincoln and Kate threw one of their parties—when a pair of muscular arms snaked around her from behind and she heard a gravelly voice in her ear. 'Hello, Sexy!' The breath against her earlobe made the skin on the back of her neck tingle.

'Lincoln Scott.' She rolled her eyes, but gave the forearms a squeeze before stepping forward out of the embrace and turning to face him.

Lincoln was the most handsome man Alys knew. Where Jack was classically good-looking, his appearance seemed flat and conventional in comparison to Lincoln's more complicated, imperfect face. He had high, angular cheekbones and a long, pointed nose that had a slight kink at the bridge. His eyes were a deep grey and slightly too close together, and yet there was something about them. He had a full mouth that was always smiling.

He was grinning lasciviously at her now. 'You're a sight for sore eyes!'

'Stop it, you devil.' She slumped against him for a moment, letting him take the weight off her legs. 'Oh my God, Linc, look at the state of me. I'm literally wearing a belt. Apparently, I'm the freak show for this evening. All of your friends are staring at me,' she finished with a stage whisper.

'You look perfectly lovely, Alys. They're not staring at you because of your outfit. They're staring at you because they've never seen a middle-aged woman this drunk at half-past eight before. What have you been doing to yourself? Where is that husband of yours and why is he not looking after you?'

'Oh, Jack...' She released herself from Lincoln's arms and waved an airy arm out towards the garden. She had lost sight of Jack as soon as the main crush of guests arrived, as she knew she would. She did not expect to see him until the taxi arrived to take them home.

However, Jack suddenly appeared at her side as if summoned. He threw his arms around Lincoln and rubbed his ribs with his knuckles whilst holding him in a headlock. Alys had noticed that he often did this to his best friend as a way of drawing attention to the fact that he was at least a head taller than him.

Lincoln casually twisted out of Jack's grip, and Jack found himself pleading for mercy with his hand twisted half-way up his back.

'Jack, me old China! Where have you been? Your wife has become a dipsomaniac in your absence.' Lincoln often affected a faux cockney accent. This amused both men because his family was old money, Lincoln had been educated at Stowe and his accent was terrible.

Jack looked at Alys and frowned. 'Take it easy, Alys.'

'I know what we need.' Lincoln took their arms and

spun them around to face the bar. He jostled the barman aside. 'Move over, mate, give the maestro some space. Alys, Jack, I'm going to make you one of my specials—so called because it always gives the imbiber what they need. Alys, this is going to clear your head and give you some Dutch courage. And Jack, it's going to loosen you up and stop you being an arsehole to your long-suffering wife. I might have to make you a double.'

'What will yours do for you?' Alys asked, her elbows propped up on the bar.

'Mine? Oh, I expect mine will give me the antidote to my cynicism, old girl. A bit of *joie de vivre*.'

'Come on now, mate. What have you got to be cynical about?' Jack waved an arm to take in the beauty of the open-plan sitting room with its split-level flooring and Roche Bobois seating. 'That sofa must have cost £10,000 alone. And you've got your own bar.'

'It's just stuff, Jack. It doesn't mean anything.'

'Then give it to me.'

'Down the hatch.' Lincoln slid a shot glass in front of each of them, took up his own and knocked it back.

Alys made the mistake of sipping hers and felt her mouth on fire.

'Down in one, Driving Miss Daisy,' Lincoln said, tipping her glass into her mouth.

Jack banged the bar with a hard palm, scrunching up his face and making loud sucking sounds.

'All that and I gave him a lemonade.' Lincoln leant over the bar and pulled their heads together against him. 'I bloody love you two.'

The evening passed in a haze for Alys after that. She found herself talking rather loudly to a German woman she had met several times before, but who had no memory of her. She vaguely remembered grazing at the buffet table, crooning to the prawn vol-au-vents. 'Where have you been hiding since 1979? I've missed you!' Around 10pm, the joke was over. She began to feel nauseous and tired, and went to find Jack, hoping to persuade him to come home earlier.

He was standing on the terrace. Kate was leaning close to him. Their heads were bowed, and as Alys watched, Kate took a smooth drag on her cigarette, then passed it to Jack. She was asking him a question and he seemed to pause to consider it, his eyes narrowing as he drew in smoke. Alys hadn't realised he'd started again. She moved closer and settled herself in one of the chairs set out along the wall. She shifted it slightly until she was half in shadow and she made herself small. She couldn't hear what they were saying, but Jack had turned serious. He shrugged and smiled a thin smile, and there were those tiny creases around his mouth that Alys used to love to kiss. Perhaps Kate saw them too, because she rested her fingers lightly on his wrist and left them there. It seemed to Alys that all three of them were holding their breath. Alys felt a dull ache in her jawbone like a yawn or a scream trapped in the sinews. She kept very still. She could not take her eyes off her husband. Jack looked as Kate's fingers played out on his skin, and he sank slightly against the balustrade. For a moment, he seemed thrown off-guard. He suddenly looked sad and very tired, then he straightened up a little and gently removed his arm from under her fingers to rub his neck. He smiled apologetically, then picked up his glass, and it was clear that he was offering her a refill as he headed back inside. Kate stayed at the balustrade, her eyes narrowing as she drew on her cigarette, before she moved off to join him. Alys went straight back to the bar.

Chapter 10

Escape

Alys woke hours later, curled in a ball on the floor between the guest bed and the wall. It was dark and quiet. She had no sense of time, but the party was clearly over. The coats that had been laid out on the bed had gone. She staggered to her feet, fighting rising nausea, and pushed her hair out of her face. She made her way unsteadily out of the bedroom onto the darkened landing. There was a light coming from the open door to the master bedroom, and she slunk back when she saw Lincoln walking wearily into the room, yawning.

'Have you locked up?' Kate called.

'Shit, no. I'll go back down in a second.'

Alys tiptoed unsteadily to the door and lingered in the shadow. She needed to make her presence known, but didn't want to startle them.

'God, I'm tired. I could have done with everyone fucking off about two hours ago.'

'You're getting old,' Kate teased. She was taking her make-up off at her dressing table. 'Can't take the pace anymore, baby.'

'I think everyone had a great time.'

Alys raised her hand to knock on the partially opened door.

'Some of us had a little too much of a good time. Did you see Alys?'

Alys dropped her hand again and held her breath.

'She was so drunk. Was she drunk before she came?' Kate barked out a laugh that was too loud for the quiet. 'Their taxi came and we couldn't find her anywhere and Jack was swearing like mad, he was so annoyed with her. We found her lying on the coats in the guest room. Out cold. Legs akimbo. She had these grey old lady knickers on. You should have seen his face.' Alys heard Lincoln sink down on to the bed and his silence must have chastened Kate, because she stopped laughing abruptly and changed tack.

'Is Alys alright?' she asked.

'What do you mean?'

'You know how she carries on.'

'Sorry.' He grunted as he tried to kick off his shoes. 'You'll have to give me more than that.'

'She's like a ghost. Like she's dead from the neck up. Is she on medication of some sort?'

'What, Alys? No. That's just the way she is. That's just Alys.'

'Don't get me wrong. I like Alys, I really do. I just wish I could connect with her, you know?' Something in his tone must have warned her off. 'She's just so spacey. It's like she doesn't even see you when you talk to her. I don't know how Jack can stand it. They are the strangest couple. What do they have in common?'

'Be kind.' He made his way to the bathroom and closed the door.

Chapter 11

The Crumbling Path

Alys sobered up in an instant. She moved quickly, taking off her shoes so that she could get down the stairs and out before Lincoln locked her in. She slipped out of the front door and streaked across the grass, avoiding the tea lights that were still illuminating the path. It was freezing and her legs stung in the chill night air. She had not thought to bring a coat or a handbag with her. She had no money or phone, and no way of contacting Jack. Jack would probably have assumed that she would spend the night with Lincoln and Kate, but after what she had just overheard, she could not imagine ever being in Kate's company again. A ghost? Half-dead? What was it that Mairéad asked her? Did she know what they called her behind her back at work? Did everyone think there was something wrong with her?

She tried to put the heels back on, but gave up. She guessed it to be about four in the morning. It was still dark, but the air smelt of early morning growth, furtive and green. A mackerel cat with a sharp, inquisitive face appeared from under a hedge, suffused with the orange glow of the street-lights. It paused, one front paw lifted, and glared at her as if the sight of her were an affront. She threw her heels over the hedge with the cat looking on, then wrapped her arms around herself and tried to pick up a brisk pace. It would take her an hour to walk home.

She had heartburn and the back of her throat was on fire. She was burning up, and she had to rub her chest vigorously as she walked to dispel the acid that burned the base of her throat. Kate had made it sound as if she were a liability for Jack. How could he stand being married to her, with her strange hobbies and ridiculous clothes? What a joke she was. She had been the outsider her entire life—shabby, odd, looking in at normal people, trying to see how they 'did' life. This was what came of being a Faulkener, with a father who had a gift shop that people laughed at, and a mother like Monica who rarely left home, and when she did, she went about her business as if she hadn't noticed anyone, as if she were floating over the top of people. Neither of her parents was a real person, when you thought about it, which Alys had. A lot. They were cartoon characters. Only her little brother, Elliot, turned into a real person because he got out as quickly as he could and made a new life and family for himself in New Zealand where no one knew what a Faulkener was.

She was twelve when she learned that the Faulkener lifestyle was not normal. She had received a rare invite to a sleepover, Jackie Grand's thirteenth birthday party. They were not particularly close friends, but Jackie had invited the whole class and someone, her mother, perhaps, must have suggested that it would be unkind not to include Alys. For her part, Alys had been delighted with the invitation. Her first. She couldn't stifle the tentative hope that it might be the first of many and that she was finally being admitted into the inner sanctum of intimate female friendship after years of peering in from the outside. The afternoon had started off well. Her mother had surprised her by buying her the same navy cords that the other girls favoured so that she wouldn't stand out. For Jackie's present, her father had given her a King Charles Cavalier china ornament that was actually a money box—not what she would have chosen herself, but she had no idea what thirteen-year-old girls liked. When Jackie had torn off the paper, a titter rose up through the ranks. That should have been Alys's first warning. She worked hard all day trying to learn the rules of engagement, but she knew none of their jokes, their cultural references, and while no one was overtly unfriendly towards her, she was the last to be chosen for games, the one who continually had to find a chair for herself as Jackie's parents kept forgetting to set out one for the 'extra guest'.

By the time they had changed into their pyjamas and set up camp, Alys was exhausted. She no longer had the energy to keep up, so she rolled on to her side away from them and closed her eyes, letting the low murmuring of the others lull her. They must have thought her asleep because they struck up a conversation in whispers about the Faulkeners. Alys recognised Sheryl Yates as she started in. Her father said that Ian Faulkener was 'a walking catastrophe', always teetering on the verge of bankruptcy. Mr Yates would know —he was the manager of the Lloyds Bank branch. He was like a gambling addict, Mr Yates said. If he had any money, it was spent before it had even hit his account. Then he'd come cap in hand to the bank, asking for an extension of an overdraft, a little leeway to tide him over until sales picked up. He was a child. Mr Yates would make him take back everything he'd bought over the previous few days. The local businesses knew the pattern. Some even refused to sell to him in the first place. Alys recognised the truth in this. It was always feast or famine in their household. A conveyor belt of shiny consumer goods on Monday would have disappeared again by Thursday without a word being exchanged. Cecilia Swanson piped up that it was a wonder that Ian Faulkener had any money at all because his gift shop was a joke and the laughing stock of the village. Anyone with any taste had to drive to Tarnley if they wanted a proper present. Jackie mumbled something about the spaniel money box and they all exploded into hysterical giggles, which they fought hard to dampen down quickly. Alys lay very still.

After a few moments, when the girls had established that Alys was indeed deeply asleep, they started on her mother. This was when Alys learned that the vague, other-worldly quality her mother exuded was due to her being 'a raging alcoholic'. Emma Wise's mother, a nurse who had ministered to Monica during several emergency admissions, predicted that she'd be dead by the time she was fifty at the rate she was going. Emma quoted her mother as saying that the woman had suffered a series of mini-strokes and still they couldn't stop her 'insatiable thirst'. The conversation had moved on to a general discussion of Alys then. They complained that whilst their mothers might feel sorry for Alys because she was obviously being neglected, they didn't have to sit next to her in class with her dirty hair and weird-smelling packed lunches.

Alys left early the following morning before they woke. From that day onwards, she became more reserved, more watchful. She made sure to wash her own hair and she went without lunch. She never lost that feeling of being measured up and found lacking.

Years later, when she and Jack had become an item, it had taken her six months to bring him back to the village. Her parents had sold up and moved to a chalet on the coast only days before, and Alys had never expected to set foot there again. She was prepared for derision and that dry, sarcastic wit of his picking over the idiosyncrasies of a rural village in the heart of Buckinghamshire, but he surprised her with his enthusiasm. He loved the village. He found it charming and had insisted that she take him around her old haunts on foot—her primary and secondary schools and the common where teenagers still loitered, swigging pilfered concoctions from their parents' drinks cabinets. She showed him the memorial centre where floristry and quilting classes took place, and the Am Dram society put on a clattering of dreadful performances. When they came to the high street that led in and out of the village, she breezed past her father's old gift shop without breaking her stride.

It took her a further six months to introduce him to Ian and Monica. Her parents had been surprised when she called to arrange the visit, as if they'd imagined that part of their lives was over and done with. They had not kept in touch with any regularity and seemed baffled as to why Alys would want to reconnect. However, when Jack and Alys arrived, Ian had clearly made an effort. There had been some attempt at tidying up. A cake had been bought. When Alys stepped through the door, her eyes went to Monica who was sitting upright at the table with her eyes on the cake. She looked composed and clean. Jack dazzled them with the forcefulness of his charm, cheering Ian with the bluster of his good humour. Monica barely spoke, but stared at him with her round blue eyes, still beautiful, and blinked from time to time as if she wasn't sure he was real. The three of them pronounced the visit a huge success. In truth, it had taken Jack and Alys three hours to drive there and they had only been there for forty minutes when Monica began to agitate and Ian and Alys immediately shifted to a well-honed choreography of containment. Ian swept Monica out of the room, and Alys ushered Jack to the front door, calling their goodbyes upstairs as they went. Jack was in high spirits on their way home, having seen nothing out of the ordinary, caught up as usual on his own impact rather than his audience. Alys, strained and exhausted, watched the drizzle on the car window and the flat landscape beyond and said nothing.

When Jack proposed to Alys, he made it a condition of their engagement that they would look for a house in the village. In fact, the Larsson's wealth had weighed in and the family had already selected an 'appropriate' residence in an affluent part of town where properties always held their value. They considered it not so much a wedding gift as an investment. Alys did not object that her first home was owned by the family and not of her choice. She complied with Jack's request because it was beyond her wildest dreams to have a home of her own, one that she would fill with her own family. Hers would be a bright, happy family full of love and laughter. So it was that Alys found herself living back in the village that had more or less spat her out, smack in the middle of all of the families who had once laughed at hers.

. . .

The cold began to seep into her bones, making her skin shrink on her frame. Her shoulders hunched, she broke into a stumbling jog, the weight of her upper body propelling the bottom half of her along. She could hear her breath rasping in her ears and had to pinch out a stitch in her side. She was weighing Jack down. She hadn't realised that everyone else saw it too. Kate wasn't being unkind. She was simply saying what others thought. She thought of everyone else, then, not just at the party but at every party they'd ever attended, the Larssons, Jack's clients, all looking at her and thinking, if not saying, 'That poor man.' The shame of it made her vomit into the kerb, retching over and over until her throat was scorched, her mouth sour.

It was starting to get light by the time she reached home. She couldn't remember ever seeing her house at this time in the morning. It rose up in the darkness, austere and unfriendly, as if it belonged to someone else. She circled around to the back of the house and tried the back door. It was locked. The spare key was not in its place. She shifted from one foot to another, any heat that she had generated through her walking quickly dissipating. She was afraid to call in case she woke the neighbours. She tried to wake Jack, but the pebbles she threw at their bedroom window fell wide of their mark and the room remained dark. Looking down at herself, her matted hair, her filthy feet, her shins splashed with her own vomit, she could only imagine what her face looked like. She decided she couldn't face Jack in this state. The garden shed was open and she crept inside, navigating stacked chairs and a patio set, until she made her way into the far corner and managed to make a nest out of chair cushions and an old bedspread Jack had thrown over his lawnmower. She watched as the sky started to lighten from inky blue to a soft aubergine, the colour of a bruise. She was hollowed out. She had come to the end of a line somewhere where the path had crumbled away before her. She didn't think she'd be able to sleep, but sleep came and took her, anyway.

Chapter 12

Empty Vessel Adrift

It was almost midday when she was woken by next door's dog barking. Alys hadn't noticed the smell of petrol from the bedspread earlier on, but it had permeated her skin and hair and made her nauseous again. She tried to throw it off her, but her limbs had frozen in strange angles and it took them a while to thaw and co-operate. She was careful to wrap up Jack's lawnmower before venturing out. The back door was open and she could hear jazz playing. Inside, the kitchen smelled of freshly brewed coffee and the Sunday papers were spread across the table. Jack had been up for some time it seemed. It was eerily normal given the evening she had passed; a warning that life could carry on perfectly well, more orderly, without her. Jack was nowhere to be seen and she tiptoed through the kitchen and made for the stairs. If she could shower and get out of her filthy clothes, she could try to pretend the night before hadn't happened. Her hand was on the bannister when he appeared from his study. He jumped when he saw her and a look of disdain passed over his face like cloud over water, replaced by a blankness that frightened her.

In the silence that stretched between them, she began to shake.

'Sorry,' she whispered.

'Look at the state of you. How did you cut your feet?'

She glanced down at the blood slick she'd left behind her. She hadn't noticed.

'I–I couldn't get in. The door was locked.'

'You'd better go and shower. You smell terrible. I'll make some more coffee.'

Under the steaming water, her tears took her by surprise. She couldn't remember when she had last cried, but now that they had started, they racked her body and she sobbed into her hands. She cried out of humiliation and shame, but more from despair because she knew now that she had broken something and the road had run out and the path had been erased and it didn't matter anyway, because wherever she went, there she was—this hulking ghost of a half-dead woman. She wept because in that moment on the stairs, her eyes on Jack's blank face, she finally admitted to herself what she had known for years, that Jack did not love her and she didn't know how to make herself lovable and above all else, she was so lonely, it was gnawing at her, turning her inside out. *'Do you know what they call you at work?'*

When she was calm again, when she had brushed her wet hair and tied it low at her neck, smoothed on some moisturiser to soothe her sore skin, when she had wrapped herself in her softest, warmest robe, she made it downstairs to the kitchen where Jack was once again immersed in the newspaper. He barely looked at her, but poured her a coffee and set it down before her. He didn't ask how she had got home or where she'd spent the night. The coffee was too hot and the smell of it turned her empty stomach, but she drank it down anyway, trying to warm herself from the inside, her sipping the only sound in the room.

'I'm sorry,' she said again to the silence.

His eyes on her face were an indictment. He studied her until she dropped her eyes, unable to face him.

'This can't go on,' he said.

'I know, I'm so sorry. I didn't mean to embarrass you.'

'You embarrassed yourself, Alys. You were a laughing stock. People were actually laughing at you, at my wife, behind your back.'

She shuddered. 'I'm sure they were. I promise that I won't drink any more. It was my outfit, I was so embarrassed. I promise that I'll always plan and run my outfit by you before we go anywhere. I promise I'll be better...' she began to stutter.

'Better at what, Alys? Better at being a wife? Better at being a person? Better at life? How will you be better, Alys?' She was on safer ground now that he was shouting.

She studied her hands. At some point last night, she had broken a finger nail at its base and a small red line of blood arced across the jagged edge.

'I can't go on. I can't do this anymore.' He ground out.

As she sat bowed over her hands, he told the top of her head how he no longer knew who she was, nor why they were together.

His voice was thick with misery. 'I tell everyone about this crazy girl I fell in love with in her salmon pink dress, but the thing is, Al, I lost sight of her years ago. I can't find a trace of her, which makes me wonder if she'd ever really existed. Did you fake her? Did I imagine her? Where did she go? It's like she was some sort of illusion to lure me in and the real Alys, this empty vessel adrift, was just waiting in the background all along.' He cleared his throat. 'I feel so... stuck. I can't imagine spending my life shackled to a woman who has nothing left inside her. How can you live with yourself like this? Don't you want more? Because I do. I want more than you're prepared to accept for yourself. I want passion and love. I want to feel alive, and you're so defeated, it taints everything. I need to breathe.'

'An empty vessel adrift' he had called her, and she found it a strange thing to call someone. She went away in her head, flew over fields and forest, until she reached the wide expanse of ocean where she imagined herself alighting on the deck of an abandoned ship. Over and over his words of disappointment, of disillusionment and frustration, crashed down on her, rocking the empty vessel that she was in their wake. She imagined herself like the Marie Celeste, that abandoned merchant ship found drifting, where once people lived, and laughed and loved each other and ate breakfast at the table together, until some mysterious calamity had befallen them and all signs of life had been extinguished. Only the superficial accoutrements of a life left behind. Perhaps he had been right to call her that, after all.

When he stopped talking, she had no words to explain herself to him, so she asked, 'What do you want me to do?'

'I want you to let me go.'

There was a slight tearing sensation inside of her, as if a tiny seam had been pulled apart. Her head nodded briefly and it was done.

He told her that he would make it as easy for her as possible. He had already spoken to Lincoln that morning and had arranged to stay with him and Kate for a few days until he could find himself a place to live. Alys could stay in the house for as long as she wanted to, although technically it belonged to the Larsson family and would need to be returned to the fold at some point, there was no need to rush. He left her then to finish packing his bags.

Alys lay back on the deck of the empty vessel and gave in to its gentle rocking, its mast creaking in the breeze as it drifted across a vast, empty ocean.

Chapter 13

Rational Adults

She was in her workroom when she heard the front door close. He had chosen not to say goodbye and this was entirely reasonable, she supposed, as he had said that he would likely come and go over the next few days. There was no need for high drama in all of this. They were two rational adults drawing their relationship to a close. These things happened. The light was drawing in, and she watched as the silhouettes of the trees that lined their garden became sharper and more clearly defined in the dusk. She thought back to The Grand Dishevelment of the Night Before and took a small comfort in the fact that she had managed some dignity, some grace in the letting go of him. She remembered her promise to help Enid get a head start with the week's book delivery at The Granary and she roused herself, her weariness leaden as she went through the motions of wrapping herself up to counter the chill of the evening air.

She kept her head down and concentrated on her feet on Miss Marple's pedals until she reached The Granary, ignoring the Closed sign and pushing her way through the heavy wooden doors. She was numb, but habit kicked in and she observed her usual ritual of pausing on the threshold and taking in the beauty of the old building before her. Enid had retained the beautiful sweep of its arched ceiling, the quirkiness of its original layout, and the narrow yellow bricks that all the old farm buildings in the area bore. These bricks gave the ground floor a warm and welcoming atmosphere, yet could barely be seen through the colourful spines of the books that lined the walls from floor to ceiling.

Comfortable old armchairs were tucked into every nook and cranny of The Granary to allow the customers to sit and browse at leisure. Alys had spent many a spare hour sitting in her favourite armchair, an old tweed highbacked chair that curved around her back like a hug, leafing through a pile of books at her side. Alys would often find herself with an empty Saturday lying ahead of her, and Enid always needed an extra pair of hands, and so it was that Alys began helping Enid with the running of the place. It was her haven. Enid was gruff and unwelcoming, but still Alys wondered how her life might have turned out for the better if she had had The Granary to escape to as a child.

The door swung back gently behind her like a pat on the back. She followed a trail of expletives until she found Enid bent double behind a large box, grappling with some masking tape. At seventy-five years of age, Enid could have passed for ninety. Arthritis had twisted her back and tipped her sideways, her gnarled hands fumbling to handle the books that made her livelihood. She never complained about her condition, but pain could make her sharp and intolerant of 'fools'. Alys miraculously passed muster. She had once saved Enid's life and that decided it as far as Enid was concerned.

It had happened not long after Alys and Jack moved back to the village. One Thursday night, Alys arrived just before closing time. Although it had rained fiercely all day, she and Jack had argued and she had needed to get out of the house. The only soul abroad in the village, it was not a night to be out in, but she took comfort from the scouring rain on her face. She had known instinctively that something was wrong when she stepped through the door, even before she saw Enid lying at the foot of the stairs. It took her a moment to register that Enid's leg was pointing the wrong way. She had skidded in her sodden shoes as she ran to her. The woman was barely conscious and Alys was scared to move her. She called 999, then lay alongside her, holding her hand, whispering encouragements, endearments even, to this bad-tempered stranger who all the same reminded her of a younger Grandmother Alys with her flint-grey eyes. She stayed with her in the back of the ambulance, only breaking contact when she had to let the paramedics in to work on her. Enid's eyes were closed, but she would not release her grip on Alys's hand. It might have been the strength in that grip that made Alys tell the admitting nurse that she was Enid's niece, signing the paperwork put under her pen without hesitation. It was Alys who drove her home a few days later to a clean apartment with a large pot of soup still warm on the hob, and it was Alys who reopened the shop whilst Enid convalesced in her apartment in the eaves, ringing a little bell to summon Alys when she needed her. Alys had been in her element—caring for Enid, keeping the shop afloat, surrounded by books, in a world of her own. As she thought about those few months now, she marvelled at how decisive she'd been. Where had that Alys gone?

'Bastarding tape. Why do they make it so bloody difficult?' Enid waved a pair of scissors at Alys by way of a greeting. Alys calmly took the scissors and scored through the plastic, tearing open the box to reveal an array of glossy book covers beneath.

'You look dreadful.' Enid screwed up her face, appraising Alys. 'What's wrong?'

'I'm hungover. I slept in the shed and Jack's left me.' Alys took the books out of the box and set them on the counter.

'Has he now?' Enid grunted.

'Yes. He can't envisage a future with someone like me.'

Enid rested back on the floor, her eyes on Alys's face. 'What do you mean "someone like you"?'

Alys shrugged. She thought it self-explanatory.

Enid sighed. 'What are you going to do about it?'

Alys blinked. Her fingers were trembling and she laid her hands on the top of a pile of books to steady them.

'I let him go.'

'Just like that?'

'It's not like I had a choice, Enid. He wants to be happy again. He deserves that.'

Enid snorted. 'Oh does he? And what do you deserve?' Her hand closed over Alys's splayed fingers and squeezed hard.

The yawning ache at the back of Alys's throat made her voice stiff. 'These things happen.' She lifted the books and set off for the shelves.

Dinner that evening was a carefully constructed cottage pie with baked beans in it as her mother used to make, accompanied by a bottle of Jack's finest Barolo. She woke some time later with the TV on, the flashing lights from a horror film playing out across her face. Her plate had slipped to the floor. She could not face their bed, so she made one for herself on the sofa and went back to sleep. When she next woke it was Monday evening.

Chapter 14

Oxtail Soup

The following morning, the sun rose pink in the sky and the air was mild. Alys felt stuffy and stiff from the sofa and didn't have the energy to wrestle Miss Marple out of the garage. The walk would do her good, and she set off at a brisk pace, as any rational adult would. By the time she'd made it into the office toilets, her pale face was ghoulish in the bathroom mirror.

'Hello, stranger.' Mairéad appeared at her side and began to wash her hands, looking at Alys in the mirror.

Alys avoided her gaze. 'Hello, Mairéad.'

'We missed you yesterday... Are you feeling ok? You're looking a little odd.'

'I'm—I'm not myself,' Alys admitted.

'Should you be in?'

'Where else would I be?' Alys asked, confused.

'Home. In bed.'

'I'll be fine. Just need caffeine.'

She backed out of the bathroom and made her way to the kitchen. Joe and Candace were looking through a schedule at her desk. Her things had been pushed aside to clear a space for them. They looked up as she passed and Joe pulled a face. 'You look rough.'

'I'm fine,' she mumbled. 'Just need a coffee.' When she got to the kitchen, her mug had been left to one side. The oxtail soup drinker had filled it with soapy water that had done nothing to clean the crusted black ring of soup around its rim. She was carefully pouring the water into the sink when she noticed the chip. She turned the cup around so that the large scrawling purple 'Alys' could be clearly seen.

'Who keeps using my mug?' she shouted across the room. Her voice sounded strange to her own ears. People stopped what they were doing to look at her. No one answered. 'No, really. I want to know. Who thinks it's ok to take my mug every day and leave it for me to clean? Who thinks nothing of breaking my mug? Who even thinks oxtail soup is a good idea?' Her voice had begun to rise and it cracked on the last word. No one spoke. 'Because I don't. I think it stinks and every day, no matter how hard I clean my mug, my coffee smells of your soup.' She waved her cup across the whole gathering, taking in Tim who had also got to his feet and was frowning now. She watched as Mairéad got up and began to walk across the room towards her, her eyes never wavering from her face.

'It's not fair. It's just—not—fair,' she faltered, her energy spent.

'Come on, Alys. Get your coat. I'll take you home,' Mairéad said gently, and she cupped a hand under Alys's elbow and steered her past the staring faces at their desks, holding a finger up to Tim as he tried to approach.

Mairéad helped her into Crispin, reached over her to plug in the seatbelt and closed the door. There was a lilac umbrella on the backseat and a small tin of travel sweets, the sort covered in powdered sugar that Alys remembered from day trips with her grandmother, in the front. She shook her head when Mairéad offered her one and leant back and closed her eyes instead. Mairéad seemed in no need of an explanation, nor did she need directions. She was one of those women who seemed to know everything there was to know. As they drew up outside her house, Alys gave a little shiver. When she got out of the car, she turned and leaned back into towards Mairéad.

'What do they call me behind my back?' she asked.

'Not now.' Mairéad shook her head.

'What do they call me?'

'Another time.'

'Tell me!'

'Alys...'

Mairéad began to pull off, but Alys kept her hands on the window until Mairéad relented.

'They call you the Weeping Angel.'

Chapter 15

Yellow Dots

Alys didn't leave the house for the rest of the week. For the most part, she slept. She was inexplicably exhausted, craving sleep and losing herself in a deep, dreamless slumber that left her even more tired. Days passed. Once, she heard the door close and realised that she had missed Jack. He had chosen not to wake her. He had cleaned the kitchen—unable to help himself, she supposed. She poured herself a glass of wine and took a slow tour of the house, looking to see what he had taken with him. This time, his wardrobe was bare. All his suits, the boxes of Church's shoes, his cufflinks, aftershave—his work armour—had been cleared. His bathroom cabinet, likewise. In his study, the photos had mostly been claimed, although he'd left the family portrait from their wedding. The bookshelves had been ransacked, small spaces where slim volumes once took pride of place. She tried to recall the books, but nothing came to mind.

As she padded around the study, she noticed small yellow sticky labels on certain pieces of furniture. His desk had one, his sound system, the Arne Jacobsen chair they had chosen together. She moved into the dining room. There too were yellow dots. He had marked the fine wines, some of the crystal, the dining chairs, but not the table. In every room in the house, she found the yellow dots. Whilst she had been sleeping, Jack had systematically inventoried their home. He had not waited a week before he had begun the dismantling. How long he had been thinking of leaving her? What had he been waiting for?

If she hadn't been such a disgrace at the party, would it have made a difference? Could she have bought herself more time with him? The yellow dot on the sofa stopped her breath in her throat. He must have leaned over her to place the dot there. She went back upstairs. There was no yellow dot on their bed. She calmly stripped the sheets, barely stopping for a moment to breathe the smell of him in from his pillowcases, before she bundled them all up in a pile and replaced them with a brushed cotton set. She went downstairs and opened one of the bottles with a yellow dot on it. Swigging as she went, she re-entered the study and chose a book at random—Hemingway—which she brought back with her to the kitchen, made herself a bowl of pasta with garlic, lemon and rosemary and settled down to read, drinking wine from the bottle, forking pasta into her mouth, relishing where the oil hit the pages. She left the dishes in the sink, an act of defiance that felt necessary to her equilibrium, and brought the novel up to the bathroom with her.

She drew a deep bath—her first in days. As she sank down into the steaming water, immersing her dirty hair in the bubbles, she was reminded of her toe stuck in the tap and resisted the urge to do it again. There would be no one to help her when she became trapped. This would be what it was like for the rest of her life now. She would have to be alert to traps for single women living alone. Ladders, faulty electrics, burglary—a list of potential threats scrolled in front of her eyes like a ticker tape. She recalled Jack's hand cradling her numb foot, and she thought that might have been the one of the last times that he had intentionally touched her. She imagined herself launching out of the bath, padding naked out into the back garden, and digging a deep narrow hole. She tucked that memory tenderly into the hole and patted the soil back over it.

Sleep came easily that night, but she woke with a start in the early hours and found that she couldn't catch her breath. She reached for the bedside light, and the first thing that came into focus was the Hemingway book cover. Tiptoeing back downstairs, she retrieved another of the yellow dot bottles and brought it back up to bed. She cracked open the book along its spine and carried on.

The sound of someone hammering on her door woke her. For a moment, she was unsure of where she was. She had been dreaming of giant swordfish leaping out of an azure ocean, the sunlight running like a strip light down their flanks. The hammering started again and beat time with her heart. It didn't stop until she'd staggered downstairs and opened the door.

Douglas was standing on the doorstep. He was scowling. It was an unfamiliar expression. She raised a hand to her hair. It was strangely sticky and would not submit to her hand as a hairbrush.

'What have you done to yourself?'

He followed her into the house, making for the kitchen

where he gently pushed her back into a chair and put the kettle on. This felt like an entirely rational act of Douglas's. He was so quintessentially English that whenever he was faced with something untoward, his first response was tea.

'I have been calling and texting you for days. Why have you not replied?'

Alys couldn't recall when she had last seen her phone. She assumed it had run out of battery at some point.

'What day of the week are we?'

'We are Friday.'

'Oh.'

He busied himself with tea-making, adding two large teaspoons of sugar to Alys's cup.

'I met Mairéad,' he said over his shoulder.

'Oh?'

He settled down beside her. 'When you didn't show up at the park, return my calls or answer the door, I began to worry.'

'What did you think had happened to me?'

He blinked at her as if she had missed the obvious. 'I thought Jack had murdered you.'

'Jesus, Douglas. He's not a monster!'

'Well, he's a very angry man.'

'He left me.' Her voice disappeared down a well and she couldn't be certain that Douglas had picked up its distant echo until he nodded and murmured, 'Who would have thought that could sound worse?'

'You're not surprised?'

'Mairéad told me.'

Alys nodded. Of course, Mairéad would have known. 'You must think I'm pathetic.'

'Must I?'

'To have clung on to him for so long when he clearly didn't love me.' Her lip wobbled. 'To have let myself go to such a state that he couldn't. I can't bear the thought of not being with him.'

Douglas took her cup and set it down before enveloping her in his arms. 'Goodness, Alys. What have you got in your hair?'

'Bubble bath, I think,' she mumbled from his shirt front and she breathed in his smell of cedar wood and wool and felt the world right itself a little. It was always the way with Douglas. He had a way of making fractured things whole again by simply being with them. At school, she would follow him out to the far reaches of the sports field to hunt for caterpillars. He was patient and methodical. She would crouch alongside him as he pulled the sleeves of his jumper down over his fingers to pluck the curled nettle leaves that would more often not peel open to reveal a bright green caterpillar writhing in the light. She would watch his face as he unearthed his find, his quiet pleasure transmitting to her. No need to speak, just a communion of sorts out by the far field—Douglas in his socks and sandals and Alys with her weird family.

They sat like that for some time, Douglas stroking her back and her taking in deep breaths and letting out little sighs, trying to master the judders that came in fits and starts.

'He's put these little yellow dots on all our things. I found one on the iroku wood salad servers Lincoln gave me for Christmas last year.'

'Whatever for?'

'Oh, you know, so that the removal men know what he wants to take when he finally goes. He's very efficient. You know the way Jack works. He always knows what he wants.' She paused. 'Or doesn't want.'

Douglas snorted. 'I don't think it works like that anyway, Al. I think you both have to agree on the dispersal of goods.'

'Well, I've polished off his Barolo, so I may have blown that.' They both eyed the chaos in the kitchen sink. 'I hate this place,' she said. 'It's like Frankenstein, all odd bits that don't fit together to make a whole. Aside from my workroom, I can't find a single place that I feel truly comfortable in. It feels like a punishment to be left here on my own.'

'We can't have that, can we?' Douglas said softly. 'You'll come home with me.' He slapped his thighs as if the matter had been decided. 'You can stay with me. You can have my room. Why don't you go and have a shower and pack some things? I'll have a bit of a clear up, then we'll go home for tea. Judging by the crust on that plate, you haven't eaten for a while.'

She didn't like to apprise him of the fact that she had eaten all her meals in bed for the past few days, in case he changed his mind about letting her stay. Suddenly, the idea of spending one more night in the mausoleum of her marriage was beyond bearing.

She quickly showered and packed the only case that Jack had left in the wardrobe—a small weekend case. He clearly had not anticipated Alys wanting to go anywhere. She was starting down the stairs when she thought about her small things. She couldn't go without them. There were no yellow dots in her workroom, she registered with a small flare of relief.

She found a large shoe box and gently nestled them side by side—the tiny pieces of furniture, the angels, the animals, the

Douglases, affirming their names as she placed them in the box. It wasn't until she was about the close the lid of the box that she noticed that Yellowstone Bear was missing. She searched for him under the table, the armchair, even squinted down the back of the radiator, but the small yellow bear had vanished.

Chapter 16

The Kindness of Strangers

Douglas lived in the Edwardian house he had grown up in. It was neat and unassuming, set back from the road and shielded by a large privet hedge. For all their friendship, Alys had only been inside Douglas's house a handful of times before. Douglas had not been allowed to bring friends home, an edict which remained in place long after his father died, and his mother suffered the stroke that would leave her powerless. Douglas's mother had been a prickly, unforgiving woman whom Alys had avoided at all costs. As she followed him in over the threshold, Alys could almost feel Mrs Weatherley's small white hand on her chest, pushing her backwards. '*Not you.*'

'Why don't you make yourself comfortable in the drawing room? I won't be a tick.' His voice was a little louder than usual. The drawing room was a study in jewelled tones; mauve, olive, and teal. There was an old leather sofa, burnished like a horse's saddle, and covered in tapestried cushions of blowsy peonies. For all her austerity, Mrs Weatherley could not help but betray her love of opulence in her work, and in the cabinet of ruby glass that she treasured above all else. Beside the fireplace, Alys noted the armchair that Mr Weatherley used to sit in, now claimed by Douglas—a Henning Mankell thriller, on the side-table alongside the chair to mark his spot.

She perched on the leather sofa, not daring to lean back on the peonies, and took a deep breath. A white cat appeared in the doorway and froze at the sight of her. Its eyes narrowed, but still it sauntered nonchalantly over to her and rubbed its face on her shins, the edge of a small fang catching as it did so.

'Hello, Soames,' she whispered. 'Long time, no see. How's he treating you?' She reached a finger down and scratched behind a ragged ear. 'Have you been fighting again?'

Douglas turned the corner, rattling a tea tray. 'The answer to your first question is, "Douglas has been treating me surprisingly well, in the face of my relentless disdain for him." The answer to your second question is, "Yes."'

Soames collapsed on to his belly and caught her finger with one outstretched claw. There was always an element of violence with Soames—it never did to be at ease with him. Even after years of careful truce, Douglas was beginning to admit that he wasn't the ideal pet. He had rescued the stray from a group of bullies who had strung the cat up and were attempting to set fire to him. For all his natural strength, it was the only time that Douglas had ever thrown a punch and he missed. It did not end well for him. They broke his arm. 'I tore a very nice pair of trousers at the knee,' he complained to Alys. The cat consented to come home with him, but had looked at him with scorn ever since.

'He thinks you're a pussy, Douglas.'

'*Pas devant le chat*, Alys. Drink your tea.'

When he left her to arrange her sleeping quarters, the sound of furniture being dragged across floorboards above sent her to the foot of the stairs, but he declined all offers of help. By the time he returned gleaming with perspiration to declare himself finished, she had read a third of his thriller.

They prepared a light supper together, working alongside each other in silence. After they'd eaten, Alys stifled a yawn and Douglas guided her upstairs to her new room. He had cleared his own bedroom for her and made the bed with real sheets and a floral eiderdown. There was a small pine chest of drawers, a matching wardrobe, and some empty shelves for her small treasures. She took her time unpacking and laying out her things, arranging the tiny figurines until it felt more homely, all the while seeing Mrs Weatherley's tightly pursed lips and the way she had of looking down her nose at Alys. On her way back from the bathroom, she noticed the door to Douglas's new room was ajar and she nudged it open with her foot and peered inside.

He had moved into his father's old bedroom. On every wall were box frames of pinned butterflies and beetles. It was a riot of dusty, muted colour, and it took a moment for her eyes to adjust to the myriad tiny bodies. She imagined the collective effort of those beating wings might bring the frames crashing to the floor. They drew her inside and she walked slowly around as if at a museum, squinting at the handwritten sepia labels that Douglas's father had so painstakingly written out—Black Arches, Argent and Sable, Cinnabar, Nut-tree Tussock, Orchard Ermine.

'Are you going to be ok sleeping with all these dead things watching you?' she called over her shoulder.

Douglas handed her a mug of Horlicks. 'I'll be perfectly fine with the dead things, thank you. They remind me of Father.'

Douglas's father had been a renowned lepidopterist and botanist. Alys had not been aware of his standing until she attended his funeral, and half of the Natural History Museum and Butterfly Conservation had shown up to pay their respects. It had been his work that had brought them to South Burling when Douglas was nine, much to his mother's disgust. She was a wardrobe designer at a theatre in the West End of London and whilst she didn't need to work, she disliked idle hands almost as much as she disliked motherhood.

Douglas could name every one of the butterflies and moths without looking at their labels. When his father passed away, his mother had banished all the specimens to the garage, and after the funeral Douglas had taken Alys to see them. Trays upon trays of powdery, silvery creatures. Through Mrs Weatherley's eyes they were unsettling, through Douglas's they were magical. His father had been a gentle man, never happier than when spending time amongst his butterflies with his son. Douglas said that his father had taught him how to be still.

As she looked at the frames in Douglas's room now, she saw not the gruesome debris of a dead man's obsession, nor the ethereal creatures of Douglas's childhood. She saw how trapped they were, stuck forever against their will in an unnatural place, and the thought of those powdery wings battering against the glass made her queasy.

She settled easily into life with Douglas. At some point, she imagined Douglas would have called Seagull to let them know she was sick, but she couldn't bring herself to care. It was as if she had been placed into an induced coma. When Douglas was at work, she slept. When he returned, they cooked comfort food, read books, and barely spoke. Jack had not attempted to contact her, and she was afraid to try him. She reasoned to herself that it would be good to give him time—a little space would give them both some perspective—but as the days dragged on, she feared the unravelling would become something permanent, and that they wouldn't be able to find the way back to each other. He would get used to life without her. For what did she bring to the party, really? He'd been carrying her for so long. She couldn't blame him if he had to set her down now. This she kept to herself, willing herself to sleep when her grief became too vast to contain. If Douglas noticed anything wrong, he declined to comment.

It was towards the end of the second week that Alys was woken from a dreamless sleep to the sound of the doorbell ringing. The visitor kept a finger on the doorbell for as long as it took Alys to shrug on her dressing gown and make it down the stairs, only ceasing when the door swung open and away from their hand.

'You took your time.'

'Mairéad... what are you doing here? What time is it?'

'Your friend Douglas found me and suggested a visit. It's 2.30pm on Thursday. Only sinners are in bed at this time in the afternoon.'

There was a moment when Alys contemplated not letting Mairéad in. She knew she was being childish, but a part of her resented this pushy, know-it-all, who she barely knew, muscling in on her ragged life with her bluntness and her pragmatism. While she was weighing up this act of resistance, Mairéad stepped past her and into the drawing room. She glanced around, taking in the detail, and sniffed when she saw the ruby glass cabinet. 'My mam has a thing about ruby glass. Douglas said to tell you to make me tea and that he has a coconut cake in the parrot tin—top shelf.'

Baffled, Alys prepared a tray as Douglas would have liked. If Douglas had invited her, she must be alright. They seemed a very unlikely combination. She found Mairéad bent over the bookcase, her eyes squinting at the spines of Douglas's crime-fiction collection. 'Something we have in common.' She smiled as straightened up.

'What are you doing here?' Alys asked again.

'I'm here to see you, of course. I'm not coming for the ruby glass.'

'Is everything alright at work? Is Tim cross with me for not turning up?'

'I told him you had a doctor's note for "general debility", but that I was concerned that it might be related to workplace harassment. The man is shitting himself.'

'Why did you do that?'

'To buy you time so that you can preserve your dignity. They're vicious in that place.'

Mairéad settled herself down on the sofa, plumping up the peonies cushions before resting back on them. 'Douglas and I feel that you need to get back to work and start getting your life back together.'

'Douglas said that?' Alys blinked.

'Yes. Well, not in so many words, but I could tell he was concerned about you.'

'No one needs to be concerned about me. I've just had a little setback and I need a bit of time to get back on my feet.' Her voice wobbled.

'Forgive me, Alys, but being a lazy bitch and wallowing in bed all day feeling sorry for yourself is not what I'd call recovery. I told Tim you'd be in on Monday morning.'

'Monday? But that's, wait, what day are we today?

Thursday? That's only a few days away. I'm not ready. Seriously, Mairéad. You don't understand.'

'I understand that you need to start living.'

'I can't.'

'Of course you can. Can't is not the same as won't.'

A flare of anger surged through Alys again, louder this time.

'Who do you think you are to tell me what to do? I've met you, what, three times? You don't even know me. What gives you the right to take over my life and tell me how I should live?'

Mairéad gazed steadily back at her, nonplussed. 'It certainly seems to me that you're very happy to let other people do that. That's your modus operandi, isn't it?'

Alys opened her mouth to expel a little gasp, then closed it again.

'I'm curious to know what made you to change course and steer for inconsequentiality, Alys Larsson. Was it one cataclysmic catastrophe or a long list of disappointments that whittled away at you?'

Alys thought of the moths above them, pinned behind glass, their fluttering wings silenced for good. She managed a whisper, 'A bit of both.'

Mairéad seemed comfortable to drink her tea in silence, her eyes on the glass cabinet, ignoring the tears that had spilled over on to Alys's cheeks.

'Alys, I'm not here to cause you any more pain, but I happen to believe that you need my help to get you back on your own two feet so that you can figure out where you go from here.'

'Why would you bother with me?' Alys mumbled.

Mairéad shrugged. 'Think of it as the kindness of strangers.'

Alys snorted. Mairéad didn't seem the type.

Mairéad sipped her tea ruminatively. When she had finished, she set her cup back on to the tray and turned to Alys once more.

'What do you see when you see me, Alys?'

'Pardon?'

'What do you see when you look at me?'

Alys was afraid that was what she had meant. 'I—I see-someone who's been very successful in their career, who is very self-assured...'

'Bullshit. You see the stain on my face. That's what you see. That's what they all see.' Mairéad nodded as if she had established a fact. 'How do you imagine it was growing up in a small town in the west of Ireland looking like this?'

Alys shook her head. 'I can't imagine.'

'My mammy used to have to drag me to school, literally peel my fingers off the railings along the road up to the gates. She knew she couldn't protect me from what would happen to me once I was inside those gates. It made her brisk with me. "Sometimes we just have to face into our trials, Mairéad,'" she'd say. "There's a reason for everything on God's earth. God's made you in his image for a reason." But as much as I scoured our library books, I never found an image of a God with a face like mine. There was no reason I could see for making me so repulsive to other people. Daddy said it was character-building. My mammy forced me to school every day because she was trying to toughen me up. She believed that it would be so much harder when I became an adult. She was wrong. Children are worse. They say what adults only think.

'When I was ten, someone put a note in my desk saying that I was the spawn of the devil, branded with his mark. I believed them. I spent a long time on my knees at my bedside praying for baby Jesus and Our Lady to take me for their own and banish the darkness in me. I had no friends. I mean it. Not a single friend. The only person I hung out with was my cousin at family gatherings, and he only did it because his mammy was my mammy's sister. He always had to wash his hands a lot when he was around me, and wouldn't take his trifle from the same bowl. Once, I found him crying in the outside toilet because his mammy had caught him a slap for saying that he didn't want to play with me anymore.

'When I reached fifteen, I sent away for some pan stick that promised to cover up any blemishes and give an even golden glow. It took great glubs of the stuff to work on me and I looked orange. I don't know what I was thinking. Everyone knew what I looked like underneath, anyway. They'd spent years flinching away from me, camouflage was beyond the point. I became even more of a joke. They used to walk behind me, humming the Oompa Loompa song.

'On prize day, I was awarded the Marie Sullivan prize for Most Promising Academic. I don't remember going up to receive my prize because every girl had conspired to cover their face with pan stick, so when I faced out into the audience, all I could see was my parents' white faces marooned in a sea of orange. I nearly didn't go back to school the following year. My mammy spoke to the head, Mr O'Mahoney, and he came to see me. He was a kind old soul. He must have been pushing retirement, but there wasn't anyone to replace him, so he kept on going. I always thought his head was in the clouds, but it turned out he knew everything that had gone on—things I hadn't told anyone—he hadn't missed a thing. He listed the back catalogue of my humiliation quite matter-of-factly. He said he had decided not to intervene because, in his experience, it only made things worse. He didn't say anything about character building, or turning the other cheek, or God's purpose. He called it as it was—a great pile of shite. Instead, he gave me a copy of The Great Gatsby with one page turned down and suggested I read it in a quiet moment. It was that passage about Daisy being beautiful for the way she thought, beautiful deep down in her soul—nothing so temporary as physical beauty. That's when I realised that it was down to me to build my character, after all. I knuckled down, came out top of my year and I didn't look back. I like the life I chose for myself, Alys. It fits me well.

'Now, I haven't thought of Brendan O'Mahoney—God rest his soul—in thirty years, but when I saw you on that first day, he came back to me with that book outstretched in his hand and his eyes looking straight at mine. When I saw you, I saw fifteen-year-old me hiding behind my pan stick, praying for invisibility.' She sighed. 'Sometimes, people come to our aid from the strangest corners when we don't even know we need them. I don't presume to be your saviour, as old O'Mahoney was mine, but there's a reason he came to mind and I owe it to him to repay his kindness. Trust me, I'm not planning on stalking you. I'll stick around just until you get back up on your feet, then I'll leave you to it. Deal?' She gave a decisive nod, as if the matter were settled. 'There's more to you than meets the eye, Alys.' The red stain on her cheek tightened as she smiled. 'People like us need to stick together, wouldn't you say?'

'It's just not that simple, Mairéad. I can't go on out there on my own. I—I don't know what I'm going to do.'

'Just start walking. Trust me. One step leads to another. You'll figure out the path as you go.' Mairéad stood up and began to gather her things. 'Now, this is very nice cake. I'll be taking that last slice with me when I go, thank you.'

Chapter 17

Garbo's Jumpsuit

When Douglas returned home that night, he was greeted by the smell of spiced beef casserole wafting from the kitchen, and a tidy house. Alys had changed into clean clothes, and her hair was shiny and tied back in a low bun at her neck.

'The invigorating influence of Mairéad, I assume?' He chuckled.

After dinner, he confessed that he had intercepted Mairéad on her way into work that morning with the suggestion that Alys might welcome a visit.

'I didn't realise you were such a man of action,' Alys mused. 'Doesn't that contravene all your non-interventionist policies?'

She was lying on top of him, taking up the full length of the sofa, sipping wine and aimlessly surfing channels on the TV.

'Alas! I fear I'm ill-equipped when it comes to affairs of the heart and I was worried about you. Drastic and uncharacteristic action was required. She's very forthright, your new friend, but I think she has a point. You can't hide from life forever. This is the start of a slippery slope you can't afford to slide down. We need to nip it in the bud. Work will give you something to focus on other than Jack.'

'But that's just it, Douglas. I don't want to focus on anything other than Jack. I want my husband back.'

Douglas's eyes rested on Soames who had slunk up onto the sofa at his feet. He flinched as Soames bit him on the ankle. 'He does that because he loves me, I'm told.'

She went back to surfing channels.

'Talking to Mairéad today made me realise that I'm like an empty shell. I wish I could climb out of my skin and pull on another person. Like a jumpsuit. Someone braver and wiser who'd know what to do with her life. Someone who would have a blueprint or a route map for this next bit. Someone who knew her own mind.'

'Someone who knew her own worth,' Douglas corrected.

Alys alighted on a black and white film. 'Oh, it's *Grand Hotel* with Garbo. I love this one. You used to watch the old classics with your mum, didn't you? I used to do the same with my gran whenever we stayed with her. I loved the old black and whites. Everything was so glamorous and uncomplicated. We'd spend hours working through their dance routines, singing the old songs.'

'Mother used to watch them to study the costumes.'

'Those beautiful dresses.'

They settled back to watch and were soon lost in the drama of a celebrated ballerina facing the end of her career.

'Garbo is just sublime, isn't she?' Alys breathed. 'Oh, not at the start when she's pretending to be tired, or when she's being all gay and prancing—that isn't her at all, it's the worst ham acting, but when she tilts her head back and looks up at Barrymore and her emotions sort of ripple over her face like a breeze on a lake, when her mouth quivers or her eyebrows furrow, these tiny facial expressions, she's mesmerising. She's this complex creature that is going with her own emotions on a whim, but the strength in her... when she walks out through the Grand Hotel lobby, she's like a queen. Then when she decides she can't dance—she senses the audience no longer loves her—she runs away! Who would do that? I wouldn't. I would have to go through with the whole thing, make a fool of myself, go home with laddered tights, get drunk and cry myself to sleep, but she has enough self-preservation to run, even though she knows the disaster it will be to her reputation and career.'

A strange burst of exhilaration had caught her up, then released her, and she settled back down again and barely moved, her eyes glued to the screen. She was oblivious until Douglas complained that his legs had cramped, and he had to manoeuvre himself out from under her as if she were a dead body.

Not until the end of the film did she turn to him. 'Oh, I wish I were Garbo. I wish I could just turn up at Seagull on Monday in Garbo's shoes.'

'Garbo's jumpsuit, you mean. I think I like Alys more than I like Garbo.'

She thumped the sofa. 'But Douglas, I am tired of being Alys. You must see what a joke she is? Alys is a mistake. A half-coloured in woman. Garbo is a whole continent. She knows who she is and what she wants. Alys can't navigate through all of this, she's useless, but Garbo would know exactly what to do. She'd know how to create an independent life on her own terms and win her man back. She'd know how to turn this into a triumph!'

She got to her feet, caught up in inspiration, and began to pace.

'I get it now. I was wondering how I might fix things—I just didn't know how. As Alys. But if I could become someone else, someone like Garbo, stronger, more sure of myself, I'm sure it could turn things around.'

'To my memory, I don't think Garbo ever married. I'm not sure she would know what to do in your shoes.' He sounded wary.

'If I could just borrow Garbo for a bit, would that be so bad?' she beseeched him. 'She could run Front of House until I work out who Alys needs to be behind the scenes. No one would even know—except you and me. It would just be my own private experiment.'

'Alys, I'm not sure I'm following your thinking. You're starting to sound a little mad.'

'Oh, I'm not going to *be* Garbo. I'm not bonkers. I'm going to use her as a role model. Think about it—what role models do fifty-year-old women actually have? Who is there to tell us how to live, or to help us forge our own identities at this stage in our lives? When our bodies are starting to become strangers to us, children have left home, marriages have crumbled. When we need help the most, who is there to shine a light to guide us?'

She stopped pacing, her mind made up. 'It would just be for a little while, Douglas. It'd just be me asking, "What would Garbo do in this situation?"'

'I think you're confusing the myth with the woman. She was a recluse who spent most of her life feeling lonely. What could she possibly offer as a role model?'

'Alone is not lonely. She had her dignity intact. She only let the world in as far as it suited her. I need that. I need that distance she created between herself and other people. Half the world gawped at my old knickers when I passed out spread-eagled on that bed. I just need a little distance and some dignity.'

'I'm sorry, Alys. I don't see what's so wrong with you. I like you as you are. Why can't you just be more you?'

'Because being me got me to this point in my life, Douglas, and what have I got to show for it? My husband has just walked out on me, I have no family, no career to speak of, my colleagues think I'm a joke.'

'What happened to make you this tired of life?'

'I'm not tired of life, Douglas. I'm just tired of me.'

'So it's time for a change. It doesn't mean you have to make yourself something you're not. Can't you just do what ordinary people do when they're having a break down—get a tattoo and sleep with someone inappropriate?'

Alys shook her head, forlorn. 'It wouldn't be enough. I need something to stir in the fundaments to make me right.'

They sat in silence, Douglas with his eyes fixed on the ruby glass, as if looking for an answer from Mrs Weatherley.

'Well,' he said finally, patting his thighs. 'We want to make you right, don't we? If you're going to channel Garbo, you'll need the big guns. *Grand Hotel* won't cut it. She was a lunatic in that one. No, you'll want *Anna Christie, Mata Hari*... I'll have to roll out my DVD collection. We're going to be busy this weekend.' He rose to his feet, but then turned to her.

'I'll help you with your experiment but promise me, at the end of it, my Alys will come back home.'

Chapter 18

Form

She was still thinking of Garbo as she dropped off to sleep. She couldn't imagine Garbo ever suffering a crisis of confidence. When Garbo became a recluse, it was like life imitating art, like Grusinskaya in *Grand Hotel* refusing to dance to a half-empty theatre. Her career was starting to slump and she chose to end it on her own terms. In the face of failure, Garbo came out shining, striding across the foyer of life with her head thrown back and that long careless stride of hers, oblivious to naysayers. But then, Garbo wasn't just an ordinary woman.

Douglas didn't understand what it meant to be a fifty-year-old woman. How could he? He didn't understand how ridiculous or irrelevant you became. He hadn't seen the look of revulsion on that young doctor's face in the coil clinic, and the shame she felt for subjecting him to her ageing body and her inadequacy. He didn't know that there was nothing more invisible than a woman over fifty. No one prepared you for that. Oh, they were all free to talk about menopause, the incandescent rages and brain fog—complete strangers swapping notes on their vaginal dryness—until they were blue in face, but there were no masterclasses on how to cope with rejection on such a major scale. It was like the universe letting you know that you were surplus to requirement once you'd produced the next generation, and she hadn't even done that. The worst of it all was the loneliness. Did other women feel as lonely as she did? They likely had close relationships with their mothers, sisters, old school friends who were like sisters, even. Alys had none of these. She wasn't sure how to have a close female friend. Douglas had always filled that space.

She thought back to her own school days. Her family, the village joke, and the girls in her class soaking up the conversations they heard at home and parroting them in the playground. She tried to ignore the impersonations they did of Monica Faulkener weaving across the courtyard, or the sniggering about the gift shop, or the threadbare elbows on Alys's cardigan, or how dirty her hair was. No, she wasn't close to them. She had baulked at the thought of coming back to the village that most of them had never left. Even after all those intervening years, she felt shabby and embarrassed when she passed them in the street. It was like a stain she couldn't scrub off, no matter how different she was now. Jack had tried to encourage her to make more friends, but it seemed that they could not expunge the memory of the joke she was, and she could not forgive their cruelty. Interestingly, those girls grew up to have fairly miserable lives—adultery, battery, bereavement, brief imprisonment, and empty marriages—it read like a felony list, so perhaps their perfect lives weren't perfect after all.

She'd had friends at university, but had lost contact with them. 'Busy lives' she'd explain to Jack, but in truth, those friends liked the party girl, the clown that Alys had turned herself into. It was hard to sustain a friendship built on straw. She had form, she thought. She had reinvented herself once before—she could do it again.

'I'm going to find the real me,' she told herself, *'and when I do, Jack will fall in love with me again.'*

Chapter 19

Becoming Garbo

That weekend, Alys devoured Douglas's film collection. She barely left the sofa. From time to time, Douglas would find a space alongside her, and watch her watching Garbo. Alys would rewind the film, pause at a scene and ask Douglas to tell her what he noticed. How did she come across to him? What did he see in her? Where did her strength lie? What made her alluring? The questions came thick and fast, and Douglas struggled to satisfy her curiosity and to match her urgency.

'The thing is, Alys, and don't take this the wrong way, but you look nothing like Garbo. You're softer, rounder. She's all angles and shoulders—she looks like a heron.'

'I know that, Douglas. I'm not an idiot. But look at her. There was a reason she was the greatest screen actor of all time. There's something about her. It's her spirit. I just want a little of that spirit to rub off on me. I need to borrow some of it. I can't go back into the office on Monday as me. I know what they think of me, what they'll be saying about Jack and me. I can't face the humiliation.'

'You're going a bit mad. You know that, don't you?' he

said earnestly, and pressed the back of her hand, as if he were talking to a lunatic.

'I'm waking up, is what I'm doing. I'm going to find the real me.'

Douglas often complained that he was born in the wrong era. He wore a certain mild facial expression when he was confronted with what he called 'the nonsense of modern, urban life'. He turned this look on her now. 'All I'm saying is that I'm not sure Garbo needed to go to these lengths to find Garbo.'

Sunday morning saw Alys busying over breakfast, and the smell of bacon and coffee brought a sleepy Douglas to the kitchen door.

'This is a pleasant surprise,' he said as he tried to flatten his unruly hair.

'Me making you breakfast?'

'No, you being up before midday.'

'I am channelling Garbo's work ethic. I'm on studio hours now, baby.'

'I very much doubt that Garbo would have been allowed bacon and eggs on studio time. Those women were starved.'

'I can't work on an empty stomach, Douglas. We both know that. I need fuel to create.'

'What are we creating today?'

'Me, of course!'

She had pushed the furniture against the walls in the living room. When she saw Douglas's face, she felt a moment of remorse. It hadn't occurred to her that he would mind, but living there for the past few weeks, it was clear that nothing had changed since his mother had been in residence. It took Douglas a moment to adjust his composure.

'Sorry. I can move it back.'

'No, no, it's fine.' He rubbed his face and came up smiling again. A sad sort of smile that didn't reach his eyes.

She took him by the tips of his fingers and led him to the sofa and stood before him.

'In order to integrate Garbo, I need to...'

'To what?'

'To assimilate all the desirable attributes of the screen goddess. I'm obviously not able to transform into her...'

'It looks like you may have tried.'

'... obviously not going to be able to transform into her,' Alys said firmly. 'It's more a question of studying her mannerisms, her style, her language, her approach, philosophy, and copying them. It's her essence I'm after. Now that I've made a deep study of her, I just need to put that into practice. For example, her walk.'

Alys moved swiftly over to the fireplace. 'She has this long stride, she walks quickly, leaning backwards with her head moving from side to side. She has this bony body, with big hands, and feet too big for her weight. Watch.'

She launched herself into a loping gait with such abandon that she caught a picture frame with her right hand and sent it flying.

'It's not broken,' she cried and returned to the other side of the room, swooping down and catching up the picture as she passed, setting it down with a flourish.

'What do you think? Do I look like Garbo?'

'I think you sound a bit weird.'

'That's my Garbo voice.'

'Oh, Alys, really. I'm afraid I'll have to draw a line.'

'Ok, ok. I won't do the accent, but perhaps I could work

on lowering my tone. That would give me some gravitas, don't you think?'

'I think—' Douglas got to his feet and straightened the picture frame. 'I think we need to take this outside. There isn't room to swing a cat in here.' Soames glowered at them, his tail flicking from side to side.

They went to the park and found a clearing between the trees where Alys pranced backwards and forwards. At first, she was self-conscious and her chin kept dipping down. Douglas would call, 'At me, Alys,' and she would raise her eyes and keep them fixed on his face, blinking furiously.

'I can't walk forward if I can't see where I'm putting my feet.'

'Don't be ridiculous—of course you can. How do you normally walk?'

'Um, looking at my feet.'

'What would Garbo do? That's better. Stop sticking your tongue out. Put your tongue back in, but part your lips slightly. No, forget that. Just try to look normal. Tongue, Alys! At me!' At one point, she thought she was starting to fall into the rhythm of Garbo's stride—she felt something flicker to life in her, like a flame catching—but then her foot caught on a tree root and she was sent flying. Her hands broke her fall and she lay for a while in an ungainly sprawl, her wrists throbbing with the impact, trying to gather the energy to stand up again. What was she doing? Douglas was right. She was losing her mind. This was ridiculous at her age. Fifty-year-old women didn't go into method acting to try to make themselves lovable. This was something only she would conceive of—no wonder people thought her so odd.

She was trying to blink her tears away when she caught

sight of an indistinct figure standing before her. It hadn't been there a second before, Alys was sure of it. Was it a floater? She wiped her eyes. Greta Garbo was lounging nonchalantly, gazing down at her. She blinked again. Garbo hadn't moved. She was wearing her Anna Christie costume —a cloche hat, a black ribbon tied around her neck, a black cardigan with a hole in it, a cream frilly blouse that lay open to her breastbone, and a black skirt. She was tapping a cigarette out of its box and inspecting Alys's prone state with a look of haughty indifference.

'Stand up, dummy.'

'W-who are you?' Alys stammered.

Garbo raised a perfect eyebrow.

'I mean—are you a ghost?'

'No, dummy. You think if I were a ghost, I'd waste time on you? I'm a figment of your over-active imagination.'

Alys gawped at her as Garbo put the cigarette in her mouth and lit it, her eyes still appraising Alys.

The sound of running feet interrupted them. Douglas appeared at her side and pulled her to her feet, patting her down as if reassuring a dog. 'You alright? Don't cry, Alys. You don't have to do this, you know. There's no shame in changing your mind.' Alys looked to see if Garbo had disappeared, but she was still there. This time her raised eyebrow suggested amusement.

'How about a coffee? Stay there and I'll fetch you a cup.' He turned and ran in long, slow strides back to his rucksack.

As soon as his back was turned, Alys began. 'So, what, I just conjured you up, is that it? Is that even possible?'

Garbo shrugged. 'Looks like it, kid.'

'Why would I do that?' A thought crossed her mind. 'Am I going mad?'

'No, no.' Garbo waved her arms at her. 'Nothing like that. Just accept that you conjured me up because you need a little help, that's all. Everyone needs a little help sometimes. You've had a rough ride.' She stamped her foot and screwed her hands into fists around her cigarette. 'It's all men's fault. Giving you a wrong start.'

'That's a line from *Anna Christie*, isn't it? You're being Anna Christie?'

Garbo's face became blank and she shrugged. 'Sorry. Occupational hazard.'

Douglas reappeared at her side with the lid of his Thermos flask. 'Here you go.' It was clear that he couldn't see Garbo standing right next to him, and when she stood behind him and Alys's eyes followed her, he turned around to see what she was looking at, but looked right through her.

Garbo grinned. 'I told you—a figment of your imagination. Here to get you back on your feet. Now drink up and watch me. When you hand the cup back, I want you to look at Douglas like this.' She tilted her head back and straightened her shoulders and looked down along the length of her nose.

Alys breathed in a jerky sigh and did her best to imitate her, and Douglas was dumbstruck. 'Actually, Alys, you might be on to something here. That was really very good.'

He gave her the thumbs up, then jogged to the edge of the clearing as if he were a director clearing the set.

'I'm not sure why you picked me as your role-model.' Garbo sniffed. 'We're really nothing alike. I'm tall and broad-shouldered and slim and you are curvy and small. You're more womanly than me.'

'But you're so feminine!' Alys exclaimed. 'They called you the most beautiful woman in the world!'

'In a boy's body.' Garbo laughed. 'All that smoke and

mirrors. I played to the screen, as all we women must. We need to start afresh. You're going about all this wrong. Now, what do you notice about me when I walk? Forget the mechanics of how I hold my shoulders, or what I do with my feet. What do you *notice*?'

Garbo strode out across the clearing, towards Douglas, as if she were walking across the lobby at the Grand Hotel. She held her hands at her waist and swung her hips slightly, her head held high. She turned and walked back towards Alys.

The thing about Garbo's walk was its confidence, Alys decided. It didn't matter that she was about to perform to a waning audience, or that she had double-crossed a lover, she walked with such insouciance. She rolled the word around her mouth before setting out. This time, Alys walked leaning backwards, so that it looked like her hips were carrying her forward. She broke into long fast-paced strides, her eyes trained on Douglas, a haughty tilt to her head.

'By Jove, I think she's got it!' Douglas clapped his hands. She spun around to catch Garbo applauding politely before she disappeared.

Chapter 20

Play Acting

'I think you've got the walk down now,' Douglas spoke through a mouthful of ham sandwich, his manners forgotten in a rush of excitement. 'We need to work on the facial expressions and her language.'

'And her philosophy,' Alys reminded him. It wasn't about the superficial things. It was her essence that Alys craved. Perhaps, as Douglas had hinted, Garbo was a woman like Alys, floundering and miserable, hiding from life. Alys hoped not, and that Garbo was as sophisticated and worldly-wise behind the scenes as she was in front of the camera. She wanted fervently to believe that Garbo would have answers for her that would allow her life to coalesce smoothly into a shape that made sense to her.

'I hope you don't mind doing this, Douglas. You're not bored, are you?'

'Bored? I haven't had this much fun in years. It's not often you get a ringside seat at someone else's unravelling. Believe me, Alys, I lead a very dull existence.'

'Well, you're surprisingly good at all this.'

He laughed. 'I must have inherited it from mother. It's funny, she could never tolerate what went on with the theatre crowd, their louche ways, you know, yet she loved the art in a very pure sense. She knew all the lines. She said she had to inhabit the characters herself to know how to dress them. In some ways, what we're doing isn't so very different.'

'Douglas, did you ever mind the way your life turned out? The business, I mean. Did it ever bother you that circumstances dictated who you became?'

Douglas appeared to ponder this. 'I don't think I thought much of it at the time,' he confessed. 'Father was gone and we needed some stability in the family. Mother did. It was just what needed to be done. Afterwards, when Mr Rushton invited me to join him, I made the decision with clear sight. I knew what I was doing. I think family has always been the most important thing in my life, and the choices I have made reflect that.'

'What did you want to be?'

'Oh, I don't know. A history teacher, I think. Yes, I would have liked that.'

'I'm sorry.'

'It is an unusual occupation, I grant you, but then, I am not what you could call a usual man. In many ways, I landed the perfect career for myself. I have always valued tradition and I enjoy being part of the ritual of a passing. I must admit, the theatricality of a final send off appeals to me, and I like to think I'm good at what I do. I am respectful. I don't rush people through their final farewells the way some directors do. I have come to think of my work as an act of love for people I've never met. I am walking alongside them on the last stage of their journey. There aren't many careers that carry with them such privilege.'

'You are a very sweet man, Douglas Weatherley, and I love you very much.'

Alys leant forward and kissed him on the side of his head, leaving a lick of moisture in the dent of his temple, which he quickly wiped away.

After lunch, Douglas became business-like and efficient. Alys was to choose a particular role, "Grusinskaya, *Grand Hotel*" and try to imitate Garbo's facial expressions.

'I'll say a word or give you a circumstance, and you give me Garbo, ok?' There was a theatrical pause before he shot 'Happy!' at her.

Alys raised her eyes up to the sky and gave a wide grin.

'Not bad. Bit over the top, but not bad. How about angry?' he asked.

Alys tried to think of something that made her angry. She couldn't summon anything. Why wasn't she angry? Surely in all of this, she could come up with something? She knitted her brow and tried to make her eyes blaze as Garbo's did.

'We'll come back to that one,' Douglas said.

'This is harder than it looks.' Alys rubbed her hands over her face.

'Perhaps you picked the wrong film. What about one of her silent films, "Flesh and the Devil". Remember her playing Felicitas? Let's take the scene when she and John Gilbert have their first kiss. What does she do to let you know she wants him?'

Alys thought for a moment. 'She looks at him with those eyes. She looks straight through him as if she were looking at something at the back of his head, but on the inside.'

'Disturbing. And so?'

'It's like she's peering into his soul. Like he's the only man that exists in the whole world.'

'Very good. So, bit of a stretch, but try to imagine that I am Gilbert. I want you to look at me with that intensity. Garbo lowers her eyelids and she doesn't blink. Tilt your head back and look up at me. You're blinking. Stop blinking. Ok, have a good blink and get it out of your system and then try again.'

Alys blinked furiously for a moment, then looked up at Douglas and fixed her eyes on his. She noticed how brown his eyes looked against the grey backdrop of the park in winter. They were a deep, rich chestnut brown, almost velvety in their darkness. He had lovely eyes. It was their gentleness and kindness that made them so, the little laughter lines that curved away into his hairline. Douglas was a very attractive man when he wasn't being Douglas. He was looking down into her eyes, and Alys forgot to blink. She lowered her eyelids and continued to stare at him until there was only Douglas in the universe, with his kind, brown eyes and the curl that had fallen across his forehead. Her lips parted.

'Get a room!' Two teenage boys on skateboards swerved past them, jeering, and their eye contact snapped in half. The spell dissipated.

Douglas was puce. She felt a bit hot herself.

'That appears to have been effective,' he said, and he busied himself with the buckles on his satchel.

'You might want to study Felicitas again, and watch when she's being bad or selfish. It's all in the eyes.'

Alys wondered whether Garbo had been watching them. Could she conjure her up when she wanted to? She tried by thinking very hard about her, holding her breath and squeezing her stomach muscles. She ventured some pelvic floor exercises. Nothing. Garbo, it seemed, would only come when Garbo chose to.

Chapter 21

Tiny Cogs

There were six missed calls from Jack when they returned home. Alys was shocked to hear from him, but unconcerned about the number of attempts. On the odd occasion when Alys was out of reach, Jack would call relentlessly on repeat until she finally remembered to look for her phone. The record was twenty-four.

'He must want something,' she said.

'I hadn't liked to point it out, but you don't have many clothes here, Alys. Had you thought about what you were going to wear tomorrow? You're going to have to go home and collect some work clothes. Maybe it's a good excuse to see him and talk things through?'

'I'm not ready. I haven't got my armour—I haven't integrated Garbo.'

'You can do silent Garbo. You never managed to get a word in with Jack anyway, so he won't notice the difference.'

There was no sign of Jack when she arrived, and his car was not in the driveway. She used her key to let herself in and couldn't resist looking over her shoulder, as if she were a cat burglar. The house was silent. She had intended to make it a swift operation. Straight upstairs, fill the empty suitcase Douglas had lent her with whatever she thought she'd need for the next few weeks, then head back, but instead she found herself in the kitchen. Her kitchen. She wouldn't have recognised it in a line-up. Gone were her precious jars of spice blends, her colourful Kilners of pasta and pulses, her plants. Facing her now were glossy waste-lands of granite, an alien landscape unblemished by Alys's things.

She stood, pressing a fingertip against the surface and trying to catch its print in the weak light of a late afternoon sun. Jack had erased her. She had been away for two weeks, at his instigation, and not once had he called to see how she was holding up. Not until he needed something. In the meantime, he had eradicated her from their home. It was as if she had never existed. She pressed all her fingers on the surfaces now, swiping, smudging, licking her fingers and wiping them back and forth. This was what anger felt like, and she knitted her brow and worked her mouth like Garbo as she flung open the kitchen cupboards, lifted every tin and jar she could find and set them out, their jaunty labels at odds with the sleek linearity of the backdrop. She reached to the back of the cupboard and located the family size jar of Nutella that was Jack's dirty little secret, half tore off the gold seal which she knew would annoy him, and stuck a knife into it, gouging out the chocolate spread over the top of the foil, wiping it over the surfaces like mud slicks. She left the knife upright in it like a stabbing.

She was in a sort of frenzy now, practising her Garbo expressions as she went. She spun around to make for the study.

'Alys?'

Jack was standing in the doorway, bare-chested and in his pyjama bottoms, rubbing his face of sleep.

His eyes widened as he saw the mess behind her. 'What are you doing here?'

She jumped at the sight of him, but quickly tried to recover her composure, tilting her head back and looking down her nose at him. *What would Garbo say?* She reached for the right level of hauteur. 'Surely I don't need an invitation to come into my own home?'

Jack's eyes moved between her and the kitchen surfaces. Her gaze followed his. The open cupboards looked like a row of shocked mouths, and she turned back to face him.

'Sorry,' she mumbled, and then because he seemed unable to speak, 'It's not you, it's me.'

Despite her contrition, she couldn't bring herself to clear up. She wanted to leave her mark. She wanted to show her anger, so she left the mess as it was. After Jack had shown her where her spice blends were kept, they sat in the living room.

'Is Douglas looking after you?'

'How did you know I was staying with Douglas?'

He shrugged. 'Where else would you go?'

Her life was so predictable to him. She was a creature of limited imagination. Of course, she would have fled to Douglas. Where else could she go? She thought of Garbo as Grusinskaya, fleeing the theatre and heading out into the city, leaving everyone to wonder where she'd gone. A truly wild woman, she could have been anywhere. Alys was pedestrian by comparison.

'I didn't think you were home. Where is your car?'

'At the garage, being fixed up. I had an accident.'

'When? What happened? Were you hurt?'

'It's fine. Some ninety-year-old woman forgot which side of the road she was meant to be on. She and her old banger were unscathed. I've had whiplash and a sore shoulder. That's why I'd gone back to bed. I'm fine, though, really.'

'Why didn't you tell me?'

'Honestly? I wasn't sure you'd be that interested. You left without a word, Alys. I interpreted that as a clear request for me to leave you alone for a bit.'

'You told me you wanted me to let you go. I thought that was what you wanted.'

'I did, I do. I didn't expect you to disappear.'

'You thought I would just wallow here in a house I don't like until you decided what to do with me?'

'It wasn't like that. I would have liked to have taken care of you, checked in on you. It's not like I don't love you, Alys. I just don't love—us. This version of us.' He cupped his hands in front of him to show the smallness of what they amounted to before letting them fall into his lap.

Alys opened then closed her mouth, as if she were coming up for air. She had forgotten how gentle Jack had been in the early years. She was afraid she might cry. In all of these weeks, apart from in the aftermath of Lincoln's party, she hadn't once broken down, but now she thought she might crack and any last vestige of dignity would be gone.

What would Garbo do? She would demonstrate restraint, she decided. She would decline to engage. People always made Garbo nervous, and when things got emotionally fraught, she would hide like an ostrich. Silence was definitely the best weapon in the armoury when you were about to lose your shit. She distracted herself from the ache in her throat by looking at Jack with her Garbo eyes. At first, he seemed disconcerted, but after a moment he was caught in her gaze, drawn in by that mesmerising focus. She held them both like that, in suspension, even after a small tear slipped out and made its way to her jawline. It was calming when there was nothing to be said. He leaned in slightly towards her as if he might kiss her, but then winced and his hand flew to his shoulder and the moment was lost, and only when he had turned away did she understand how much she had wanted him to.

'Actually, Alys. I'm glad I got to see you. I've been trying to reach you.'

'I saw that.'

He looked sheepish. 'I need to ask you a favour. A big favour.'

Silent Garbo looked on.

'It's about next weekend.'

Alys looked blankly at him.

'Mum's birthday party? Had you forgotten?'

'It may have slipped my mind.'

'It's all anyone has been talking about for the past six months. It's worse than a bloody wedding. It's like a military operation.'

Hannah Larsson was the commander of the Larsson family. She had given birth to her four boys by the age of twenty-two, a fact she never failed to remind Alys. She ran her household like a well-oiled machine, with her boys as tiny cogs. She was fuelled by thwarted ambition, and turned being a stay-at-home mother into a career. Her job was to set her boys up for success. Their job was to excel. She would brook no dissension. Before the boys could walk, she had decided that Linus would be a doctor, Jack would practise at the Bar, and the twins, Otto and Eric, would be the business brains and bankers. If Hannah had decided that her birthday would be the event of the century, then she would have it so, and her little cogs would dutifully turn with her direction.

'The thing is, Al, I haven't told them about us. What with the party and everything it didn't feel like the right time.'

She trained her eyes on him. Was it a timing issue, or was he just avoiding the inevitable showdown with Hannah? Hannah Larsson might despise her daughter-in-law, but she was a stickler for tradition and respecting the sanctity of institutions. No matter that her son had married beneath him to a woman who hadn't borne him a child, she would insist that he lie in the bed he had made for himself.

'And the favour?' Alys prompted.

'I need you to come on Saturday and pretend that you are still my wife... I mean, that we're still together.'

'Absolutely not.'

'Alys, please...'

She shook her head.

'It's just one day, then I promise we can go back to our arrangement, and I will find the right time to tell her our decision.'

'Your decision,' she mumbled.

'Please Alys. It will break her heart. We can't do it this close to her birthday.'

Try as she might, Alys could not imagine the steely Hannah Larsson broken-hearted.

'You know how I feel about lying.'

'It won't be so much a lie as an evasion—a delaying tactic. If there's any lying to be done, I'll do it. You'll just need to turn up, stand by my side and look happy.'

'I'll never be able to carry it off for a whole day.'

'Not unhappy, then. Alys, please. I wouldn't ask it of

you if it didn't mean so much. I promise, this is a onetime event. I will tell them afterwards.'

She hesitated. It was unlike Jack to say please. The truth was, she didn't want anyone to know that her husband no longer wanted 'this version of us'. If no one knew, perhaps there was a chance that he would realise that this was just a mid-life crisis and get over it. It would just be a pothole in the otherwise harmonious marital path. This was normal. It happened all the time to people of their age. Sometimes they got back together even stronger than they were before. This could happen to them. She would try harder to be a better woman, and he would learn to love her again, and she wouldn't feel scratched raw every time she looked at his beautiful face and felt the depth of her loss.

'I'll think about it.' She nodded.

Chapter 22

Excuses

Alys spent the rest of the day hanging her clothes in Douglas's old wardrobe. It had been intended for a child and was narrow and short, but her clothing was sparse and tired and fitted in without complaint. She told herself they could be moved back to the house she shared with Jack at a moment's notice, but couldn't shake a sense of finality, and it struck her that with her clothes and her small things removed, there was very little left that she would lay claim to. It was as if she had been in transit for a decade. She brought her spice blends down to the kitchen where Douglas had cleared a shelf for her, and set about making a spiced vegetable tagine, filling the kitchen with aromas that would have made the plain-eating Mrs Weatherley wrinkle her nose and fan the door. Douglas sat across the table from her as she chopped vegetables, only stopping to take a sip from a large glass of wine. She was calm when she told him about her afternoon with Jack. She confessed to the kitchen vandalism, which made him chuckle. She didn't tell him how painful it had been to see Jack bare-chested and sleepy, and how she had wanted to curl up against his bare skin and breathe in its scent. She didn't tell him that she hadn't been able to shift the hollowed-out feeling in her stomach that the loss of him brought, nor the renewed sense of shame that she had been responsible for this crisis in her marriage.

'Will you go to the party?'

'Do I have to?'

'Not if you don't want to. Not anymore. You don't have to do anything you don't want to.'

'I don't want to go to work tomorrow.'

'That's different.'

'I told him I'd think about it.'

Douglas snorted.

'I don't want to cause him any more trouble. He doesn't deserve it.'

Douglas opened his mouth and closed it again.

'Really, Douglas. It's not his fault we've come to this.'

'Why do you always make excuses for him?' Douglas shook his head in wonder. 'He can be a complete cad, and you always make out it's your fault?'

'I don't always...'

'Yes, Alys. You do. Every time.'

She considered this. 'I'm not an idiot. I know he's not perfect. Isn't that what love is about, though? Accepting one another's flaws? Taking the rough with the smooth?' She thought about Ian and Monica, still pushing on after all these years. Jack hadn't accepted her imperfection, though. He'd given up on them. Some flaws were just too big to surmount.

Chapter 23

Eyebrows

The evening had ended on a mellow note. She had distracted Douglas by reminding him of a late-night opening at The Granary. Enid had miraculously persuaded the famous local crime writer, Alastair Cummings, to give a book reading, and Douglas had talked of nothing else for days. Still, she slept fitfully, disturbed by vivid dreams of struggling to run on dusty ground where deep fissures suddenly appeared underfoot. She had only just gone back over to sleep when the alarm went off, and the face that stared back at her from the bathroom mirror was haggard and bleary-eyed. Monday had finally arrived.

She was still sombre when she and Douglas left the house. She had forgotten to retrieve Miss Marple, so they walked part of the way together before Douglas had to turn off.

'Remember Garbo'. He kissed her cheek.

She tried to keep the parting image of his face in her mind as she trudged to Seagull Publishing. Each step closer brought an increased dread, and by the time she rounded the corner and slipped down the alleyway beside the building, it was as if she were wading through porridge.

She paused at the bottom of the stairs, in her father's old stockroom, one hand pressed against the wall to hold her up, a light sheen of sweat on her forehead. She couldn't face these people. If they had suspected that she was odd before, they would know without doubt now that her husband had left her. It was there for all to see. Like old knickers. There was no hiding it. She wished that she could be Garbo, holed up in her New York apartment, surrounded by her beautiful things and free to admit only those closest to her. What would Garbo do now?

'I'd climb those stairs with my head held high as if I couldn't care less.'

Alys opened her eyes and there was Garbo sitting on the step alongside her, her arms resting on her knees. She was wearing a man's shirt, wide legged trousers, and black pumps, and was picking her teeth with a toothpick.

'You!' Alys gasped. 'Where have you been?'

'Oh, here and there.' She shrugged.

'Why can't I summon you when I need you?'

'I'm here, aren't I?'

'But I've needed you all weekend. If you're a figment of my imagination, why couldn't I make you appear like a genie?'

Garbo frowned. 'I don't know. I'm not sure it works like that. Anyway.' She got to her feet and tossed the toothpick to one side, 'I would go about my work as if no one existed for me. I would please myself and if I had to have dealings with anyone, I would look them bang slap in the eye. Now, up you go. Show them your mettle.'

Alys wiped her face with her cuff and started up the

stairs. Garbo took each step in time with her. 'That's the spirit,' she urged.

As she reached the top of the stairs, Alys's movements became studied and languid. She pushed through the door at the top and, calling to mind her walks in the clearing, she tipped her hips forward, tilted her head back and aimed for her corner. Candace was leaning over Tim at his desk, they both straightened as she approached, but Alys strode past them without a sideways glance.

The state of her desk caught her in mid-stride. It appeared as she had left it, but she was taken aback by the disorganisation and chaos of the manuscripts, stacked at right angles to each other. It looked like a crabbed pokey hole. How had she found this a healthy place to inhabit? She took her seat, banging her knees on her desk and her elbow on the wall. When she came to lift the manuscripts off her desk surface, she found she could not fully pivot on her seat. She was trapped between the wall and the desk corner and her body twisted violently to free the trajectory of the seat.

Garbo sat perched on the corner, a slight smile tugging at her lips.

Alys caught herself, breathed deeply, and shifted back into character. A coffee would calm her nerves. She was waiting for the kettle to boil when she suddenly noticed Tim loitering close by. His anxiety revealed itself in a series of twitches, a furious blinking and a curious spasm that threatened to dislocate his shoulder.

'Alys! Great to see you.' He gave a thumbs up. The kitchen galley was narrow, and Alys was alarmed at having to share it with her boss for the first time in her memory. 'I trust you're well? Not that I'm prying, of course. Just wanted to, you know, touch base with you and check that you are functioning... I mean... feeling normal... not that you weren't normal before, just what with... and everything. Good. So all good. Glad we've that sorted. Goodo.' He attempted to pat her shoulder, then withdrew his hand as if he'd been scorched.

He shuffled backwards in an awkward imitation of the Moon Walk, and she turned her attention to the mug cupboard.

There was her Alys mug, only it wasn't her Alys mug. It was a replica, without the chipped handle and the soup stains.

'The piranhas had a whip round and replaced it.' Mairéad appeared at her side. Alys stood with the cup in her hand, then she turned and hugged Mairéad. It was like holding a plank wrapped in bones and gristle. Alys wasn't sure if she was hugging her out of gratitude, or holding on to a life raft. She wanted to wail, 'What am I doing here?' Instead, she said in her Garbo voice, 'That's terribly kind of them.'

Mairéad looked at her curiously. 'You ok?'

'Yes, yes. I'm splendid.' The effort to keep her tone light and her voice deep was harder to maintain than she'd expected.

Mairéad followed her back out to her desk and looked on as Alys proceeded to clear every piece of paper on to the floor and then wipe her desk down with her sleeve. She sat down at her chair and tried to shift it forward, but the wheels caught on a wrinkle in the carpet and she humped fruitlessly to shift it. Mairéad watched her with a raised eyebrow.

'I cannot bear this!' Alys cried and put her hand to her cheek for good measure. 'Something must be done.'

'Who are you and what have you done with Alys?' Mairéad said stoutly.

'Too much,' Garbo murmured, over Mairéad's shoulder.

Alys ceased humping and slumped back in her chair. She was exhausted herself.

'Alys is taking some time out,' she said in her best gravelly tones.

'What's with the weird accent?'

'Yes, I hate the accent too. I don't sound anything like that.' Garbo peered at Mairéad. 'I like this one.'

'Sssh.' Alys silenced them both and casting wildly around her.

'Are you hearing voices, Alys?' Mairéad looked concerned.

'In a manner of speaking.' Alys looked out of the window. Mairéad seemed to have a way of making her divulge her innermost thoughts. It was very disconcerting.

'Look at me!' Mairéad turned Alys to face her. Alys trained her eyes on Mairéad's chin. If she didn't engage in eye contact, she might just avoid having to tell her anything.

'These voices—they're not telling you to do something stupid, are they?' Mairéad growled.

'No!' Alys let out a laugh. 'Nothing like that.'

Alys gave in at the sight of Mairéad's obvious relief. 'It's Garbo.'

'Greta Garbo?'

Alys nodded frenetically.

'You're pretending to be Greta Garbo, or it's actually Greta Garbo?'

'I know you're teasing me. I'm not up for humour at the present time. I'm channelling the spirit of Garbo to get me through this... episode.'

'I'm not going to ask why. For the record, from the off, I

always thought you were on the edge of going completely bats.'

Alys glowered at her under knitted brows.

'So how's it working out for you?'

'Not good so far. Not good.'

'You want to give me a demonstration? Go over there and tell Tim you want the desk over there by the window.'

'I'm not ready.'

'Pff. I thought you were Garbo. Stop being such a pussy.'

'Yes, Alys. Stop being a pussy.' Garbo pinched her arm.

Alys tried to stand up and banged her thighs on her desk again. How had she never noticed how uncomfortable her working space was? Had she grown two inches? Why did she no longer fit?

She manoeuvred past Mairéad and broke into a lope, head lifted high. Tim started when he saw her in front of him. His eyes began to water. She jutted her left hip against his desk and stared down the length of her nose at him. 'I need to move desks. That corner space is unsatisfactory.'

Tim glanced over at Candace for support. 'I'm not sure where we could find to move you, Alys.'

Alys faltered, but then caught sight of Mairéad nodding purposefully at her from the corner and she tried again. 'You misunderstand me. I am not asking for permission. I'm just informing you that I'll be relocating to the desk by the window.' She followed this up by gazing at Tim and lowering her eyelids slightly. She might have been overdoing it, but it seemed to have the desired effect because he nodded mutely and Candace shot up and offered to help her move. 'I watered your plants whilst you were away, Alys', she tweeted.

Candace's earnest desire to help made Alys uncomfortable, but she managed a low 'Thank you,' and was touched to see a pink flush of happiness suffuse Candace's face.

'Actually, Candace, we do need your help, but with something else altogether. Bring your handbag and follow us.' Mairéad joined Alys and pulled her back towards the bathroom. Candace followed meekly, her head pecking backwards and forwards in distress. Once inside, Mairéad flashed an old screenshot of Garbo on her phone at Candace and said, 'I'll need you to pluck your woman's eyebrows so that they look like these. Maybe not as thin, but make sure you get the shape.'

Alys tried to protest by putting her fingers over her brows, but Mairéad assured her that it was the difference that was needed to transform her. She peeled her fingers off her face one by one, placating her as if she were a frightened child.

With trembling fingers, Candace diligently worked at Alys's brows, pausing to check the photograph or peek at Mairéad who was standing with arms folded, overseeing the operation. When she'd finished, Alys was tickled by a light flurry of hair on her cheeks.

'Jesus. It was like topiary. Fair play to you, Candace. That was no easy job.' Mairéad patted Candace briskly.

Candace blushed with pleasure as Alys peered into the mirror, turning her face one way and then another.

A triptych of faces peered back at her, with Mairéad and Garbo on one shoulder, their eyes squinting in critical appraisal, and Candace on the other, so full of apprehension she looked as if she might cry.

Candace had worked a miracle. Alys looked different, fresher, younger. She looked like a different woman. Gone were the thick straight eyebrows she had grown up with, replaced with finer, shapely brows, slightly arched over her eye socket. They were thicker than Garbo's, and yet they gave Alys the same piquant, challenging expression which was offset by the softness of her eyes. Jack used to call their colour 'pepper grey', and for the first time she understood what he had seen in those days when he thought nothing of spending time staring deeply into them. She tried out a few Garbo expressions—a beguiling gaze, a calculating sideways glance. Her eyes filled with tears.

'Not bad,' Garbo conceded.

'Thank you, Candace, you've made me look...' She couldn't finish.

Candace clapped. 'You look just like her!'

'Well, I wouldn't go that far,' Garbo prickled.

It hadn't occurred to Alys that she would tell anyone other than Douglas of her experiment, and now here were two women in on it. What was happening to her? Garbo would never have allowed her private affairs to be dragged out in such an undignified fashion in a public toilet.

'Good work, Candace.' Mairéad placed a hand on her shoulder. 'If you say a word of any of this to anyone, I will sew your lips shut with a needle and thread, is that understood?' She handed a pinched-looking Candace her handbag and guided her to the door. 'Alys will be out to join you shortly. You might want to make a start moving her things over.'

'Was that absolutely necessary? Candace wouldn't hurt a fly,' Alys protested.

'No, but she can't keep her trap shut, so unless you want everyone talking about your business... As your agent, I considered it a precautionary shot across the bow.'

Chapter 24

The Granary

Mairéad appeared at her desk later that afternoon. 'You've a hair appointment on Thursday after work.'

'I didn't make an appointment.' Alys frowned. Or had she? It was possible that she'd forgotten. She was prone to forgetting appointments.

'No, I did, and I'm coming with you to make sure that you don't chicken out and ask for just a trim.'

'I can't make Thursday. I'm going out with Douglas.'

So it was that Mairéad accompanied Alys on her first trip to the hair salon in over a year. Alys, mystified by Mairéad's ability to ignore any obstacle placed in her way and assume control of a situation, felt obliged to invite her to Enid's book reading at The Granary in return. Mairéad accepted with equanimity, as if she had intended to join her all along.

True to her word, she cajoled Alys into accepting a shorter, softer cut, which brought out her natural curl. Alys's shorn hair looked like a bedraggled fleece. She had to resist the urge to push it out of view with her foot. By the time they met Douglas in front of the bookshop, she was giddy with the recklessness of her acquiescence. The early evening air lay a cool hand on the nape of her neck.

'You look—beautiful,' Douglas murmured. To Mairéad, he extended a courteous nod and then, offering both of his arms, he said, 'Shall we, ladies?'

Once inside the bookshop, Douglas escorted Mairéad to the crime fiction shelves. Alys nestled just inside the door. The shop looked particularly magical as garlands of tiny lights hung from the rafters, illuminating the tops of customers' heads with a soft glow. Alys took a deep breath, absorbing the familiar smell of paper and the earthy, old stone smell of the barn beneath.

Enid was perched on a stool, looking every bit the bookseller, behind the large haberdasher's counter that served as her cash desk. In front of her were silver trays bearing wine and canapés with salmon paste garnished with chunks of cherry tomato that Enid had hacked at. Alys made her way over to the diminutive woman and leaned over the side of the counter to kiss her cheek.

'It looks beautiful in here tonight.'

Enid grunted, but her eyes twinkled when they rested on Alys.

'Hello, stranger. Haven't seen you around these parts in a while. You've made a bit of an effort I see. Not bad looking when you scrub up. That bastard, Cummings, is late. If he doesn't turn up, it'll be the last thing he does on this earth.'

'Is he coming far? Don't worry, if he's a no-show we've always got Douglas. He's read every one of his books and in this light, he could pass for the cover photo. Most people are only here for the wine, anyway.'

Enid let out a throaty crackle then winced.

'Your back playing up?' Alys touched her shoulder

lightly, feeling bones under thin skin. Enid's head dipped briefly.

'I'm afraid I'm going to have to call time here soon.' Enid cast a wistful glance over her beloved shop. 'I'm not sure how long I can keep the show on the road.'

'Nonsense. We'll find you holed up behind a book delivery when you're a hundred.' Alys teased, but Enid grimaced and her mood turned sombre. 'Everything has its season, Alys. You know that. Nothing lasts forever.' She patted her hand pointedly. 'Time for a new chapter.'

She might have been speaking of either of them. Alys interlaced her fingers with Enid's and rested her head against hers. Both of them started as the door flew back with a bang and the star of the evening, Alastair Cummings, appeared in the doorway, shouting apologies to the floor and Enid, and bustling towards them.

'Fool,' Enid muttered before slipping off her perch to take his coat.

The evening was a great success in the end. As if to make up for his tardiness, the author made every effort to connect to his fans, writing personal messages in each book he signed and sharing intimate details of his writing process and the upcoming book in his new series. Douglas and Mairéad were rapt with awe. Alys took a seat in her favourite corner and let the sound of laughter wash over her head. She watched Enid as she struggled to find a comfortable position for herself. It made her sad to think of Enid retiring. What would become of her without the shop to keep her busy? Who would take care of her? Come to think of it, what would become of *her*? The Granary had been an anchor for Alys. All the threads that kept her stable were being snipped one after the other, and she didn't relish the thought of being cut loose.

When the author left, he took the crowd with him, leaving Alys, Douglas and Mairéad to help Enid clear up. Enid, slumped with exhaustion, insisted on celebrating with a whisky and she rested a weary hand on Alys's forearm and nodded to the stairs. Enid lived above the shop, in the eaves of the barn. As far as Alys knew, she was the only person allowed in Enid's inner sanctum and, had it not been for the accident, even she might not have seen it.

Enid was like Garbo, content in her chosen seclusion, surrounded by treasures, and like Garbo, her apartment was an astonishing explosion of colour; dull pink, sand and a dusty blue in her bedroom, a rich olive green in the living room, a sunshine yellow in the kitchen. The exuberance of her home was a closely kept secret, as if it were a reflection of her soul. Alys hunted for the whiskey and found a half empty bottle beside the tiny wood burner, whose silver flue stretched up and out of the roof of the barn. It was cosy and intimate in Enid's world, and Alys took her time looking for the whisky glasses. She lingered over a group of photos that lined the stairwell as she went back down the stairs. Enid as a young woman, laughing on the seashore after a swim with friends; Enid, sitting at a desk, thoughtful in a black polo neck, pen in hand; Enid kissing the side of a man's cheek, her eyes squeezed shut with intense pleasure. This was a life, and wherever she looked, she could see Enid's imprint. Enid had never been married, never been a mother either, and yet here was evidence of a rich and adventurous life, full of love and meaning. Alys traced the smile of the young woman whose eyes were squeezed so tightly in pleasure, and pressed a small kiss on her lips with a finger.

She found them sitting in a cluster of armchairs down-stairs, eating the last of the pretzels and laughing as if they'd known each other for years, as Enid regaled them with stories of Alastair Cummings' racier youth. Hunger clawed at Alys's stomach. She hadn't eaten since lunch. She poured out the whisky at the counter, with 'just a smidgeon' for Mairéad who needed to 'get up the road', and hesitated before pouring her own, the bottle hovering over her glass for a second before she set it back down. She was starting to notice how often she reached for a drink to calm herself, and there was no need here. It was easy being in their company—these misfits and oddities, these people who felt like her kind, who counted her as their friend. A tremulous pride lifted the corners of her mouth.

If her life had been intact now, if Jack hadn't left, would she have ventured out tonight and shared this evening with her friends? Evenings were reserved for Jack. More often than not, though, his client drinks would run on and she'd be home alone, drinking wine on an empty stomach, dinner kept warm until he burst through the door, having already eaten. When Jack came home, the house would spring to life, like a faithful spaniel at the sound of his owner's foot-step, as if it had been dozing when it was just Alys. She would have been waiting too, waiting for Jack to come home and—what? Breathe life into her? No, she wouldn't have made it to an evening like this. How much of life had she missed, waiting for Jack to come home?

Chapter 25

Privacy

Douglas and Alys declined the offer of a lift from Mairéad, preferring to take the long walk home. It had rained earlier and they fell into step, the pavements wet underfoot.

'You're quiet,' Douglas said.

'I'm just realising that I'm not a very good friend to you.'

'Nonsense.' He put an arm around her shoulder and pulled her close.

'I haven't been around for you, always so wrapped up in Jack and what he needed. I realised tonight how unavailable I've been. Availability is literally the most basic requirement of a friend.'

'You have a marriage. You have to commit to your husband and put the effort in. That's what happens.'

'It feels like I've put a lot of effort in, or maybe not enough, or maybe a lot, but in the wrong places. I'm starting to wonder how it could have been different, if I'd had more of a life of my own. What would have happened if I'd had more adventures with you, as I would have liked to have done? I think Jack came to resent my dependence.'

'What do you imagine we would have done if you'd been more available?' Douglas sounded amused.

She floundered. 'We'd have gone to Enid's literary evenings.'

'They happen once in a blue moon. You don't think Enid would be shelling out the Reisling if they happened every Thursday, do you?'

'We'd have done more rambling.'

'Ah, rambling.' Douglas nodded appreciatively.

'I'd hate to be the cause of you missing out so much,' she sighed.

Douglas stopped and turned her to face him. The streetlight caught the line of his cheekbone.

'Alys, you don't imagine that I've been sitting at home waiting for you to come out to play with me all these years?'

Put like that, it did sound a little ridiculous. Did the whole world revolve around her?

'I haven't missed out on a thing,' he reassured her. 'As a matter of fact, I've thoroughly enjoyed every one of Enid's book signings. I'm the member of the Botanical Society of Britain and Ireland. The local rambling club. I play cricket. I sign up for various evening courses—remember the coffee spoon I whittled you?'

'Yes, I know all that, but—'

'I have—companions, of the romantic variety, if that's what you're referring to.'

'Do you?'

He inclined his head, throwing his face into the shade. She could just catch the hint of a smile.

'But why don't you talk about them? Why have I never met them?'

'Because I value my privacy. I'm a simple man, Alys. I like a simple life.'

She wracked her brain to try to recall some of Douglas's acquaintances. There was a man, Brian, Bri, who went on field trips with Douglas. She'd met him once when he'd come to collect Douglas from her house. How did she know so little of the details of his life outside of their relationship?

'Do you have a—friend—at the moment?' she asked tentatively.

'Not at the moment, no.'

He gently nudged her forward. The subject was closed.

She had always thought him transparent. If anyone had bothered to ask her, she would have claimed to know all there was to know about her best friend, and yet now it turned out that he had been keeping secrets. Had she known he was so private? She would have called him shy, a little socially awkward outside of work, perhaps, but not capable of such evasion. Still, it couldn't have been easy trying to maintain a love life with Mrs Weatherley's pinched face, watching his every move, determined to let her son know just how disappointing she found him. Ever respectful of his parents' wishes, Douglas must have learned to be discrete about his friends. Perhaps he did it to protect himself from her disapproval.

'I've been so self-absorbed. It's like I've been sleep-walking all these years.'

'Good grief, Alys. Stop overthinking it. You are absorbed in trying to punish yourself. This is not about you. It's about me and my preferences. I like order in my life, and I don't like things to get complicated. I like to keep things separate and discrete from one another. Had I wanted it any other way, you would have been the first to know.'

'I'm not sure we get to choose,' she mused. 'I mean, whether it's orderly or not. I'm not sure life works like that.

In my experience, it's messy and blurry. It's a riot of the unexpected.'

'Perhaps that's why I'm still single, and you managed a marriage of nearly 30 years.'

'I'm not convinced that's much of an achievement,' she murmured.

That night, she rolled their conversation over in her mind, trying to acclimatise herself to the thought of Douglas having an intimate relationship. She didn't know how she felt about it beyond a vague discomfort, a hazy jealousy for someone who didn't exist. Douglas had always been there for her. She had thought she had done the same for him. She had never discussed his love life because it never came up. She'd imagined that he was just one of those men who preferred his collections to people. Now she saw that his life was one of his own careful curations, with people, events, experiences carefully pinned, distinct from one another in a configuration of his choosing. She imagined him as a boy, bent over his father's box frames, his tongue out sideways, the hair on the back of his neck lying soft and sleek as he concentrated on his arrangement of his specimens. She rested a tentative fingertip on the skin above his collar.

Chapter 26

The Day Before

Her mobile woke her on Friday morning before the alarm went off. It was Jack, apologetic but insistent. 'It's Friday, Alys. The party's tomorrow. You said you'd think about it, but I haven't heard from you. If you're doing this to punish me, there are other ways. Don't punish my mother.'

Alys struggled to sit up and push her hair from her eyes. Her new haircut behaved differently in the mornings, it seemed.

'I'm not punishing you, Jack. I just forgot.'

'Forgot?' He sounded exasperated. 'How could you forget it again?'

'Perhaps I didn't forget. I haven't been able to make up my mind.'

Jack pushed on. 'It would mean the world for her to see you.'

'No, it wouldn't.'

'I think you misunderstand Hannah.'

'No, I don't.'

'I don't understand why you're being so difficult. This is so unlike you.'

'Is it?' Alys pondered. What was 'like' her? Acquiescence? Submission? 'I don't mean to be difficult. I just… I find it difficult spending time with your family under normal circumstances. I find *them* difficult, to be honest.'

Jack gasped. 'What has my family ever done to you, save accept you into their arms and put a roof over your head? A roof, I might add that you have never shown an ounce of gratitude for in all the years you've lived in it. What exactly has been so difficult about that?'

Alys shrank back into her pillows.

'Don't you think, Alys, that for once you could be a little less selfish?' he hissed.

Her alarm took the opportunity to ring shrilly, as if in agreement. Her shaking fingers struggled to stop it. In the silence afterwards, she heard the faint echo of its ringing and Jack's deep breathing down the phone, his way of trying to suppress his irritation. 'Please, Alys. Do this one thing for me? I think you owe us this much.'

Did she? What did she owe him, and for what? What was fair recompense for her sin of not matching up to expectations, for the disappointment she caused? Had she really shown such ingratitude for the security that the Larsson money had provided her?

'Ok,' she mumbled. 'This one thing.'

His relief was palpable. A switch had been flicked and he laughed and chattered as if they were lying side by side in bed together, reminding her of other Larsson events, memorable for the spectacular location, or the incredible food. He was like a spoilt, needy child. Now that he had his way, he was trying to make it so that he hadn't bullied or belittled her to get it, choosing to believe that they were both as excited as each other. When he finally let her go, she rose stiffly from her bed, her bones aching as if she'd been shaken.

She told Douglas over breakfast.

'I thought I could hear him throwing his toys out of the pram.' He grimaced.

'Jack always gets what Jack wants,' Alys muttered. Resentment caught her askance.

'Not for much longer,' Douglas comforted her. 'You're going to learn to stand up for yourself again, Alys. You've never liked bullies.'

'If you're referring to the Russell Planchett incident again, can I remind you that was a onetime response? Most of the time, I rolled over and let them kick me.'

'Nonsense. You've never liked injustice. It wouldn't take much to reawaken that fierce little girl.'

Sadness caught her throat. Where had that fierce little girl gone? What made her decide that she'd never win the fight?

She left for work, only to return moments later, out of breath and in a state of panic.

'What will I wear? I have nothing, and I mean nothing, to wear to the party tomorrow.'

'We'll figure something out,' Douglas soothed her. 'Go to work. We'll sort it out tonight.'

Chapter 27

The Dressing Room

There was a large box waiting for her when she got home that evening. It had been propped up against the front step, shielded behind the privet hedge from the main road with its opportunistic passers-by. A card tucked in beneath a red satin ribbon read, 'Thought you might need this. J.'

She had to turn the box on its side to get it through the door, and she left it on the kitchen table, unopened, averting her eyes each time she passed it, until Douglas came home.

It was Douglas who broke its spell by using the card as a taper to light the fire and unceremoniously snipping the ribbon. Inside, nestled in crisp tissue paper, lay a red silk dress and a pair of black heels in their own cotton bag.

'Ah, this is what Jack's wife is supposed to look like,' he mused as Alys lifted it carefully from the box.

'Jack's other wife.' Garbo appeared at her shoulder. 'It's two sizes too small.'

Alys let it drop gently back into the tissue paper. 'It'll be perfect when I've lost my tummy. A kind thought.'

Garbo sighed.

'Do the shoes fit?' Douglas asked.

Alys couldn't help but glance at Garbo's own shoes.

Garbo started. 'What are you looking at? You're looking at my feet, aren't you? Always it's the feet with you people! My feet are a size seven, perfectly in line with my height. Of course, they made me out to be some freak of nature with huge planks for feet, and you know why? They couldn't think of anything else to hit me with. They couldn't control me. I wouldn't let them! Ha!' She tilted her head back triumphantly. 'The shoes are fine,' she sighed. 'Take the shoes.'

Douglas tucked the dress back in the box and closed the lid.

'Come with me, Alys. I have another idea.'

He led her upstairs and continued past her bedroom to the end of the corridor. They paused for a moment outside a door on the right—his mother's bedroom. He swallowed. 'I think we might find what we're looking for in here.'

Alys had always supposed the door to be locked, but it was more the foreboding presence of Mrs Weatherley that had kept her away from exploring this part of the house.

'Is this where he keeps the heads of his ex-wives?' Garbo yawned at her side.

They sidled into the room, and Alys gasped. Mrs Weatherley's bedroom had been converted into a dressing room. Gone was the heavy, mahogany bedroom furniture Douglas had always complained to Alys about, and in its place were rails of costumes, coats, dresses and skirts in silk, tweed, velvet, sprigged cotton. Below, boxes of shoes. Above, shelves showcasing hats, bags and belts. All of them pristinely kept. It was a textile library. Alys crept into the middle of the room and turned around slowly, taking it all in, conscious of Douglas's eyes on her face, gauging her reaction.

'I rearranged it all after Mother died. I couldn't bring myself to give her things to the charity shops, I'm afraid. I know that sounds selfish, but it didn't seem right at the time, so I brought it all in here until I could decide what to do with it and, well...' He cast an eye over the room.

'Jeez.' Garbo whistled. 'It's like a shrine to his dead mother. It's worse than the heads. There are some very nice pieces in here, mind you.'

'I was afraid to tell you before, in case you thought it was odd,' he said sheepishly.

Alys ran her hand across the clothes on the rail.

'It's amazing. It's like a museum or one of your beautiful collections.'

'Mother did have an eye for quality.'

Alys nodded. She remembered Douglas's school uniform. It had been made of wool, of a more stylish cut than the standard polyester version that the rest of the school wore. When it rained, he smelled like a wet dog. Mrs Weatherley had made the uniform larger than Douglas's thin frame, and because of the quality of the fabric it lasted for years—marking Douglas as an outlier for most of their time at Maltings.

'I think we should be able to kit you out for tomorrow at any event.' Douglas smiled. 'The question is, what would Garbo do?'

Garbo blinked at Douglas. 'Is he talking to me?'

'Rhetorical question,' Alys murmured.

'Well, I wouldn't do these for a start.' Garbo dismissed a row of thick tweed suits with a sweep of her hand. 'But this is sublime.' She pointed out a black jersey dress in a 1940s style, with buttons to the neck, a fitted waist and a flared skirt. Alys lifted it from the rail.

Garbo proceeded to point to outfits at intervals along the rails. Alys pulled out the clothes—long silk dresses with beaded necklines, tea-dresses, wide-legged trousers and baggy shirts, polo-necks and pencil skirts.

'Do you want a hat?' Garbo gestured to a cloche hat similar to the one she was wearing.

'No hats,' Alys demurred.

'No, could be a bit much, couldn't it?' Douglas said over his shoulder. He was busy creating a space for Alys's selection on another rail, reaching out to take what she was holding.

'Do you remember that time you went to the Larsson hog roast evening?' Douglas chuckled. 'Hannah had told you that all the women were to wear formal dresses, and you wore that long dress with the sash?'

Alys groaned. She had found the dress in a secondhand shop. It felt nice, soft and forgiving, and the sash that ran from under the breastline to the hem detracted from her stomach. It had rained heavily on the night of the party. In the dash to the taxi, Alys had managed to trap the sash in the car door and it trailed along the road in the mud and rain all the way to the party. She had to spend a frantic few minutes dabbing at it with a dried out wet wipe she had found at the bottom of her bag. Worse was still to come. It seemed that Hannah's instruction had not been given to the other guests. Some girls were wearing light dresses, others jeans. Hannah herself was wearing a sleek trouser suit.

'I looked like Katherine Jenkins popping in for a surprise visit. I said to myself, "You can either get drunk, or go home."' She shuddered. 'It was the longest night of my life. Actually, give me back the long dresses, I can't face that again.'

Douglas fetched a long oval mirror from his room and left Alys to try on the remaining dresses. Garbo lit up a cigarette and stretched out on the floor, propped up by an elbow, as Alys stepped out of her clothes and slipped the first dress over her head.

'You know, Larsson, you're not bad looking. This boy likes what he sees.' Garbo wiggled her eyebrows.

'I'm not sure you should be smoking in here,' Alys whispered.

'Why?' Garbo waved her cigarette. 'It's not like I'm going to set fire to the place.'

'It's the principle. It's disrespectful.'

Garbo sighed and stubbed it out on a shoe box.

'You two are as odd as each other. Not that one. You need my height to carry it off.'

Alys tried one dress after the other, marvelling at the beauty of the fabric and the cut. Why didn't they make clothes like this any more? Each one was rejected by Garbo, who was beginning to fidget.

'You need something elegant but understated.' She tapped out another cigarette, ignoring the dark look that Alys gave her. Clamping the cigarette between her lips, she muttered, 'Try the black one.'

Alys pulled the black jersey over her head and turned to inspect herself in the mirror. Garbo narrowed her eyes and appraised her. 'Put the shoes on.'

Alys almost didn't recognise herself. Her hair, with its new shape fell in soft curls around her shoulders. The tiny seed buttons and the fitted bodice minimised her breasts and showed off the curve of her waist. The skirt fell to just below the knee. It was structured, but soft, and she had never felt more feminine. She turned this way and that, letting the skirt twirl gently against her.

Garbo nodded approvingly. 'That's the one. You can let your boyfriend in now. I can hear him breathing outside the door.'

'He's not my boyfriend,' Alys corrected as she opened the door to Douglas, who tried to look as if he had been inspecting the lintel.

'Very nice.' He smiled.

'Not too funereal? Alys asked.

'If I may...?' he asked, and he rummaged through a few boxes until he found a turquoise brooch that he pinned to her shoulder, just above her heart.

'Mother would approve.' He nodded.

Chapter 28

Pillow Talk

That night, Alys tried unsuccessfully to get to sleep. The more she worried that she wasn't sleeping and would look peaky and baggy-eyed for the party, the more alert she became. The jersey dress hung on the back of her door, and she tried not to look at it, or imagine how she and the dress would behave themselves at another Larsson gathering. Garbo lay sprawled on the bottom of her bed, the amber flare of her cigarette tip glowing as she drew on it.

'What are you worried about?' she asked. 'You don't owe these fools anything. Just go, get a few free drinks and some food, and then do something outrageous.'

Alys snorted.

'Why not?' Garbo shrugged. 'You'll never see them again.'

'Need I remind you that I am fighting for my marriage? If I can just pull this off, Jack and I might still have a chance.'

It was Garbo's turn to snort. 'Men!'

Alys sat up against her pillows and tried to pick out

Garbo's face in the darkness. She could just see the outline of her profile in the inky light.

'Have you ever been in love?'

'Oh, sure.' The amber tip flared.

'But never enough to want to marry?'

'Marriage felt like a such a big step. I don't think someone like me would suit it. I don't like to be led. I want to be free to be on my own. Besides, where would I have met someone? I was working, always working, until it got so that I couldn't bear to be around anyone anymore.' She laughed briefly, then fell silent. 'I never met someone I could give my freedom up for. I wouldn't have minded if it had been a man or a woman, but I never found that one.'

'Did you never want children?'

'Me?' Garbo sounded astonished. 'People make me nervous, Alys. What sort of a mother do you think I would have made? Children need to eat, don't they? I can't even boil an egg!' She sat up and faced Alys then. 'Remind me why you thought I would be a good role-model for you?'

Alys thought for a moment. 'Do you remember that line of yours in *Anna Christie* about living in the fog? It goes—'

'I like this fog, honest. It makes me feel as if I was out of things altogether,' Garbo said.

'That's the one. In the film, the fog is a cleansing thing for Anna. It helps her feel that she can leave behind her old identity to the fog, and start afresh with a clean slate. For me, though, it's like I've been living in the fog for so long, I couldn't see any part of me. I had just got used to seeing a few feet in front of me. Everything else was this sort of dense, white cloud. I abdicated my life. I let other people make decisions for me, about me. I was invisible. Life was just becoming one long series of daily humiliations I allowed to happen to me, and because I kept my eyes on the ground, it didn't matter. Wait long enough, and all the unpleasantness will just be subsumed by the fog.'

'I was always the ostrich, you know.' Garbo grimaced and picked at a thread in the duvet. 'I told myself when things get tricky, get your head down and if you can't see them, they can't see you.'

'You! You were strong!' Alys protested. 'You knew how to preserve the mystery of being a woman. No one could ever have humiliated you. You took control. No one ever knew about your private life—only what you wanted them to know. You were so aloof and private, and I want to learn how to be in control of myself like that, not collapsing into tears everywhere or making a fool of myself.'

'And you hope that I can teach you that? It's true, I have always felt that we lose a little something of ourselves in the telling. It is better to keep some things for our own. Why this modern need to bare all? It's a lack of discipline I don't admire, but my dear Alys, I think, like so many people, you confuse me with the myth. You imagine that I sat in my ivory tower over everyone, collecting my art, holidaying on the Riviera, having a gay old time. That couldn't be further than the truth.'

'But that's how the press portrayed it,' Alys said.

'Oh, sure they did. The truth is, I led a very restricted life in many ways. I always had this thing about wanting to be left alone. I needed my solitude to make the world right, you know? But when I look back on my life, I am sorry that I did that. I wasted the best years of my life like that, when I should have reached out and gorged myself on all those fascinating people, all those adventures. Such beauty!' Garbo sighed and her mouth turned downwards even further. 'All that abundance and I missed out on everything.'

'But, but your dignity, the mystery around you...' Alys tried to keep the dismay out of her voice.

'There is no great mystery, Alys, just deep unhappiness. Don't make the same mistake I did. Don't wait until you've made yourself someone else. This is your life! Jump in! The truth is, we are always in the fog. So what if you can't see ahead of you? Do something, anything, and then make it up as you go. Let yourself go and do something outrageous.' Garbo leaned forward and clamped her hands on Alys's ankles, her long fingers wrapped around them, and she squeezed them gently. An entreaty. Alys heard the loneliness in Garbo's voice.

'You will come tomorrow, won't you? You'll be there with me when I have to face them?'

Garbo stubbed her cigarette out on Alys's duvet. 'Always worried about what other people think of you, aren't you, kiddo? That's your ivory tower.'

'But you'll be there?'

'Sure, sure.' Garbo waved her arm airily. 'Now go to sleep.'

Alys did not remember her head hitting the pillow.

Chapter 29

Disembodiment

Jack came for her the next morning, early. She had dressed herself in a trance and was just putting the finishing touches to her make-up when she heard the knocking below. Her eyes widened and her hand shook as she reapplied another layer of the red lipstick Garbo had insisted on the night before.

When she joined them, Jack was telling Douglas about his new extreme hiking kit, and Douglas was looking at a plant on a shelf just behind Jack's head. They both turned when she appeared, and she would have been delighted by the look of astonishment on Jack's face had she not felt like throwing up the porridge Douglas had force-fed her earlier to line her stomach.

'You look very—nice,' Jack said finally. 'Did you get the dress I sent you?'

'Oh, I almost forgot.' Douglas disappeared and brought back the box. 'All these years, and you still don't know your wife's size.' He was joking without smiling.

Alys stepped in. 'It was a kind thought. I kept the shoes. Thank you.'

Jack was still looking at her as if trying to see what was different. Try as she might, whenever she was around Jack, she couldn't channel Garbo. She forgot her movements, her style, and old Alys appeared, apologetic, shabby, ashamed. She could see how she was even now trying to propitiate Jack, to dispel the tension between the two men as she always did, and stopped herself from talking. She trained her face into one of Garbo's aloof expressions and tried a slightly amused smile at the same time.

'Shall we?' Jack said, and she smiled again as he struggled to get the box back through the front door.

'I'll be there in a second,' she called, making her voice low and firm. Douglas shut the door on him and turned to face her. She was starting to tear up and looked at him in panic.

'You have everything you need to get through this day, Alys Larsson.'

She hugged him and the turquoise brooch pressed into her skin, like a pledge.

'If the wheels come off, I'll come and get you.'

'You don't drive.'

'No, but I have friends who do,' he said mysteriously, and he wiggled his eyebrows to make her laugh.

'I love you, Douglas.'

'And I love you, Alys. Always,' he said gravely. Alys opened her mouth to speak, but he opened the door and, putting his hand on her low back, he gave her a firm push over the threshold.

Chapter 30

Something Outrageous

It was an hour's drive to the Larsson Homestead as Hannah liked to call it, although 'homestead' would imply cosy warmth and the sort of place people loved coming back to after a hard day's work. Hannah's residence was neither.

Jack and Alys exchanged small talk as if they were playing the old Atari game, Pong, two short lines batting a small dot between them with an audible plock each time the dot touched a line. Jack would say something then, after a short pause, as the dot travelled across the court, Alys would respond. Sometimes there would be a longer pause and it would be Alys's turn to serve up a titbit, something she'd read in the news, perhaps. She was reminded of how narrow her life was when her only contribution to the conversation was other people's exploits.

How had their conversations gone when they still lived together? It would have depended on Jack's mood that day. She knew when to talk and when to keep out of his way. Sometimes, if work had gone well and he was feeling pleased with himself, or if she stretched her memory back further to those heady days when he sought her out, when he just wanted to be with her, she could remember the laughter. He was funny when he chose to be, and she would delight in him finding her funny—bent back, hands on his stomach, eyes squeezed shut as if he'd explode. She could recall those lazy mornings with the weekend papers strewn between them—no need for talk then, just contentment. One word here or there to express a thought, and the other knew what was meant and could finish the sentence.

She tried to pinpoint the exact moment in their marriage when she became aware that his appetite for her and her conversation had waned. His attention span was the first to go. She saw that she only had a short window in which to keep him with her. The anxiety made her work harder to catch his attention, filtering out anything he might consider trivial, adopting a fast-paced, sarcastic tone that might pass for smartness and hook him so that, even to her own ear, her conversation sounded contrived. Emotions irritated him. Recounting office news, adventures with Douglas, progress on a series of short-lived hobbies—quilting, wild food foraging, the choir, her work at the animal shelter, things that were personal to her—were boring. After a while, she found that it was easier just to listen to him.

Even the small talk couldn't last today, however, and they spent the second half of the journey in silence. It was as if neither of them had the energy for it when the real conversation between them still needed to be had. By tacit agreement, that had been shelved until after today's ordeal.

When they eventually turned in through the front gates of the Larsson estate, her stomach churned and contracted with familiar dread. She slipped a peek at Jack's profile and noted a tightness in his face. The Larssons did that to you—put you on your guard. She imagined she and Jack silently preparing for a medieval battle, putting on their armour plates together and, in spite of everything that was happening, she was glad that he was with her.

The driveway meandered between twin rows of sentinel larches and would have been beautiful had Alys not always associated it with a visit to the family. The drive was longer than the house merited. The original house, dating back to the early 1800s, had been flanked by two wings, but the East wing had taken a direct hit from a stray bomb in 1942 and had never been rebuilt. Where the gardens were landscaped and structured, the asymmetry of the house was experienced like a misstep by visitors, despite the beauty of the remaining house with its crisp white stones and wide, low windows.

'Shit. We're late.' Jack slapped the steering wheel. A Maserati, a Lexus and a Porsche had already taken pole position, and he had to park his car on the other side of the archway that led to the stable block.

'How can we be? We left early.'

His silence made it clear that he blamed her, and she hurried to join him on the drive. The gravel dragged at her heels, and she had to tiptoe at a fast pace like a show pony to keep up with him without losing a shoe. By the time they had reached the portico and the wide oak door, she was flustered and off-key. Where was her composure? Where was Garbo? She scanned the driveway. Garbo must have found something better to do. It was just like her to please herself. Hadn't that capacity for self-preservation been the thing that had drawn Alys to her in the first place?

'Showtime,' Jack muttered as he rang the bell. Alys drew herself up to her full height and arranged her face. The door opened as if a curtain were being drawn back, and in the light that streamed from the hallway, she became

Grusinskaya at the Grand Hotel at once—graceful, elegant, comfortable with being in such social circles. Linus, Jack's eldest brother, stood in the open doorway. He was wearing a white shirt, open at the throat, and faded blue jeans, and was carrying a full champagne flute in his left hand.

'There you are!' he shouted and threw an arm affectionately around his brother. Taller and broader than Jack, he always manhandled him roughly, and Jack accepted the blows just as affectionately.

All the Larssons were tall. Jack was taller than the twins, but an inch shorter than their older brother, Linus, a fact that rankled him. It was said that they resembled their grandfather, Papa Larsson, and that they descended from a long line of Norwegian Vikings, which lent them their fierceness and size. Jack liked to play on his Viking heritage, particularly with newcomers, but the family tended not to make too much of the connection. Papa Larsson had ended up blowing his brains out, and not much was said about that.

Linus handed Jack his glass to hug Alys, and he held her at arm's length to examine her as if she were a patient of his and he wanted to check the whites of her eyes.

'Look at little Alys all growed up,' he said approvingly and kissed her lightly on the cheek. She decided to go silent for the time being, but smiled gratefully. Linus had always been her favourite of the brothers.

'Are we late?' Jack whispered. His eyes travelled to Linus's bare feet.

'No, you're early. I was just going up to shower and get dressed for the main event. Everyone stayed over last night. Mum wanted a "last supper" with us.' He lifted his glass from Jack and made for the wide staircase in front of them. 'They're all out the back. See you in a mo.'

Jack took his time wiping his feet backward and forward on the mat. A burst of laughter from the back of the house gave him pause. He examined his feet, head down. Would he have been included in the "last supper" if they'd known that he was no longer with her? No doubt, the same thought had crossed his mind.

He set off, and she followed behind, making use of the wide hallway and its marble floor to practise her long strides. Occasionally, the edge of a heel would cause her to skid a little, but by the time she reached the living room, she had found her rhythm and almost crashed into him. He had stopped just before the threshold. He was stock still, except for the thumb of his right hand which began to work the pocket seam on his trousers. It was as if some invisible force was holding him in stasis. His jaw was clenched tightly. She had never noticed before such uncertainty in him. Was he always this tense around them and she had been so caught up in her own terror that she hadn't noticed his unhappiness? Was that possible?

It was Otto who first noticed them and gave a shout. Jack straightened as if he were entering court. She reached out and stilled his worrying hand. 'Showtime!' she reminded him.

He smiled then, a big, genuine grin at the sight of his little brother, bounding over with his bullish charm. Otto barrelled into them and enveloped them both in a bear hug that crushed Alys's face to Jack's shoulder. She caught Jack's eye as they straightened up and he winced by way of apology. They had become co-conspirators in a battle for survival. They both needed to emerge from the day intact. Otto was pulling them into the room and she was tripping over her feet and overlapping kilim rugs when Hannah, who had been standing with her back to them, turned to greet them.

'There they are!' she said, as if they had been waiting for them to start the party, and held her arms out to Jack. She was wearing another of her trouser suits—an immaculate white one—as if she were a bride. Alys cast a quick glance around the room. Where was Garbo? She'd promised she'd be here to help her.

'You look peaky, Jack. Is your wife not feeding you properly?' Hannah was holding Jack at arm's length, inspecting his face.

'No, she isn't.' Jack smiled at Alys. Co-conspirators.

Hannah moved over to Alys as if she were majestically bestowing blessings on a line of congregants.

'You, on the other hand, Alys, look radiant. You've done something different to yourself. What is it?' She turned Alys this way and that. Her eyes were cold on Alys's skin, her mouth downturned, as if she were trying to decide whether or not to buy an ornament with a crack in it.

The thought popped into her head and immediately she leaned back and gazed directly into Hannah's eyes, unblinking. It was enough to make Hannah release her arms. 'I'm wise to you,' Anna Christie would have said. 'I know your type.'

'How was last night?' Jack asked tightly.

Hannah spun around and laughed out loud. 'Oh, it was The Best, darling. Just as those little intimate suppers can be. We had a marvellous time, didn't we, boys?' she called to Max and Jack's father, Tom, who had appeared at the French doors, tucking their cigarettes into their pockets.

'Where were you two?' asked Max, the quieter of the twins, and he picked his way through an assortment of occasional tables and cream modular sofas to offer them each a shy hug.

'Where indeed?' Jack murmured, and the hurt in his voice and the small vicious smile Hannah had reserved for Alys sparked something in her. Anna's defiance was still in her veins. *No. You don't get to do this to us.*

'I'm not sure we were invited, Max,' Alys said in her lowest voice. 'Sometimes those intimate little suppers are best left small. In fact, we couldn't have made it anyway, could we, Jack? We were at a crazy birthday party last night.' She gave a laugh. 'Insane. It took me an hour to scrub the gold paint off my body this morning. We didn't really make it to bed, so apologies Hannah if you catch us yawning today. We'll do our best not to doze off.' A rush of adrenaline gave her pins and needles. Hannah caught off-guard was a new experience. Alys had willingly, eyes-wide open, thrown herself off a cliff, accepting the consequences that would inevitably come her way, and the recklessness of it was enthralling.

Hannah looked at Jack, who was standing open-mouthed, no doubt wondering who this woman was beside him—with her vintage dress, her strange accent, and her bold lies. His wife who didn't like lying.

'Whose party was it?' Hannah asked suspiciously.

He was lost for words.

A vision of Anna's Irish lover came to mind. 'Matt Burke,' Alys said firmly. 'You wouldn't know him, Hannah. He's a friend of ours.' She put her hand on Jack's arm, closing Hannah out. 'One wild Irishman. He's like a furnace engine.' She let out another hoot of laughter. 'Insatiable. Jack ruined a perfectly good suit in the pool and I'm covered in bruises from head to toe. It's a miracle we managed to make it here.' She'd leave it there. No sense overdoing it.

The silence was profound. It was as if she had thrown a pebble down a well and they were all waiting to hear the distant splash.

Otto burst out laughing.

'You old dogs. You spent the whole night worrying that Jack would feel left out, Max, and all the time he was living it up in a pool orgy. Now, that's how I like to party.'

'Can I offer you a hair of the dog?' Tom said drily, and he drew Alys over to the bar, leaving Jack to Otto.

'Gimme a whisky, ginger ale on the side, and don't be stingy, baby!' Alys drawled in her best Anna voice.

Tom raised an eyebrow.

'Please,' she mumbled.

He deftly prepared her drink, taking his time. She watched his hands, still strong with the long, slim fingers that Jack had inherited. Her father-in-law was a mystery to her. She remembered being in awe of him when Jack first brought her home. She had heard all the stories of how driven he was. To hear Jack tell it, the man was a machine, wired for work, unaware of his young sons, content to leave their upbringing and care to his ambitious wife, who drove the boys hard. Academic excellence was the only thing that could draw a smile from their father. He had retired a year before at 75 and, by all accounts, was now "beating the shit out of the golf course". Linus had predicted that he'd be dead within the year. People like him didn't cope with retirement. The twins were laying bets on it. No love lost there. Alys had always found him distant, but polite.

'You look very nice, Alys.' he said gently as he handed her a drink, and they turned to face out across the living room.

'Thank you, Tom. The place looks well.' She gestured across the room with its high ceilings and wall of French windows. Everywhere was white and cream, throwing into relief the riot of colour from the rugs.

He looked as if he were noticing his home for the first time.

'Hannah,' he said dismissively. Interiors were not his thing.

She took a sip of her drink and then a larger one, welcoming the warmth.

'How's my son treating you?' Tom asked. She glanced up at him, but his face was equanimous. Jack had clearly told no one of his decision.

'Fine,' she said.

'It can't be easy for you, being the only daughter-in-law in this family,' he went on, his eyes focusing straight ahead. 'I had thought the other boys might marry—perhaps not Max—but the others... I suppose Hannah and I mustn't have been a great advertisement!' He smiled ruefully and went on, 'I'm afraid it must be quite lonely for you here.'

Alys, unused to this level of intimacy with her father-in-law, emptied her glass. Without looking at her, Tom took it from her and turned back to the bar, fixing her another with the same focus and precision as before.

'Jack was always my favourite,' he murmured. 'He was a sensitive boy, you know, like Max. It was Hannah's idea to toughen him up by sending him to St Cadmum's. You know all about his time there?' He looked up at her and took her silence for acquiescence. 'Brutal place. Still, he survived it. He was sensitive, but he had such spirit. He's a fighter. He was good at sport, the running was his thing, of course, but he was quick with his fists too. I suppose the bullying settled down quickly enough once he'd broken a few noses. It toughened him up, perhaps prepared him well for a career at the Bar. That grit of his has made him a success, but I was always sorry to see it. I've often wondered who he would have become, what career he would have chosen for himself, if we hadn't intervened. I put a stop to Max following him to the bloody place, but I was too late for Jack.'

They watched Jack laughing with his brothers across the room. Linus had joined them, and the four of them were ribbing each other as if they were teenagers.

'I always thought that being a father meant providing a good life and the best education for your family, but these days I think back and I rather wonder.'

Alys ached for Jack. He would never have known that Tom felt that way about him.

'I was very happy when he brought you home for the first time, Alys. He was so in love and I thought that things hadn't turned out so very badly for him after all. I could let myself off the hook at last. You were what he needed—soft, feminine, kind. Of course, it drove Hannah crazy. She is a jealous woman, I'm afraid. She likes to keep the boys close—you see that, don't you? All that business about last night... Still, I know you have made my Jack happy over the years and I thank you for that.' He tapped her glass with his own.

She didn't trust herself to speak at first and when she did, her voice was gruff.

'I don't think I made him all that happy, Tom. I think he might have been happier with someone else.'

'Nonsense. You were, and are, exactly what my son needs, if he has eyes in his head. You don't imagine that marriage is easy, do you? Marriage is tough—you need all the grit and stamina you can muster. You need faith. So you've hit a blip.' He shrugged. 'This happens in life. It will pass.' He put his hand on her elbow to guide her back to the centre of the room. It had been the longest conversation she had ever had with him. Jack looked at her quizzically, but she shook her head briefly.

Jack chose the moment to pull a small box from his pocket, his gift for his mother, shifting from one foot to another like a little boy. When Hannah tossed it unopened on to a table that was laden with large gift-wrapped boxes, Alys had to turn away from the crestfallen expression on his face. His eyes went to Hannah constantly as they ate the beautiful lunch that the caterers served—asparagus tarts, poached salmon, chocolate fondant. The boys kept up a regular banter of their own, which drew Jack in and made him laugh, but he was always watchful. He was like a stray dog, hoping for scraps.

Alys had always thought of these giant men as boys, and now she saw that in many ways they still were. They had created a family of their own between them, and there was comfort and security in the easy love they had for one another. They had survived because of each other. She thought of her own brother then and how they had survived in their own way, but theirs had been a strategy of avoidance and isolation, rather than leaning in towards each other. All too often, Alys felt the weight of Hannah's scrutiny, and each time she made sure to keep her mask of slight amusement and nonchalance. A Garbo showreel ran behind her eyes, and she could slip easily now into character without trying too hard. Her borrowed dignity and restraint allayed her self-consciousness. The wine flowed around Jack—the only sober one at the party—the others would be staying on, it seemed.

Hannah had largely excluded Alys from the conversation throughout lunch. It wasn't until they had been invited to retire to the sofas for coffee, that she turned her attention to her, and Alys could sense that she was building up to something as she went to stand in front of the mantlepiece and tapped her champagne flute for silence.

'I'd like to make a speech.' She made a point of waiting until she had their full attention.

'I'd just like to say how very moved I am to have my beautiful sons and my loving husband here to celebrate this special day with me. It has been a remarkable weekend so far.

'I hope you know that I am very proud of you all for the success you have had. It was always my ambition that you would make something of yourselves and here you are—Titans in your respective fields! I like to think that I played a small part in your achievement.' She laughed lightly, pausing to allow the boys to thank her. Alys's eyes flickered to Jack, who was quieter than the others in his response.

'Regrets? Only that it seems that the Larsson name will rest with you boys. I had hoped that we would create a dynasty that would do your Viking lineage proud, but only Jack managed to find himself a wife and, unfortunately, for all her loveliness, one who has been unable to provide him with a child.'

It was as if a paper knife had been slipped between her ribs and Alys let out a little gasp. Jack studied his hands. The boys shifted awkwardly in their seats, their eyes on Jack, awaiting a rebuttal.

It was Tom who spoke. 'Hannah. That is uncalled for.'

'Is it, Tom? You said yourself you would have loved a grandson to carry on the name.'

Alys felt Hannah pull the slim shank of the knife out, twisting it as she did so.

Tom winced. 'It's none of our business, Hannah. You

shouldn't pry into other people's marriages and their reasons for things. Those are private.'

'What reasons could there be for not having a child?' Hannah scoffed. 'Surely that was the only reason that Jack would have considered marriage to her?' She gestured to Alys with an impatient flick of the wrist.

'Perhaps you would like some more coffee?' He rose to his feet. But Hannah would not be silenced.

'I'm not drunk, Tom, I'm just stating facts. You marry a woman like Alys for one thing only. So, where are they? Your heirs, your grandchildren? You're not trying to suggest that Jack has anything to do with it?'

Jack closed his eyes. 'Say something!' Alys wanted to shout. 'Don't let her do this. Tell them, Jack.' But Jack had shut down. They were co-conspirators no more. His brothers sat aghast, but Hannah was just getting into her stride.

'The Larssons have always made big families and there are no barren women on my side of the family. I don't need to remind you, I was barely 18 when I had Linus. The fault doesn't lie with us, Tom.' Hannah was triumphant.

Alys thought of all her false bravado, all that walking up and down and practicing in the mirror, of the time that Douglas and Mairéad and even Garbo had put into building her up, only for Hannah to see through it all and bring her to her knees. She was a little girl playing in the wrong league, but the unfairness of it galled her. She should tell them the truth, present her case, make them understand. If this was the reason that Hannah had thought her unlovable, she could fix it. Her legs were trembling when she rose to her feet, words scrambling in her mind, stuttering over each other. A flicker of movement distracted her momentarily. Garbo was lounging over by the table that was still laden with Hannah's unopened presents. She was looking at Alys intently, and suddenly her words from the night before came to mind. Why this need to justify herself, to blurt out their intimate secrets? This was the gift that Garbo offered —her dignity. She was with her at the last. Alys smiled back at Garbo and the trembling stopped. Let Hannah think what she liked.

Garbo put a finger to her lips as she carefully picked out Jack's birthday present to his mother and slipped it in her pocket. Alys watched as she faded out.

Do something outrageous.

'Do you know, Hannah, it's funny to hear you talk about getting knocked up at that age as if it were a badge of honour, as if it makes you more of a woman than me. Just because you became a mother, it doesn't mean you're a good one.' She turned to retrieve her bag. 'Tom, thank you for hospitality. Boys, always a pleasure. Jack, time we went home, I think.' She didn't wait to see Hannah's face. She hauled a stunned Jack to his feet and, gripping his hand tightly as if she were dragging him out of a wreckage, she strode out. She had to help Jack into the car, buckling him in like a child. Then she opened the back door and dragged the unwieldy box with its red dress from the back seat, tearing a corner as she did so. She kicked it into the centre of the driveway, where Jack reversed over it as they left.

Chapter 31

Dignity

Neither of them spoke on the way home. Alys drained by her performance. The exhilaration that powered her as she marched them out of the Larssons' had worn off and she wanted nothing more than to climb into bed and sleep for a long time. Jack was lost in his thoughts, his mouth working, his eyes on the road ahead. Her mind circled and picked over the candidness of Tom's revelations and the empathy she felt for young Jack, being made to toughen up and become someone else to win his mother's love. His hurt at Hannah's rejection wounded her. She couldn't count the number of ways that woman must have broken him over the years.

She relived that moment earlier that day when she had touched his hand and they had been united in force. How nice it felt not to be alone, to trust that someone had your back. She wanted to weave her fingers into his as they rested on the wheel. Surely Tom was right, this blip in their marriage would pass. What had he said about her being perfect for Jack? She was so caught up in this revelry that she was surprised to see that they had arrived at Douglas's house. She had assumed that after all they had been through, Jack would take her home.

His eyes were red-rimmed when he turned to her. 'I'm sorry,' he said.

* * *

'He's seeing someone else.'

Alys sat in the bath, her knees drawn up, and her head resting on her kneecaps. She wasn't sure where her tears ended and the bath water started. Douglas was sitting on the floor on the other side of the bathroom door, and she had to say it twice before he could hear her.

She had thrown herself into the house in such a state, shivering all over, the colour drained out of her, unable to speak. At a loss, Douglas had run a deep bath and put her in it to warm her up. She'd only just managed to reach the bathroom when she vomited. She was still shivering, in spite of the heat of the water. Great judders would roll up her spine and over her head like a cat whose fur had been rubbed up the wrong way.

'She's 30, Douglas. She's practically a minor.'

Douglas did not reply.

'Did you know?' She lifted her head. 'Oh God, did everyone know?'

'No,' Douglas soothed, his voice muffled through the wood. 'No, of course not. It's just that I suspected as much. What would motivate a man like Jack to walk out on his marriage, if not for someone else?'

'He swore he only started seeing her after I moved out, although I don't believe a word he says. Can you imagine if she'd been there the day I went to get my clothes? I can't believe he would move on so quickly. I can't believe he would make me go through all that today, knowing that he had no intention of getting back together.' Her crying started again. 'He said he couldn't handle the guilt after what I'd done. He felt I deserved the truth.'

'So it was only because of today that you deserved the truth?'

'I don't want the truth, Douglas. I want blissful ignorance and for my life to be as it was. I want to be home, sleeping in the same bed as my husband, making him toasties and curling up on the sofa, listening to his war stories. I—I can't bear the thought of some other woman being with him, kissing him.' She began to claw at her wet cheeks in anguish, grabbing at her skin and tearing at it to make the pain less.

'I can't bear that I lost him.' She began sobbing in earnest now, raw visceral cries, howls, hurt beyond repair and a desperate yearning to turn the time back, back to when he loved her.

Douglas bore silent witness. He rode it out with her as she screamed and sobbed. When she was exhausted and quiet, the door opened and he appeared with his jumper over his head to spare her modesty. He managed to locate a towel, emptied the now cold water, and pulled Alys out of the bath. She let him wrap her up like a papoose and lead her to her bedroom. Between the vomiting and the screaming, she was a hollow shell.

'Garbo would have been proud of me,' she mumbled. 'I was all calm detachment and then I gave him the look, Douglas, and I know it worked because he looked all confused and miserable. He had expected me to go to pieces and freak out. He didn't know what to make of me. I let myself out of the car and walked away. I didn't lose my shit until I got inside, honest.'

'Alys, you're just—just perfect as you are. It doesn't matter to me,' Douglas said.

'It matters to me,' she insisted. 'Garbo would have been proud.'

Chapter 32

Wax

'I like to be alone, not always with some other person. There are many things in your heart that you can never tell another person. They are you. Your joys and your sorrows. And you can never, never tell them. It is not right that you should tell them. You cheapen yourself, the inside of yourself, when you tell them.'

Garbo

When Alys walked into the office on Monday morning, she wasn't sure who she was. She remembered Stiller, Garbo's first mentor, marvelling that Garbo was special because she was like wax, able to be shaped and moulded at will. Alys felt like wax. Formless, blank, but without a guiding hand to carve spirit into her. She had pinned her hopes on having a day with Jack where she could prove to him how much better she could be, how much she'd changed. It had been too little, too late.

She hadn't eaten since Hannah's birthday lunch on Saturday afternoon. Her eyes were scratchy and a dull throbbing headache beat time with her as she climbed the stairs. She remembered then how Garbo had walked those steps with her and she straightened up, dampened down her grief and squared her shoulders. She would not wear this sorrow on her sleeve, spilling distress. Now she realised what comfort there could be in making an island of yourself. When she reached her desk, she was subdued, but contained.

Mairéad had not made it into the office, but Candace was staring so intently at Alys her eyes had started to bulge, as if she were trying to reach her telepathically. Sighing, Alys gestured over to the kitchen and it was all that Candace could do not to sprint.

'Well?' Candace asked, bursting with anticipation. 'How did it go?'

'Not good.' Alys declined to elaborate.

'He didn't go for Garbo, then?'

'It would seem not.'

She made herself a coffee and took it back to her desk.

The subject remained closed until Thursday when Mairéad cornered her and accused her of feeling sorry for herself.

'It's not that.' Alys shook her head. 'It's just that I don't know where to go from here.'

Candace, hovering in earshot, coughed and Mairéad begrudgingly moved over to let her in.

'All I'm saying is that I'm not sure that Garbo was the right choice for you.' Candace had been Googling. 'The woman was practically alone her whole life. I mean, let's face it, she was a bit uptight, wasn't she?'

'She was sublime,' Alys murmured.

'Astonishingly, I'm with Candace.' Mairéad shook her head in wonder. 'I think next time round, you need a fresh role-model, something different.'

'Next time?' Alys asked. 'I don't think I can reinvent myself again.'

'You're not going to give up now, are you?' Candace said indignantly. 'You've only just started. I think you need someone who's more of a woman. Who's lived a little.'

'Walked the hard road of womanhood.' Mairéad nodded sagely.

'Someone who's a little bit, well—open-minded,' Candace prompted.

'Up for it.' Mairéad nodded.

'Slutty,' Candace finished.

'Who did you have in mind?' Alys asked.

'Ava Gardner,' they chorused.

Chapter 33

The Work

On Saturday, Douglas set off early with his rambling club. Feeling at a low ebb, Alys meandered through the village to the old granary. She tried not to visit Enid too early on Saturday mornings, because the bookshop was usually invaded by a group of sleepy fathers. Sure enough, when she pushed open the vast double doors, the place looked like a men's club, every armchair taken. The occupiers were scratching tousled, unwashed hair and yawning loudly, and the air smelt of stale morning breath and fart. Some of their children were playing hide and seek and running relays, but a few were sitting on the story rug, engrossed in books. Yellow morning light streamed in from the slatted windows high up in the rafters and bestowed a golden glow on these children. Their sunlit heads were angelic, their little mouths working as their fingers traced the large print on the pages before them. Alys knew that it was for these special few that Enid tolerated the fathers.

Enid was scowling at them from her perch, like a malevolent old crow, waiting for them to fall asleep so that she could peck their eyes out.

'You're going to have to work on your poker face,' Alys said as she approached and kissed her cheek.

'Fools,' Enid growled, not taking her eyes off them. 'They think this is a bloody crèche. That's what our libraries have become, you know. In my day, libraries were temples– venerated for their silence. Not anymore. They're full of inconsiderate yummy mummies who think that everyone wants to hear them read to little Isabella. They don't talk, they shout, these people. Their kids are horrible, too.'

Alys fetched two mugs of steaming fresh coffee, tracked by the envious eyes of men who hadn't had a good night's sleep in months. Enid slipped off her perch and led her to the back of the shop,

'I don't think we're going to find any spare chairs.' Alys scanned their favourite corner in amongst the history books. Enid sidled up to two men, who were engrossed in large hardbacks they had lifted from the shelf beside them. 'Are you going to pay for those?' she barked. Within moments, the books were back on the shelves and the armchairs emptied. 'Works every time. If you listen carefully, you can hear their wheels spitting gravel in the yard.'

They settled in and Enid wrapped her hands around her mug, sighing as the heat reached her aching joints.

'Your hands bad?' Alys queried.

'So, so,' Enid brushed her off. 'What's new with you?'

'Oh, you know, the usual. My husband has taken up with a woman young enough to be his daughter. I've become a cliché. I supposed you've already heard?'

Enid grunted. 'Do you love him?'

'Blunt as ever.'

'It's the only question worth asking. Do you love the man?'

Alys took a long sip of her coffee, choosing her words carefully. 'Sometimes. Does that make sense?'

'What do you love about him?'

'I suppose when you've been with someone for thirty years, you just love the familiarity of them, don't you?'

Enid looked unimpressed.

Alys tried harder. 'I admire his intellect. I always think competence is very attractive.'

Enid grimaced.

'His skin smells very nice. He always puts the seat back down after he's been to the toilet. Look, it's not all passion and reckless abandon, or even spontaneity. It just settles into something—not complacency—it's contentment.'

'Are you content?'

'I haven't given it much thought.'

'Surely, that's the only thing worth thinking about.' Enid took a loud slurp of her coffee.

They were silent for a moment as Alys tried to remember when she last felt content. It was on the bench, swapping sandwiches with Douglas. Before that? When Jack had been out with a client and she had spent the evening singing along to an old Barbara Streisand album. She'd felt something then, hadn't she? She couldn't sing when he was home. It upset him.

'Those photos of you on your stairs—who's the young man you're kissing?'

'Who *was* the young man,' Enid corrected. 'His name was Barclay Shawcross, a ridiculous name for a beautiful man. That was one thing we had in common. Ridiculous names. Can you imagine if we'd got married—Enid and Barclay Shawcross?' She let out a hoot.

'Barclay came from a long line of Barclays, but my mother named me after a spinster aunt of hers, no doubt hoping I'd also inherit her presbyterian ways. Mummy would roll over in her grave if she knew what Barclay and I got up to. That was the other thing we had in common.' Another hoot, then more soberly, nodding over her coffee, she murmured, 'He died a few weeks after that photo was taken. A diving accident that broke his neck.'

'I'm so sorry.' Alys took one of Enid's hands in hers.

'Long time ago.' Enid settled back in her chair, trusting her hand to Alys, letting her trace the tendons that stretched taut between knuckle and wrist.

'It looks as though you loved him very much.'

'I did.' She nodded. 'Banged everything that moved, mind you. The man was insatiable. Couldn't keep it in his trousers. He was showing off in front of a new girl when he dived off the cliff. Two days after he'd gone, I discovered he'd given me the clap. Filthy bastard.' There was a grudging admiration in her voice, and when she caught Alys's surprise, she leaned forward and said, 'I tell you something. No man ever loved me the way Barclay Shawcross did.'

Her small, grey eyes glittered like old coins.

'I suppose you think you're the only one who's been dragged through the wringer, girl? What did you think? That you could show up here with your broken wing, and I'd be like some wise old crone that would hand you the secret of life?'

The thought had crossed Alys's mind.

'Doesn't work like that. Even if I did have all the answers, I wouldn't tell you. You have to do the hard yards yourself, or it doesn't work. The only thing I know is that if you want to have half a chance of having a happy marriage, you have to be someone yourself. Otherwise you just merge into the other, and you know how that works out, don't you?'

'But how do you become someone yourself? I don't know what that means. How do you learn that?'

Enid smiled mysteriously. 'That's the work.'

When Alys left The Granary, she had a biography of Ava Gardner under her arm, and Enid's fierce defence of her erstwhile lover on her mind. Alys was very sure that she had never felt such passion. To have been loved so deeply, that even after all those indiscretions and the passing of 50 years, that Enid still felt its imprint disturbed her.

She ducked under the arm of one of the fathers who was opening the door for her and absently returned his smile.

'How does Jack make you feel?' she asked herself as she cut across the old threshing yard.

Terrible.

Chapter 34

Beautiful Animal

'Hollywood used to call her the world's most beautiful animal. She really is a magnificent creature, isn't she?' Candace breathed, reaching over Alys for the popcorn that Mairéad was inhaling. She had been hoarding the bag since they sat down.

In the darkness, Ava Gardner's green eyes glared down at them from the screen. She was like a cat, angrily flicking her tail back and forth.

'I don't fancy his chances,' Mairéad's muffled voice this time.

They were watching *The Night of the Iguana.* Ava was Maxine Faulk, a fiery, free-spirited hotel-owner in Puerto Vallarta, Mexico. She couldn't be more different than Garbo. Her passion was uncontrolled, wild, her temper volatile and violent, yet she also had a devil-may-care approach to life and a loose-limbed sensuality.

'She's going to let your man have it with that drinks trolley, I'm telling you.' Mairéad came up for air. 'Someone take this bag off me, I can't help myself.'

'Ssshh,' Alys hissed. She was studying Ava intently as

she attacked Richard Burton in a fit of rage. She envied Maxine Faulk. She envied her sensuality and her freedom, and most of all, she envied her place. She had her own establishment that she ran successfully. She could help herself to a Coke from the ice-chest without having to ask permission. She had the run of the place in her bare feet. This was what Enid must have meant about being someone yourself.

It was the way she moved that caught Alys's attention. She was loose and open. Some people—and she counted herself in this category—were bound tight, close-chested, only occupying as much space around them as was entirely necessary to breathe and function. But Ava was expansive and unrestrained. With her head thrown back, she was earthy, gleeful, joyful. Rather than moving away from people, she moved towards people—even if that meant sating her "biological urges" with a couple of beach boys. Ava was abundance.

There was bravery in her too, living alone on the hill, chasing her demons, fighting back the loneliness with rum cocos and the beach boys. She seemed indestructible, but it was her vulnerability that eventually caught the man. Alys was transfixed. So lost was she, that when the lights came on, she was blinded and momentarily confused as to where she was.

'That's that, ladies.' Douglas had pulled open the curtains and looked bemused to see Mairéad crumpled in the corner of his mother's good settee with what looked like a pound of popcorn stuck to her jumper, and an emotional Candace tucked under her arm.

Alys blinked up at him. 'This is the one, Douglas. Ava has the answer.'

'I've forgotten the question.' He grimaced.

'Now, don't be a party-pooper, honey.' Alys kicked off her shoes and wriggled her toes. 'Let's make some rum cocos and get this place swinging.'

Candace clapped her hands and a confetti of popcorn rained down between the sofa cushions.

'What is a rum coco?' Alys paused. No one knew.

'I'm guessing rum and coconut, neither of which we have,' Douglas said drily.

'What else did Ava drink?'

'What didn't she drink?' Mairéad expertly tipped the contents of her jumper into the empty popcorn bag.

'She drank tequila in Mexico.' Mairéad glanced at Douglas, who shook his head.

'Champagne?'

Another shake.

'Whisky? Gin?'

'It's two o'clock in the afternoon, ladies.'

By the early evening, when Douglas's drinks trolley had been laid to waste, when Douglas himself had to be put to bed on the sofa, the talk turned to tactics. Alys was rustling up what she called a fridge-ends supper for them to settle their acid stomachs, and Mairéad and Candace were addressing their comments to her back.

'This is going to be a bigger stretch for you, Alys.' Mairéad nodded. 'I'd say it was no trouble for you to play a closed off, uptight, anti-social woman of mystery, but Ava Gardner? You're going to need a rocket up your arse.'

'Now, Mairéad, it won't be as hard as all that,' Candace protested. 'She looks a bit like her for a start. She has her wide mouth, and if we leave her hair to its natural curls...'

'It's not about the looks, Candace. Gardner was the hottest, most famous movie star of the 50s and 60s. She was a star, and she behaved like one. Alys is going to have to learn how to behave like a woman who was used to having her own way as a God-given right.'

Alys turned to see them both looking doubtfully at her.

'I get it. I do. Oh, I'll watch her films, read the book and copy her mannerisms and try to live as close to the woman as I can. But even I can see it's—it's more than that.'

Alys set their plates down. She had prepared a medley of roasted vegetables, goats cheese, basil and pine nuts, and it smelled wholesome after the popcorn and gin.

'I get it. I just don't know how I'll go about it.'

'Start small. Loose hair, red lipstick, big gold earrings.' Candace forked up a piece of griddled courgette. 'What?' She looked at Mairéad. 'She gets the look right, the behaviour will follow. Trust me on this.'

'You've become awful gobby since you joined our club.' Mairéad shook her head. 'I only let you join because I thought we could do with a general dogsbody.'

'There is no club,' Alys said firmly.

'There most certainly is. How else do you think you're going to survive the wreckage of your life to date? There is definitely a club and you're looking at it. In fact, it's more like a SWAT team, a small cell of expert operatives whose mission is to "Find Alys".'

'Oh, I like that. I'll be in charge of the Looks Department,' Candace crowed.

'If it stops you talking,' Mairéad relented. 'I'll obviously be Chief Executive and Chief Operations Officer. Now, looking back over the Garbo period, the Asset—that's you, Alys—only really became Garbo when she was out in the field. Oh, she practiced like mad beforehand, but it wasn't until she was exposed to threats on the front line, facing down the enemy, that she found it in her. It's what I'm calling the exposure method. I think it could be highly effective in this next stage of the operation—The Gardner Experiment. I suggest we set a target a week from now and work towards that.'

'A target?' Alys queried.

'A social event, a happening, when you can put your practice into action. We need a party with a lot of good-looking men. Oh, what can this be?' Mairéad jumped up and plucked a card from the fridge door. 'It looks like an invitation to a party for good-looking men and it's in two weeks' time.' She smiled guilelessly.

'Lincoln is having a party,' Alys mumbled. 'I was going to decline. I don't feel like partying. I can't go now, anyway. Jack will be there with his new woman.'

'All the more reason for you to be there. You don't imagine Gardner would turn down a party, do you? She could have an arm falling off, and she'd rock up with her ice luge and a bottle of tequila. You don't need to go alone. Take Douglas.'

'He doesn't like Lincoln's parties.'

'Take one of us.'

Candace looked as if she might cry. 'Oh please, take me. Take me.'

'Sorry, Candace. The answer is no. There is no way you could drag me to that party. No way.'

It was decided. Alys would go to the party.

Chapter 35

Meeting Miss Gardner

Tap, tap, tap.

Alys, drifted in and out of the light and insubstantial sleep that was always the consolation prize after a big night on the booze. She caught the sound and stirred. Her bed was too hot, and she kicked off the duvet and rolled on to her side.

Tap, tap, tap.

There it was again. She opened an eye. Was that a mouse? She strained to hear it repeat, but all was silent, and the effort to keep her eye open was too great. She rolled onto her back and pulled the duvet up to her shoulders.

'For Christ's sake, are you going to keep me here all night? Wake up, Sleepy Bones.' A husky drawl at the foot of her bed made both of her eyes snap wide open and she shot up, her back tight against her headboard.

There was the silhouette of a woman, perched at the end of the bed. Alys reached for the bedside light.

'Oh, please. Leave the light for a little, honey. It's too harsh on my eyes.'

The voice had a southern accent, soft and honeyed, as if

she were singing rather than speaking to Alys. It was familiar and Alys fuzzily tried to place where she had heard it recently. *Rum cocos. It couldn't be.*

'M-Miss Gardner?'

'Call me Ava, baby.'

Alys's mouth fell open. Stupefied with sleep and drink, she left it there, lantern jawed. It was happening again. How was this happening to her?

Ava seemed to read her thoughts.

'Don't worry, baby. You're just having a little figment visitation.' This said as if it were the most natural thing in the world to have happened.

'What time is it?' Alys asked.

'Oh, I guess it's a little after three. I couldn't sleep.'

'And so you thought it would be a good time for a —visitation?'

'I wanted a little company.' She sounded like a petulant child, but there was an edge to her voice too, and Alys thought back to what Mairéad had said about movie stars expecting to have their way.

She was awake now, and suddenly aware that it wouldn't do to annoy the very woman whose help you needed.

'It's a pleasure to meet you, Miss Gardner,' she said.

'Ay-vuh.'

'Ava.'

'That's better. We can't get past first base if you keep calling me Miss Gardner, can we?'

She paused and lit a cigarette. Another smoker. It was different this time, though. Alys could actually smell the freshly lit cigarette. If Douglas ever made it off the sofa, he'd kill her.

'So tell me, baby, why am I here?' Ava blew smoke as if she were blowing bubbles.

'I'm not entirely sure,' Alys stammered.

'You dragged me up for something, honey, what is it?'

Alys thought for a moment.

'I'm on a sort of quest. To find myself. I know that sounds a bit cheesy, but I have made a bit of a mess of things—mainly my marriage—but more generally, my life and...'

'And you thought you'd ask me how to fix it?' Ava burst into laughter, a rich, raucous cackle. 'Oh, that's good, honey. You sure picked the right girl for that, with my three husbands, my over-familiarity, shall we say, with the bottle, and my career lying dead in a ditch. You're a hoot!' She cackled again and moved further up the bed towards Alys. 'Hey, move over. I want to get in.'

Alys obligingly moved over across the bed and squeezed herself in against the wall. She heard Ava kicking off her heels before climbing in awkwardly beside her and spreading herself out. 'Move over, I said.'

'You have all the room. There is literally nowhere else I can go,' Alys protested, but she squeezed herself smaller, all the same.

In the darkness, close up, Alys could just make out Ava's face. She looked older than she had imagined. Alys still had Maxine Faulk in mind, but this version of Ava was in her mid-sixties. She had a Thermos tucked under her right arm. 'Open this for me?'

Alys took the Thermos and unscrewed the cup and the cap. She could just see enough to pour, but hesitated in case she burned herself.

'What are you waiting for? I'm dying of thirst here!'

Alys filled the cup with what appeared to be gin. 'Oh, I thought it was coffee.'

'Beefeater's. I swear to god, I might as well own the company.' She laughed again and Alys felt a light pitter-patter of gin as it spilled over her duvet. Ava took a sip, gave a deep sigh and then pronounced, 'I'm ready. Hit me. What are we doing?'

Alys floundered. She hadn't had to explain anything to Garbo. Garbo just knew what Alys was trying to do. As she was fond of repeating, she was just a figment of Alys's over-active imagination. So why would Ava be any different? Yet, she genuinely seemed at a loss. Alys sheepishly explained her experiment, gabbling over the words to describe it—a project? A transformation? A journey?

'You're on a journey, alright, honey, an adventure. You're just looking for a map of the territory, right? Only it's not X that marks the spot, it's Alys. And you think somehow that I am going to be able to fill in some of the map for you, is that it?'

Alys nodded, reluctant to go on. In spite of the warmth in Ava's voice, and her interest in her predicament, there was something about her that set Alys on edge. It was as if she were being held between the silken paws of a panther, who was drowsy and playful, but who at any moment might unsheathe its claws and maul her.

'Well now, how do you know that any map I might share with you is worth its salt? You might not like the territory.' The swipe of a paw. She was waiting for Alys to say or do something, but what would a Hollywood legend want from Alys? The woman was an icon, a goddess, a powerful, sensual force of nature, vaunted as the most beautiful woman in the world. What could Alys offer? She wracked her brains as Ava, seemingly content to wait, leisurely sipped her gin.

Then it came to her. Homage. She had to pay homage.

'I—I wanted to learn from you, er, Ava. I want your map of the territory because you were—are—so full of spirit and life. I know I'd never match your beauty, but it's your spirit, your joie de vivre, I'm interested in. You know how to enjoy life...'

'Your friends called me slutty.' Ava pouted.

So she had known what it was about all along.

'They meant it as a compliment, believe me. You're an icon of—of—sexual freedom and equality. You were no different than the men.'

Ava sniffed and took a sip of gin, mollified.

'I loved being physical, honey. I was beautiful, why wouldn't I?'

'You were just enjoying being yourself.'

'Exactly. Don't get me wrong, my life was its own kind of crazy. Took a lot of wrong paths, made the map up as I went, but I loved every minute of it. I wouldn't change a thing.' She paused and then continued more thoughtfully. 'You know, maybe there is something I could teach you after all. Maybe I could help you loosen up. Be a little more yourself. Live a little. Just go with the biological urges, you know?'

'I'm not sure I'd recognise a biological urge, Ava, I'd have to be honest.'

'Honey, when was the last time you had a really great roll in the feathers?'

Alys blushed, and Ava let out another roar of laughter.

'If you're riding with me, you'd better get used to that. I don't beat about the bush when it comes to sex. Look, you have to let your body drive for a bit, you know what I'm saying? You're all in your head. You need to remember that you're an animal, and animals have biological urges, baby, and woe betide you if you don't let that animal roam from time to time.'

'I don't think I know how to be an animal, Ava.'

'You leave that to me, honey. We've got a party coming up, right? We're going to get you in training, starting today. You leave it *all* to me. Now, I need to get some shut-eye. All this talking is wearing me out.' She handed Alys her cup and shuffled down under the duvet and after a moment, Alys felt herself pulled in against the warm side of Ava's body, cocooned. She lay there for a moment, breathing in Ava's perfume, rose petals and bergamot, and felt her eyelids become heavy.

'Ava?' she murmured. 'I can't remember when I last had a great... roll in the feathers.'

Ava rested her chin on the top of Alys's head. 'I know, honey.'

Chapter 36

Animal Training

Douglas was lying where they'd left him. His broad shoulders spilled slightly off the sofa, and one of his arms trailed along the floor. Alys marvelled at how he had managed to sleep in such an uncomfortable position. His face looked different when he slept. Where had those creases at the corners of his eyes come from? He was a funny man, but his laughter was always contained, dignified, as befitted a man of his profession. She had never noticed the planes of his face, nor the strength of his cheekbones and jawline; his bone-structure more chiselled without the large brown eyes to soften it. She was still tired from her nocturnal visitor. She would have loved to curl up into Douglas's sleeping form and let herself nap, but she couldn't see how she could do it without lying on top of him, which would undoubtedly give him heart failure. Instead, she settled herself alongside him on the floor and lay the back of her hand in his open palm. It fitted perfectly. He roused slowly and, though his eyes stayed shut, his hand closed over hers.

'Am I dead?' he croaked.

'I don't think so.' Alys leant up and put her head on his chest. She could hear his heart beating slow and steady.

'You're the picture of ruddy health,' she confirmed, and she stayed there because it was comforting to hear Douglas's signature tune played out over again.

He brought his arm up to rest on her back, holding her to him, and they dozed for a while.

'I want someone to set up a drip and purify my whole system. I've been poisoned.'

'Don't whine, Douglas. You were a rock star last night. That's the price we pay for stardom, baby.'

'What did I do?' he groaned.

'You were the perfect host and partner in crime,' she soothed. 'You were the life and soul, and then suddenly you disappeared. We found you in here, picking off the popcorn from your mother's sofa in case it made her cross, so we rolled you on to it and you passed out.'

Douglas groaned more loudly. 'I hate this sofa. When I was a boy, my mother wouldn't take the plastic wrapping off it, so we had to sit still or all you'd hear was the crackle of the plastic. It was purgatory to sit through a tv programme. In the summer, it would make the backs of my legs sweaty. Father and I celebrated when the bloody thing finally disintegrated. I still hate this sofa.' He sighed. 'And I hate the ruby glass,' he whispered. An afterthought.

'You could sell it and start again. Decorate the place as you'd like it.'

'Oh, I couldn't do that, Alys.'

'Why not? It's your place now. You could get rid of all this heavy furniture, and you'd be surprised how beautiful this room could be.'

'No, I couldn't do that.' He had stiffened underneath

her. He was uneasy and she regretted disturbing him, spoiling the mood.

'Or you could just leave it as it is. Also nice.'

He patted her back. The subject was closed. 'You're going to have to get off me, Alys. I can't feel my left arm, and your hair is tickling my nose. It's making me feel rather nauseous.'

She helped him to sit up and fetched him a coffee and some dry toast.

'I know what will make you feel better. You need to come on an adventure with me today.'

'No, I don't think that would... what sort of adventure?'

'I'm beginning my training today, by the end of which I will have turned into a magnificent animal.'

'Ah, the influence of Miss Gardner, I assume? Will this training require drinking copious amounts of whiskey? I don't think I'm able for it.'

'No. I have decided not to pursue that line of training at the present time on account of the hammering in my temples. I am talking about tuning into my body and learning to listen to its needs.'

'We're not talking about biological urges, are we?' He looked alarmed.

'All I'm suggesting is that you help me find some open water—a nice pond or stretch of river without much of a current—so that I can swim. I want to do some exercise in the open air. Nothing salacious, I promise. Come with me. It'll be fun, baby.'

'Please refrain from calling me baby, Alys. There is nothing alluring about infantilisation.'

. . .

The water was colder than she expected. It had taken her a while to find a part of the bank where she could step down and test the water with her bare feet. She had eventually found a lip of shingle and, gripping on to a tussock of grass, she stepped down gingerly into the water. The chill sent a tingle up the length of her body, and she felt her skin tighten and her nipples harden.

'I don't think I can do this,' she called back to where Douglas was fixing his bike chain. He straightened up and gave her a hard stare. He had to pull over twice to be sick on the way there, and still had a slightly clammy sheen to his face.

'If you think we've come all this way for you to chicken out now... You're going in if I have to drag you.'

'But it's hurting my skin.'

'Believe me, that's nothing in comparison to what you'll be feeling if you don't go in.'

She turned back to face the water and edged in slightly. The shingle beneath her feet began to soften, and a putty-coloured sludge squelched between her toes. She glanced down at the black 50s style swimming costume she'd borrowed from the dressing room. She hadn't thought to try it on first. It clung to her curves, but covered her flesh and its strange combination of prudery and allure made her feel womanly.

'I can hardly see the bottom. How do I know it's safe?' she squeaked.

'It's safe. I swim here all the time.'

'How come you've never brought me?'

'To be honest, Alys, I didn't know you could actually swim.'

It was a fair point, for which of her parents would have had the interest or the energy to teach her?

'I can swim very well, thank you. I have my 25 metre badge somewhere. I'm just used to warmer water. I don't think I can...'

There was a sigh behind her and Douglas dropped down on to the bank. He had stripped his clothes down to his boxer shorts and he waded past her, grabbing her hand as he went and pulling her in after him. Terrified of losing her footing, as the ground on which she had been inching forward fell away, she didn't have time to register the cold as she splashed in alongside Douglas. He held her within the curve of his arm, and she put both hands on him as if he were the bar in the local swimming pool. It took her a moment to let go.

'Just breathe out, Alys. Breathe right out. Catch your breath.'

She did as she was told, keeping her eyes on his collarbone with its light sprinkling of hair that was suspended just above the waterline.

'I didn't know you could swim either,' she grumbled.

'I couldn't. I was an adult learner. Took some classes a couple of years ago.' He launched on his back and swam out to the centre, spinning back on to his stomach to take a few strokes upstream. As he'd reassured her, this part of the river was like an offshoot, a backwater, with less of the current of the main body of the river. She turned and swam in the other direction. Her skin was acclimatising to the temperature. Her hands and feet were numb, but her skin elsewhere had taken to tingling, almost burning, and she felt a bubble of excitement and daring as she struck out. The old Alys would never do this. She spun around in the water like an otter, making little eddies of bubbles rise to the surface around her. It was intoxicating. She lay on her back and tried to float. From this angle, she began the homework that

Ava had set her. She looked closely at her shoulder, the rise of her breasts, and the water trickling between them, she pushed her hips higher and admired the way her hip bones jutted out and the swell of her stomach. From this angle, it looked soft, feminine. She straightened one leg, pointed her toes, which she had painted red that morning, and traced the line of her thigh muscle, as droplets of water fell from her leg to rejoin the river. Ava was right. All this time, she had felt embarrassed of her body, but when she looked at it through the lens that Ava had shown her, there was only beauty. She really was a magnificent animal. No, that was a step too far. She let her leg fall back. Perhaps "magnificent animal" was something she would have to work up to. Still, she arched her back out of the water, feeling a thrill as the back of her scalp began to sting with cold. Tipping her head back, she let the river pull at her hair. When she straightened up and opened her eyes, Douglas was watching her. He swiftly turned on to his stomach and swam hard further up the river, following its line as it meandered away from her.

They swam until their strokes became languid and careless, and when they stepped up on to the bank, the skin on their arms and thighs was fiery red. They each turned away from the other to change, their clothes sticking to damp skin. Alys had given up on her bra. Her clothes had to be dragged—and in some cases—rolled on, and she sat on the blanket Douglas had brought, feeling as if every item of clothing was somehow put back on upside down or inside out. The air was warmer than the water, yet she couldn't stop the juddering that set her hands shaking and teeth chattering. Still, she was grinning like a mad woman and Douglas reached into his backpack, brought out his old Leica and took a hasty photo of her.

'Not fair,' she cried.

'I am the official recorder of this journey. You'll thank me later.'

'Then let me take one of you, partner in crime.' She snatched the camera and lined him up in the frame. In the flat afternoon light, his eyes looked almost black as he gazed intently at her.

'Smile!' she called and he offered her his official photo smile, featured in all of their school year photos—polite, noncommittal, his eyes darting away to the side as if he'd rather be anywhere than in front of the lens. He took the camera back and exchanged it for a cup of something from his flask.

'Is this gin?' Alys asked.

'Good lord, woman. Who have you been hanging out with? Don't be ridiculous. It's hot port. For medicinal purposes,' he added sanctimoniously.

It was delicious. She tasted cloves, orange zest, and sweet honey. It was dense and heavy in her stomach and almost immediately she felt herself relax, her muscles tense from shivering, settling themselves as she pulled the edges of the blanket up and over them both.

A robin flew out from a nearby bush and alighted beside them, spry and alert to their movements. They stilled. After a moment, he began to sing.

'Do you know that the robin sings all year around, but that his spring song is brighter than his autumnal one?' Douglas whispered. She could feel his warm breath against her neck, where her hair lay in wet strips like seaweed. She was hunkered against him, the warm port in her belly and her skin was tight and sticky, the air fresh and marshy around them. She felt like a wild thing, elemental, washed clean and spare, alive to everything around her. Something she no longer wanted had been left behind in the river.

'I'd like to come here again,' she whispered into the blanket weave, as much as a promise to herself as a warning to Douglas.

She didn't shower that night. The river had anointed her and she wanted to keep it with her for as long as possible. Her hair had dried in curls, and she tied it roughly to keep it out of her eyes as she prepared a rich beef casserole with wine that the women had left the night before. Douglas lit a fire in the living room and they ate their stew from bowls on Mrs Weatherley's sofa and watched *Mogambo*.

Chapter 37

Pleasure

'Hey, honey, what's new?'

Alys woke to the smell of cigarette smoke again. Ava was sitting in the middle of her bed, her bare feet tucked up underneath her. She glanced at her alarm clock. 'Ava, it's two in the morning.'

Ava shrugged. 'I couldn't sleep. Besides, I never get up before 4pm. I guess you'd call me a night owl, baby.'

'I have to get up for work in, oh, five hours, so can this wait?'

'No! I want to hear how the swim went. Did you love it?'

Alys rolled back on to her pillow and smiled up at the ceiling. 'It was wonderful.'

'You see, honey? It's as simple as giving your body what it needs.'

'I couldn't believe how free and alive I felt. I felt...' She searched for the word.

'Horny? Did you feel horny?'

'Ava!' She feigned shock, but when she thought about it, there was something arousing about feeling such freedom in the water, her legs slippery against one another.

'I gotta tell you, I would have pounced on that Doug. Now, he's a real man. I like my men like that.'

'Douglas?' Alys scoffed. 'Believe me—he's not your type.'

'How would you know what my type is, honey?'

There was an edge to Ava's tone, but Alys ignored the warning. 'Well, let's see, he doesn't sleep with anything that moves, has no known affiliations to the criminal underworld, would rather die than knock you around. Besides, I think he, ah, prefers the other side, if you catch my drift.' This last was said discreetly.

'You mean he's gay?' Ava cackled. 'Honey, trust me. I know gay when I see it, and he ain't it.'

'I don't want to disappoint you, Ava, but the man has been my best friend for my entire life. I think I'd know.' She paused. 'Besides, I have never seen him with another woman nor heard of a girlfriend. He's very "private" and you know what that means.'

'It means the guy's very private.' There was a silence as Ava lit another cigarette and drew on it. The flame ghoulishly illuminated her face, turning it purple and dark green before she blew it out. For a moment, Alys was struck by its curious asymmetry.

'Honey, remember Deborah Kerr's line in *Iguana*, something like, "It's only his circumstances, it's not the man himself?" I'm telling you—that is a fine man, going to waste under our very noses, and if you aren't going to partake, move over, sister.'

'How can you be so sure of yourself?' Alys marvelled, ignoring for a moment that, as a figment, Ava was unlikely to have much success. 'Did you always get your man?'

'Well now, Alys, let's not forget I was beautiful. And I did love sex. I was very good at it. I guess you could say that I certainly lived life in the expectation that I would get my man.' She sniffed and paused to lift a tobacco flake from her lip. 'It's tough, getting older, you know, and it's even tougher when you used to be beautiful. No one prepares you for how irrelevant you become, when your looks fade.' She sniffed again. 'You young women—I don't know what you're waiting for, what you're saving yourself for. It's like you've got both arms around the crown jewels in your lap, and you'll growl at anyone who comes near them. What the hell for? They ain't that special. You have to make hay while the sun shines, you know what I'm saying, honey? While you still got what they want.'

'I'm hardly a young woman. I'm 50, Ava.'

'That's a helluva lot younger than me. You've still got it. Don't waste it, baby. Oh, I'm not saying you put out for every guy you meet, but it's about listening to your body. Taking what you want when you feel like it. When it feels like an adventure. When it makes you feel alive. When you can't wait to feel your skin on his.' She gave a little shiver of delight. 'Please yourself, honey.'

Chapter 38

The Eye of the Storm

The day of the party loomed and Alys was still in two minds whether or not to go. Mairéad called the party Alys's reemergence into the world. The project had taken on a life of its own, buoyed along by others' enthusiasm, and she was afraid that she was losing track of why she had started it in the first place. Part of the problem was that she was exhausted. Every night, Ava appeared at the foot of her bed to share her secrets, but none of them brought Alys comfort. She was conscious of the bags under her eyes and had fallen asleep at her desk on two occasions. For all of her kindnesses, Ava only served to show Alys how less like a real woman she was.

Douglas, too, was causing her concern. Since their swim, he had been distant and morose. He had started to leave a room when she entered it, and she was beginning to worry that she'd outstayed her welcome. For such a private man, it couldn't have been easy having to share his life with a friend he barely recognised in the midst of her breakdown. She resolved to get the party out of the way, and then perhaps Ava would leave her to sleep through the night.

She'd be able to plan for the future if she could survive the ordeal and get some decent sleep.

Her stomach churned at the thought of facing those people again, knowing that most of them had witnessed her downfall and those dreadful knickers, but Mairéad insisted that facing down the demons of her shame was the only way to move on from the experience.

Alys thought there must be some truth in this because a tiny shard of self-preservation bothered at her, like a splinter in her heel that wouldn't let her walk on until it had been addressed. Before Garbo, she might have been happy to pretend that nothing had happened, but now she saw how destructive that was. She wanted to show those people that she wasn't a joke, that she was an interesting and vibrant woman. More than anything, she wanted Jack to look at her across the room and wish she were his.

His new relationship had shaken her hope from its tree. In quiet moments, there was a faltering in her. She was less certain that she might win him back, but she wanted him to feel that he had lost something. She wanted his respect and in acknowledging that, she had to admit that she wanted to respect herself again.

Ava came early the night before the party. Alys was making a tiara for a mouse Cinderella, and was absorbed in twisting some wire around a tiny piece of turquoise sea glass, when a faint trace of gardenia perfume made her look up. Ava was standing by the door, affecting nonchalance. It was the first time Alys had seen her in the light, and although Ava had angled her face away from her, she could see how the left side of her face dragged.

'Party's tomorrow, honey,' Ava said casually, examining the cuff of her ivory silk shirt.

'I know.' Alys went back to her tiara.

'You got yourself a frock?'

'Not yet.' Alys tied off the wire in a small knot and clipped it with sharp scissors.

'Leaving it a little late, aren't we?' Ava settled alongside her and picked up the felt mouse, whose beady little eyes seemed to be watching for her tiara.

'How 'bout a little gin martini?' She wiggled her Thermos in front of Alys. 'Keep me company?'

'Why not?' Alys said. 'Since you're a figment and I'm likely drinking air. What harm can it do?'

Half an hour later, Alys was struggling to see Ava over the tip of her glass. 'What did you put in that flask?'

'They hit the spot, don't they?' Ava said gleefully. 'I learned how to mix them at the Cocoanut Grove. The finest education a girl could get. I had to drink them under the table out of coffee cups because I was underage.'

'Did you always like booze?' Alys thought for a moment that she might have stepped over the line—she was never sure where the line was with Ava—but, after a thoughtful silence, Ava answered her. 'Not always. I think I was like you. I used to drink to get over my shyness.'

'You were shy?'

'Of course. I was a tobacco farmer's daughter, trying to find her way in Hollywood. Do you think that was easy?'

'But you always looked so confident.'

'Perhaps I was a better actress than they said I was.' Her laugh was low and husky. 'When you get to the party tomorrow, the trick is to have one or two for courage, and then stick to the soda water. There's nothing sexy about a fall-down drunk.'

Alys shuddered at the thought of her last performance. 'Will you come?'

'To the party? No, honey. It may have slipped your notice, but I'm not up for partying these days. Not since that goddamn stroke nearly killed me.' It was the first time Ava had acknowledged it, and Alys was touched by her bravado.

'You're still very beautiful. No one would see you anyway, remember? Please, Ava. I don't think I can go alone. They all saw my knickers last time.'

'At least you were wearing some, baby.' Ava patted her hand. 'No, I'll tell you everything you need to know tonight, and you'll be fine. First off, you want that husband of yours on the hook, don't you? You want him squirming. You know what the secret is, honey? Indifference.'

'Indifference?'

'It drives them crazy when you look like you don't give a fig. Ignore him and play the field. Find some schmuck to flirt with. It'll kill him.'

Alys looked uncertain.

'Trust me.'

'Oh, I do trust your experience. It's just that I don't think I know how to flirt.'

'Sure you do. Every woman knows how to flirt. It's innate. You just, you know.' Ava turned her green eyes on to Alys and tilted her head back. She stared intently into her eyes and gave a laugh. 'See? You have to look like you've just had sex and you wouldn't mind going again. When you move, roll your hips, put your shoulders back. Walk like you love yourself. It's easier in bare feet,' she added, lighting a cigarette.

'Lastly, you need my killer shot. This will floor them, trust me.' She took a long drag on her cigarette and, fixing her eyes on Alys, she blew the smoke through her nose and mouth. She looked like Medusa, with the smoke tendrils curling around her red mouth and her almond-shaped green eyes, luring Alys into her spell.

'Every. Time,' she mouthed to Alys. Then she snapped upright and passed the cigarette to Alys. 'You try.'

'But I don't smoke.'

'Honey. Where have you been?'

Alys took the cigarette and took a short puff, which resulted in a coughing fit. Ava raised an eyebrow. 'Now, sugar, we both know this isn't a real cigarette. Leave the dramatics to the professionals, please.'

Alys tried again and managed to breathe it out. The next time she breathed it in, she managed to blow it out through her nose, but she couldn't sustain the look of sexual intent that Ava carried off so perfectly.

'You're not taking it seriously.' Ava frowned.

'I'm trying.' Alys whined. 'I just feel a bit silly. I don't look like you, for a start. If I looked like you, I'd walk around with those sexy eyes and the smoky halo all day, believe me.'

'You look fine.' Ava rolled her eyes. 'Try again.'

Alys tried hard to compose her face into something that resembled seductive allure, but a giggle made a brief escape before being slapped down by Ava.

'You make me sick, Alys Larsson,' she shouted. 'You spend your life moaning about how people don't take you seriously when all the while it's you who acts like a joke. How can you expect anyone else to treat you better? Now, smoke that goddamn cigarette, and look at me like you want to fuck me.'

Like a scolded child, Alys did what she was told, replaced the cigarette between her lips with shaky hands and took a deep drag. This time she looked at Ava who, even with the damage left by her stroke, was still the most beautiful woman she had ever seen, and she imagined what it would be like to slip her tongue between those red lips and feel the flicker of Ava's tongue welcoming hers.

The smoke drifted upwards between them and dispersed over their heads.

'That'll do,' Ava croaked. 'Let's get you kitted out. What are our options?'

Alys took Ava to Mrs Weatherley's room. Douglas was out for the evening and she felt some qualms about not asking his permission, but she was running out of time and as she appeared to have no say in when Ava appeared—Ava being the force of nature that she was—she had to take her chances when she could.

Ava took a turn around the room, limping slightly but still holding herself like a movie star and nodding approvingly. 'You got some fine threads here, lady.' Suddenly, she stopped short and stripped off her clothes to a silk camisole. She pulled out a pink lace dress with a black belt and stepped into it. 'Now, this is my kinda gown. Zip me up, sister.' She looked beautiful.

'*Barefoot Contessa.*' Alys nodded wisely.

'You know they wrote that character after me?' Ava called over her shoulder, admiring herself in an oval floor-length mirror.

'I don't mean to interrupt your reverie, but any thoughts on what I should wear?' Alys asked.

'Sorry, honey. It's been a while since I dressed up.' Ava threw an arm across the rails without taking her eyes off her reflection. 'Wear what you like.'

'That's all you have for me?' Alys asked incredulously.

'But that's everything, baby. When you wear what you like, you become yourself, and that's when the show starts.

Have you listened to anything I've said? It's *Barefoot Contessa* all the way. When are you going to stop being such a pussy? Pick something, for Christ's sake.'

Alys kicked off her own clothes to her bra and pants and strode to the railing. 'Why does everyone call me that? I'm not a pussy. I just thought with your vast experience of being a bit slutty you might have an opinion.'

'That's low.' Ava sunk into a small green velvet tub chair beside the mirror and kicked her bare legs out in front of her.

'What about this one?' Alys lifted a little black dress. Ava shrugged.

'Something a little racier, then. The red?'

Alys tried another. Ava looked away.

'Ok, I'm sorry. You weren't slutty, you were a total legend. What about this one?'

Ava cast a conciliatory eye towards her and inclined her head.

'Yes? The green?' Alys stepped into a forest green fifties-style dress with thin stripped sleeves that lay across her collarbone and shoulders. Nipped in at the waist, it fell just below her knee. She couldn't reach the zip at the back, but even half-open she couldn't help admiring herself in the mirror. The dress was exquisite. The skirt wasn't as full as a traditional fifties dress. It was softer and clung more to her hips. She fingered the fabric reverently. It was the most beautiful dress she had ever worn.

'Will you zip me up?' she called to her left.

'You look lovely,' Douglas said. Alys whipped around. Ava was no longer in the tub chair and Douglas stood in the doorway, tugging off his tie.

'I'm sorry, I hope you don't mind that I helped myself, but I was running out of time and...'

'Don't be silly,' he said, throwing his jacket and tie wearily into the tub chair and unbuttoning the top button of his shirt. She turned back to the mirror and again was caught in the thrall of this perfect dress. She felt Douglas approach behind her and was suddenly aware that her back was bare to him. Her skin prickled with the touch of his fingers on the base of her back as he struggled to find the start of the zip. It stuck at first, and then he gently coerced the slider up her spine, his fingers trembling lightly against her skin. When he got to the top, he rested his fingers between her shoulder blades and met her eyes in the mirror.

'You don't have to go through with this, you know.'

'I sort of do, Douglas.'

'You've nothing to prove to anyone but yourself.'

She smiled. 'Well then, maybe that's what it's about. Come with me, please.'

Douglas looked away. 'I'm afraid I can't.'

'Please, Douglas. I can't do it on my own. You don't even have to talk to anyone. We won't leave each other's side, I promise.'

'I'm sorry, Alys. It's not that I won't, it's that I can't. I... I have a date.'

'Oh.' Alys sank into the chair, shifting only to let Douglas rescue his jacket. He couldn't look her in the eye.

'With a—lady?'

'I hope not!' His head sank lower under the guilty weight of his confession. The silence stretched on until Alys exhaled the breath she had been holding. Ava had been right about Douglas after all. How had Alys got it so wrong? She was annoyed at the pang of betrayal she felt. Surely, Douglas was free to live his own life. He certainly didn't need her permission to see someone else. It wasn't as if she and Douglas were an item just because he had offered her a roof over her head in her time of need, for God's sake. His discomfort rolled off him in waves, and she rallied to reassure him.

'How lovely. I hope you have a wonderful night.'

'Are you sure you're ok with it?' His eyes flickered back up to her face.

'Of course! Why wouldn't I be?'

'Because I suppose I could cancel...'

'Please don't. It'll do you good to get out and have some fun.'

'It's just that I wouldn't want to hurt anyone's feelings...'

'No, you couldn't do that. You should go.'

'If you're sure...'

'Absolutely.'

'Good. That's settled.' She caught a hint of relief in his voice, but something below that she couldn't place. He faked a yawn. 'I think I'll take myself off to bed, then. Goodnight, Alys.'

'Goodnight,' she called after him.

The room felt empty when he left. Alys cast around for a moment, gathering her thoughts. Ava had thrown her pink dress on the floor, and Alys set it gently back on the rack and then took herself to bed.

The last thing she saw when she turned out the light was the little mouse Cinderella on her bedside table. The tiara had fallen over one eye, but the other gazed beatifically back at her. An easterly wind had whipped up. It sounded as if huge, white-crested waves were crashing down against the house. The casements creaked and the windowpanes rattled lightly, but stayed put. In the house that Alys had shared with Jack, she could never hear the wind, so well-insulated, hermetic was it. Jack loved the dense silence that descended once the doors were closed against the night, but it always made Alys clammy with claustrophobia, and she would inch open the window in her work room and press her face against the cool glass to catch her breath. Here, she listened to a light rippling on the roof tiles and burrowed deeper into her duvet. Whatever challenges the party would bring, she was in the eye of the storm now.

Chapter 39

Going with the Flow

In the morning, well-rested, she rose early. She fried eggs with sage leaves and toasted a few slices of the sourdough bread she had baked the day before. She and Douglas ate in companionable silence, with coffee brewing on the hob behind. She'd filled his kitchen with her favourite cookery books, some plants from the office, and her collection of handmade ceramics. Two wonky mugs waited hand in hand on the surface, and the sight of them made her smile. She watched Douglas's face, intent on his breakfast, accepting, steadfast, and felt a well of tenderness for this kind, gentle man and his unerring faith in her.

'I was thinking.' Something clawed at her throat and she coughed and had to begin again. 'I was thinking that I should probably get out of your hair one of these days.'

Douglas frowned. 'Have I done something wrong?'

'No, of course not. You've been my saviour.' She reached for his hand. 'I clearly did something amazing in a past life to deserve you. I just think you've done enough, and it's not fair on you to have me knocking around. My crazy ideas have caused far too much trouble. I feel like I've sort of taken over. You would probably like your house back and your, er, privacy.'

He looked confused. 'What's brought this on?'

Alys's throat closed over completely and her eyes welled up.

'Is this because I said I was going on a date?'

She couldn't speak.

'Alys. It's just a date. It means nothing.'

She shook her head. *Yet*, she thought. *It means nothing yet.*

'Alys. Look at me. You're my best friend. Nothing will change that. Nothing ever has.'

She knew she was being irrational, but perhaps it was the lead up to the party. She wanted everything else in their lives to be the same. It was as if the house of cards she had built around her was starting to teeter.

'Please don't. You know I don't like it when you cry.' Douglas looked exasperated. 'You got married, Alys, for Christ's sake. You didn't see me crying when you took off and married that awful man. I'm just going on a blind date.'

'Jack's not awf—wait, what? You're going on a blind date?' She snapped to attention.

'Yes. I have finally allowed my friends to set me up with a single lady of their acquaintance called Dawn. Before you say anything, know that I am not comfortable with the concept of "Dawn and Douglas", but there we have it. I believe it's quite acceptable when you reach our age, Alys. I am "going with the flow". Please close your mouth.'

She was dumbfounded. Douglas, so risk-averse, so proper, throwing caution to the wind. 'Perhaps your attempts at reinvention have inspired me.' He smiled and got up to pour the coffee. 'We were both a little stuck, I fear.' He handed Alys her mug and, tapping his gently against it, he murmured, 'Time to move on, Alys.'

She repeated that line as she got dressed that evening. Candace had appeared on her doorstep around 6.30 with a small pink vanity case. 'I thought you might need a hand.'

At the kitchen table, Candace set out her brushes and makeup palettes with the seriousness of a heart surgeon.

'It's very kind of you to think of me,' Alys ventured.

Candace waved her off. 'Mairéad sent me.' She perused Alys's face. 'Besides, I do love a challenge.'

Candace slowly and expertly began to paint Alys's face. Alys tried to engage her in conversation, but so focussed was she on her work, it was clear that she wasn't listening and her responses were out of sync with Alys's questions. There was the foundation, then the concealer, the setting powder, the pink blush high on the cheekbones, the brow brush, the sheer eyeshadow pressed into her eyelids, the liner, the mascara, then another liner for the lips, and finally a glossy red lipstick. Alys had long since lost track and knew with certainty that she would never be able to recreate what Candace had affected. She was not sure she wanted to, either. It felt like cheating, putting this amount of camouflage on your face. She could imagine seducing someone, spending the night with them only to have to witness their horror when they saw the real her—wan, washed out, looking five years older—the next morning. Ava didn't wear much make-up, Alys had noted. Didn't need to. She was surprised then when Candace held up her hand mirror and showed Alys her finished work. The make-up was subtle, but glamorous. Alys just looked a fresher, more colourful version of herself.

'I look normal,' she marvelled.

'The red lipstick really shows off your eyes,' Candace mused. 'I'll leave you it for touch-ups.'

'Thank you, Candace.' Alys squeezed her arm. 'You didn't answer my question. What are you up to this weekend?'

'Oh, nothing much. A quiet one for me.' Candace smiled ruefully.

'You know you could come to the party? It's not too late.'

'Thanks, but I want to make a head start on some work Tim's left me, so I wouldn't mind an early night.'

'Surely Tim doesn't make you work weekends?' Alys frowned.

'Of course not!' Candace flushed. 'It makes me happy to help. Besides...' She leaned in towards Alys, her teeth worrying at her bottom lip, but Douglas appeared in the doorway and Candace pulled back and began to tidy away her brushes.

'Goodness, Alys. You look just like Ava. I don't suppose either of you could help me with these cufflinks, I can't seem to get my fingers to do what I ask.'

'Douglas has a date,' Alys explained. 'With a woman.'

Candace went to his aid, her eyebrows in her hairline.

Chapter 40

Both Sides of the Coin

"When I lose my temper, honey, you can't find it any place."

Ava

They shared a taxi. It was unclear who was the more nervous.

'We look like we're going to the Academy Awards,' Alys joked.

'I'm not overdressed, am I?' Douglas fretted. 'I had other options.'

'No, I just mean, we're both so nervous.' She took his hand and squeezed it. 'You look very handsome, Douglas.' She meant it. He always looked well in a suit. He moved well in a suit. Alys gave herself a little shake. She would have to stop thinking of Douglas as a man. That was Ava's doing. She was beginning to regret not bringing a guest. It was her own fault. She'd been undecided up until the last minute. She wished Ava were with her. Alys fervently wished for that. She didn't think she could do this alone, and as they pulled up in Lincoln's driveway, Alys was reminded of the last time she'd been here with her Gandhi tunic and her wet hair and her sneering husband with his disappointed eyes. Patting the sleek curls that Candace had coaxed into shape , she breathed out a long, slow sigh.

'You could always come out with me tonight,' Douglas said quietly.

'Dawn, you and me?'

'Oh, I'd forgotten about her. Well, I'm sure she wouldn't mind. I'm told she's very kind.'

'You forgot about the woman you're taking out to dinner? Douglas, you have been on a date before, haven't you? You told me you'd had—friends.'

'It's been a long time.' Douglas looked terrified. 'I've never been on a blind date before.'

'And I've never been to a party on my own. Another first.' She smiled, drawing courage from his nervousness. 'Look—we are both going to go out and give tonight our best shot and if it's terrible, we'll make our excuses and rendezvous back at yours for a cup of cocoa. If it's really terrible, we can dine out on our stories for years to come.'

She could feel the imprint of his fingers on her hand even after the taxi had driven off and she was alone on the doorstep. She was about to ring the bell when Kate opened the door. The party was in full swing behind her.

'Oh, it's you, Alys. I thought you were someone else.' Kate's eyes were slightly glazed, but they sharpened as they took in Alys's appearance. 'You look—different,' she said, and Alys heard surprise and displeasure in her voice. What had she ever done to make this woman dislike her so? Before she met the figments, she tried to propitiate her, to bumble along apologetically and make herself small so that Kate might accept her. Tonight, though faced with Kate's rudeness, Garbo's aloofness suddenly came to mind and she fixed Kate with a vague smile and looked past her at the people beyond.

'Hello, Kate. It's nice to see you too.'

'Are you all alone, Alys? You don't have a plus-one?' Kate made a show of looking around the driveway as if Alys's date might be lurking in the bushes.

'I did have, as you know, but unfortunately he's left me, so I'm on my own tonight.'

'I was so sorry to hear the news.' Kate leaned in, her eyes glinting.

In the lightest tone she could manage, Alys replied, 'Well, I say "unfortunately", but to be honest, Kate, it was three weeks before I'd even noticed he was gone. You know how "spacey" I can be.'

'If it isn't Alys Larsson looking all grown up!' Lincoln appeared at Kate's side and pulled Alys into his arms. 'You look stunning.'

'Thank you, Lincoln.' Alys left her kiss on his cheek. 'I see the party is off to a good start. Your signature cocktails, I presume?' She tucked an arm into his as he led her away and smouldered up at him, as Ava would do.

'Allow me to mix you one of my finest. Shut the door, would you, Kate? You're letting the cold air in.'

Alys shrugged out of Mrs Weatherley's voluminous black swing coat like a grand unveiling, and her old shyness made her look for her feet. 'You look so lovely.' Lincoln reached out and put a finger under her chin so that she had to meet his eyes. 'Beautiful, in fact.'

She was suddenly conscious that her dress exposed the whole of her decolleté, and he was looking at her in a way that made her self-conscious.

'Where are my manners? What'll it be?'

The scent of rose and bergamot enveloped her, and a voice in her ear, low and husky, said, 'Make mine a gin martini.' Alys spun around, but there was no sign of Ava. 'You came!' she said.

'What?' Lincoln looked over her shoulder.

'Sorry—gin martini please, Lincoln. Where are you?' she whispered as Lincoln moved behind the bar.

'Don't get excited. I'm at home in my track pants, but I'm with you in spirit. You were gurning at that guy, Alys. After everything we worked on. I'm not having you wrestle public humiliation from the jaws of victory.'

'Thank you, Ava. I don't think I can do this alone tonight.'

'You're gonna have to stop talking to me. You're muttering to yourself like a crazy woman. I can hear your thoughts just as clearly. Just listen to my instructions and do exactly as I say.'

'*Roger that. It'll be like one of those spy movies when the heroine has an earpiece.*'

'Straighten up and stop being so round-shouldered. You gotta show them what you got, honey,' Ava purred.

Kate had followed them to the bar. 'What are you drinking, Alys?'

'She's having a gin martini,' Lincoln said as he pushed a glass in front of her.

Kate smiled. 'I hope that's not too strong, Lincoln. We don't want a repeat of last time, do we?'

Alys took hold of the glass and toasted Lincoln.

'We most certainly do not, Kate,' she agreed. 'Particularly as I'm not wearing any pants.'

'Pah!' Ava laughed. Kate saw a friend across the room and retreated.

'*Kate hates me.*'

'She certainly does. The green-eyed monster riseth, my dear. She sees the way her boyfriend is with you.'

'*Lincoln? No, he's more like a brother. He's Jack's best friend.*'

'Not tonight, he ain't. Where is Jack anyway?'

Alys turned around and faced the room. She found him almost immediately. He was standing in the midst of his running club mates, his arm loosely slung over his new girlfriend's shoulder. She took a small uneven step backwards until she felt the bar edge digging into her back.

'*He's there.*'

He looked relaxed and expansive, laughing loudly at something the tallest of his friends—Greg? Grayson?—had said. When had he last looked so at home? She studied his face, taking in how different it looked when he wasn't frustrated or disgusted. He was wearing his dark blue shirt—her favourite because it showed off his eyes. Her eyes flickered to the woman at his side, and her stomach contracted sharply.

Wearing a little black dress that emphasised her blond hair and honey-coloured skin, Jack's new girlfriend was a younger version of Hannah Larsson. She looked impeccably clean and fresh, as if she had been in the shower for hours and had just stepped out and into her dress with her skin still damp to come to the party with her boyfriend in his dark blue shirt. They were a perfect fit; it was as if she belonged with him. She was tiny, and when Jack lifted his hand off of her shoulder for a second before settling it back down again, she staggered slightly as if she was too fragile to bear the weight of him.

Alys tried to pull her stomach in a little further. She should have gone for a dress with long sleeves.

'*It was a mistake to come here. What was I thinking?*'

'Nonsense, honey. You have to face this sometime. Better to do it with a martini in your mitt. Put your elbows back on the bar and relax. Look like you own the place. Smile.'

Lincoln appeared alongside her and followed the trajectory of her gaze. 'I'm glad you came, Alys. I was worried you wouldn't, but you're both my friends and I hate how sometimes when the marriage breaks, it breaks everything else around it.'

Her marriage was broken, then. She had broken it. She thought that it was perhaps just a little scuffed, with the odd dent in need of some attention at any rate, and that if she could just change—oh—everything about herself, balance would be restored. Things might even be better than before. Looking at Jack now and the change in him, she could see that he had found his balance without her and it suited him. He looked as if he were living the life he always should have been, and the loss of him stirred a wave of misery which threatened to dismantle her. Tears were close. Her lips trembled violently, and she put her hand to her mouth to steady them and focussed on her breathing. She thought of Garbo and of how important it was to keep her dignity tonight, and how it mattered in life not to tell people everything, how it was better to keep private things close, and she held herself in check just as Ava in a spit-filled rage screeched in her ear, 'You tell him that no-good son-of-a-bitch doesn't know what he's missing and he's lucky you haven't scratched his dick off with a rusty tin.'

'He looks happy. I'm glad for him,' Alys said quietly.

'He does, doesn't he? Still, you know Jack. He always puts on a good show.' Lincoln took a ruminative sip of his drink. 'To be honest, I don't think Jack knows how to be happy. I think that's always been his problem.' He gestured to his girlfriend. 'That won't last long. She's a sweet girl, but she's like a blank page. There's no substance to her. I don't mean to sound unkind, but Jack appreciates real women. He'll soon get bored.' She felt his eyes on her again and her skin began to feel hot. It was distracting.

'That's it, honey. Listen to your body. Feels nice to be wanted, doesn't it?' Ava cooed.

As if Jack felt the intensity of their stares, he suddenly looked directly at them. His laughter caught in his throat as Alys's breath caught in hers. He froze in mid-gesture, and his girlfriend took the opportunity to slide out from under his arm. He had clearly not expected Alys to show up, and his eyes narrowed. His face tightened for a second as if he had been caught off guard with an acute pain somewhere, but he quickly regained composure and smiled stiffly. Alys tipped her head in response. How strange it was to be at a party with your husband who happened to be with another woman. It was as if something had been dislocated and put back into place, but still ached.

She had finished her martini and it was replaced. Tonight, and for one night only, she would play Maxine Faulk, she decided, burying her pain in wild drinking and flirting. She and Lincoln held court at the bar. A group of Lincoln's old school friends gravitated towards them and Alys gave herself over to the throng and the chaos, grateful for the ground cover. In turn, she was introduced to an extremely short banker who had to look up into her face until they found him a bar stool; another barrister with a haze of slightly fluffy blond hair, but a sharp eye and razor wit; a cosmetic surgeon with the largest hands Alys had ever seen; a couple who had just sunk their savings into a vineyard in Burgundy and shared an expression of bewilderment bordering on hysteria, and—unfathomably—a mushroom grower with deep set eyes who made a fortune supplying shiitake to all the top restaurants. If she had been told their names, she'd forgotten them, but it didn't seem to matter. They swept her up on the tide of their familiarity.

'Where did Jack have you holed up? Why have we not met before?' The barrister mirrored her thoughts.

How indeed had she not met these people before, she wondered? They were Lincoln's oldest friends, after all. She thought back to all those parties where she spent the night hiding in the guest room, slinking about behind Jack.

'You having fun, honey?' Ava yawned.

'Hey, where have you been? I haven't seen you for a while.'

'Didn't look like you needed me, so I took a little nap.'

'Have you been drinking my martinis?'

'No—that's all you. Relax, you're holding your own, baby. Remind me to tell you about the time when I drank Bob Mitchum under the table.'

Another man appeared at the edge of the group, and jostled his way in the centre until he was facing Lincoln, who gave a shout and pulled him into an embrace. 'Aaron! Where have you been?' They slapped each other hard on the back, slapping harder and harder until they were knocking people's drinks and the others shouted for them to stop. Aaron's eyes slid sideways to Alys and he mouthed an apology. He was a beautiful man; tall and rangy with a wide grin showing white evenly spaced teeth against smooth black skin. His eyes were a light amber and lit up with amusement.

'I've been working, Linc. We open next week, remember? Some supplies were meant to be delivered this morning and didn't show up until seven. I couldn't leave until we'd unloaded and stored everything for the guys coming in on Monday.' Aaron's eyes shifted to Alys again. Her mind emptied.

Ava nudged her. 'Now this one is hot. Do something, honey, before he gets away.'

'Hello,' Alys stammered.

'That's all you got?' Ava spluttered.

Aaron smiled, 'Hello.'

Lincoln stepped in. 'Alys, Aaron, Aaron, Alys. Aaron is —where do I start? Only the finest pianist I know and a highly successful entrepreneur with a string of jazz clubs to his name across Europe, which is why we never see him. I give you—my best friend and our entertainment for this evening.'

Aaron laughed. 'I'm not sure about the highly successful bit, but I am the finest pianist he knows.'

'Alys here—' Lincoln planted a kiss on the side of her head '—is the kindest, funniest, most self-effacing woman I know. She also happens to be an amazing singer, although I haven't heard you sing in decades, Al, which is—' Lincoln frowned and looked over to Jack's group '—a real shame.'

The last time Alys had sung in public was about five years ago at a client dinner Jack and Lincoln had thrown at a piano bar in town. Lincoln had dragged her up to sing at the end of the evening, and they managed an improvised duet which left them both laughing and having to give in to calls for an encore. Their audience had loved them. Jack had been furious. She had thought he was angry that she and Lincoln had all the attention, or perhaps he had thought it inappropriate in front of their clients, but when they got back to the table, he had told her that her singing had always set his teeth on edge. He said it was embarrassing. Embarrassing. That was the word he used. It reminded her of being a child again and how she had unwittingly, innocently, gone about the daily business of just being Alys Faulkener, not realising how other people saw her, and how wrong she was until her peers had pointed it out. She had stopped singing after that.

She glanced over at Jack. He was watching them with a sullen expression on his face. His displeasure was always so evident when he didn't get his way, or she had done something that didn't match up to his expectations. She looked around her at this group of friends who had so effortlessly welcomed her. She had forgotten what it felt like to be liked and accepted with ease, with no agenda or conditions. She was dressed as Ava, but she was just being herself, her full self, as Ava had taught her and they liked her. They actually liked her.

'Make him see what he's lost,' Ava murmured.

Alys leaned slightly away from Aaron and gazed directly into his face as Ava would have done. He met her stare and smiled, and she found herself smiling back; a broad, mischievous smile, as if she had just agreed to let down someone's tyres or put a hotel ashtray in her pocket.

'I wonder what I would need to do to persuade you to sing with me,' he mused.

'What are my options?' She cringed as soon as the words were out. *'Oh God, Ava.'*

He burst out laughing. 'It's all to play for.'

She shook her head. 'Tempting, but I'm afraid Lincoln's

right. I haven't sung in public in decades, and in any case, I was never the finest singer of his acquaintance.'

'I don't know.' He scratched his chin thoughtfully. 'Lincoln has very good taste. He knows what he's talking about.'

His eyes crinkled and he started grinning at her again. He had a way about him, a natural joyfulness, that was infectious.

'I hate to break up whatever's going on between you two,' Lincoln cut in, 'but those ivories aren't going to play themselves, mate. You owe me.'

Aaron winced. 'I really do,' he admitted to Alys. 'Sure I can't persuade you?'

At that moment, she'd have said anything to keep him close to her with his amber eyes and his wicked grin, but she couldn't help checking back at Jack. Jack was scowling at her, oblivious of his girlfriend, who was pulling at his sleeve and trying to talk to him. In an instant she felt the spark that Aaron had ignited in her dampen and blink out.

She shrank back on the bar stool. 'I don't think I could.' She shook her head slowly as the last of her exuberance faded to grey.

'If you change your mind, you know where to find me!' Her eyes followed him as he sauntered off towards the far end of Lincoln's living room, greeting people as he went. He collected a cool nod from Jack before finally settling down behind the piano. When the music came, it was strong and soulful.

Kate appeared at her side. 'He's brilliant, isn't he?' Alys glanced at her. She looked slightly dishevelled, and her eyes were off-kilter. 'Do you know, Lincoln bought that piano just so that whenever Aaron is in town, he could hear him play—they call it the Private Sessions.'

'I find it strange that our paths have never crossed,' Alys replied, her eyes seeking him out again.

'Well, he's never here for a start. He spends most of his time in Lisbon—his main club is there.'

'But why would I never hear about him?'

Kate shrugged. 'Lincoln knows it makes Jack insanely jealous, so he doesn't talk about him. You know how Jack can be very proprietary about his friendships. Aaron couldn't care. He just has that lovely way about him—a live and let live attitude. He's a free spirit who doesn't like to be tied down. That's why women always fall so hard for him. He has a way of making you feel that you're the only woman alive, but honestly, Alys, you should know—he has a woman in every port.'

'Ah, there it is. I was wondering what she was getting to.' Ava yawned.

Alys slipped off her stool to face Kate. 'You came all the way over here to tell me that?'

A cold hand clawed at Alys's arm. 'I don't want to see you make a fool of yourself.' *Again.*

'Oh, don't worry, I get it. People like me don't get to have the fairy tale. I already knew that. You wasted your breath.'

She strode off down the hallway that led to the guests' bathroom, locked the door and leant her body against it as if expecting Kate to barrel in after her.

'Boy, that bitch is a piece of work, isn't she?' Ava appeared and perched on the toilet seat. 'And who knew you could turn it on when you needed to? I like this feisty mama! You don't need me, honey, you got it all going on in there. Let her have it!'

Alys was wringing her hands, trying to shake a rising agitation out through the tips of her fingers. 'I'm not angry with Kate, I'm angry with myself. I was standing at that bar, and I was enjoying myself for once. For once, I forgot I was me, and it felt so good just to be free to enjoy other people's company. Then I looked up and saw Jack glaring at me and I felt shabby all over again, as if it didn't matter that I had this beautiful dress and my hair felt nice, because he saw through it and it was still dirty, shameful old me cowering beneath and if that beautiful man spent any longer with me he would know too. He would see just how much of a fake I was being.' A sob caught her in check.

She was used to suppressing her emotions, compartmentalising them in small boxes in her head so that they couldn't overwhelm her. She had hundreds, thousands of these boxes, precariously balanced, each harbouring a hurt, a slight, a neglect, a humiliation stretching back years. Now it seemed as if the whole pile were teetering and threatening to burst open.

'I feel all this anger, Ava. I don't know where to put it. I'm scared I won't be able to stop it now. If I really let go, there'd be no coming back. I'm standing there, looking at Jack looking at me, and it suddenly strikes me how many times in my life people have belittled me and I let them do it. They tell me all the things I'm not, I can't do, I can't have and I just accept it. I'm so—angry.'

Ava took her hands, peeled her gently away from the door and led her to the sink. She turned the cold tap on and put Alys's hands under the stream, stroking them gently as the coolness of the water started to dissipate the heat that was rising in her.

'That's the other side of the coin when you're a passionate woman, honey,' she soothed. 'And you are a passionate woman, no matter what you tell yourself. That was always my way. I was the best lover and the dirtiest fighter. There was nothing in between. If you want to live life fully, Alys, you gotta take both sides of the coin. This is progress, baby, believe me. You get to feel.'

They stood for a while, letting the water flow around their hands. Their eyes met in the mirror, Ava in a pale grey tracksuit, her hair scraped back, her skin clear and polished. Her scent drifted between them, and Alys breathed her in. She could still hear Aaron's music, the notes slipping underneath the door, keeping time with the sound of the water hitting the basin. There was something loose and fluid in the way Aaron played as if he had a tiny thread of the tune, but his fingers wanted to stray down side-alleys. He was happy to let them explore for a while, but then she'd hear a familiar phrase and they'd be back into the main refrain again.

The balls of her feet were aching where her heels had forced her forward on to them. She hadn't realised how long she'd been standing.

'Take them off.' Ava turned off the tap and handed her a towel. 'They're such a bind. You don't see the guys having to wear instruments of torture, do you? Take them off.' Her husky voice was an invocation. Alys' feet had swollen painfully in the shoes that Jack had bought her, and it took her a while to kick them free of her. She left them where they fell and splayed her toes, feeling the coolness of the tiles beneath her bare feet.

'Feel better?'

'I didn't think I'd ever get them off.' Alys met Ava's smile.

'Look who looks the film star now,' Ava whispered and pulled her to her good side.

Alys looked at Ava, more beautiful with her ravaged face devoid of make-up than she had been in her glory days.

'It will always be you, Ava.'

'Didn't you feel it when you had all those people buzzing around you, like bees to honey? Or when the cute pianist couldn't take his eyes off you? Didn't you feel the power you have?' She looked down at Alys's feet and nodded approvingly. 'A barefoot contessa.'

Chapter 41

Barefoot Contessa

When Alys left the bathroom in her bare feet, she moved with a surety and an earthiness as if she had shucked off another layer, as wild and as natural as she had felt in the river. She made her way to the bar and asked the barman for a rum coco.

'*To us*,' she toasted Ava silently. The room was hot and crowded. She crossed it and moved out on to the terrace where Aaron's eyes and his music followed her. He was playing *In the Wee Small Hours of the Morning*. She sipped her rum and looked out across the garden—an inky blue silhouette. A light breeze joined the music as it played across her. She let herself relax into a pleasurable melancholy, her fingers following the notes absently on her leg. A brusque voice pulled her out of her reverie. 'You'll catch your death out here.'

'Hello Jack.' Alys turned to face him, resting her arm on the balustrade.

'I wasn't expecting you to see you tonight. Actually, I barely recognised you. It seems that every time I see you, you've reinvented yourself.'

'How perceptive of you,' she murmured. 'Where's your friend?'

'Sarah? I sent her home.'

'You *sent* her home?'

'I mean—it was time for her to go home.'

'And you let her leave on her own? Always the gentleman.'

'I put her in a cab with Greg. She'll be fine.' A flare of irritation was swiftly dampened. 'So, how have you been? I've been worried about you.'

'How so?'

'I was afraid I'd hurt you after mum's party.'

Dignity. She straightened a little. 'Not at all. These things happen.'

She just hadn't thought these things would happen to them. She didn't trust herself to open her mouth. He put his hand alongside hers on the balustrade and she kept her eyes on the minuscule gap between their little fingers. Aaron began to play *My Funny Valentine*.

It had been their first dance at their wedding, and they had played it religiously at every Valentine's Day and wedding anniversary since. Jack always used to joke that she was his funny valentine, with her laughable looks and her stupid thoughts that tumbled out of her less than smart mouth, and standing there in her green dress she felt the slight of those words, and she understood how sad the song had always made her feel. Weariness descended on her.

Jack looked close to tears. 'I miss you, you know.'

She nodded and looked out to the garden. She could hear Aaron singing now, a soft mellow voice that slid over the notes.

'It's not easy watching your wife across a crowded room and knowing that you won't be taking her home.'

She turned to look at him. 'This was your choice. I'm just trying to get on with life after you.' Her voice was flat.

'I know, I know,' he apologised, flinging his hands up, and for a moment she had a memory of Kate flirting with him and him gallantly deflecting her, and the loss of him stung her again. That version of him when he was still hers.

The old Alys would have wanted to know what exactly it was about her that he missed, sifting through his answers forensically for anything that would tell her definitively what was lovable about her, what was worthwhile. This new Alys was wary and tired and no longer wanted to know the answer. This was indifference.

'Are you seeing anyone?' Jack asked.

'None of your business,' she retorted.

'Sorry, sorry. It just drives me crazy to think about you with another man.'

'You have a bloody girlfriend.' She was incredulous.

'I know it sounds like double standards, but honestly, Al, she means nothing.'

Alys frowned. 'To you.'

'What?'

'She means nothing to you. But she means something. She means something to the people who really know her, who really love her. Her family, her friends. She means something to herself. She's not defined by your opinion of her.' Her voice was suddenly louder than she had anticipated.

'Calm down, Al. Get off your soap box.' Jack held his palms out in front of him, too close to her face. She stepped away.

'I'm perfectly calm, Jack. I just remembered how challenged you become when a woman appears to know her own mind.'

She made to move inside.

'You're still my wife, Alys.' Jack pulled at her arm. 'If you'd made this much effort, you'd taken this much care of yourself when we were married, we would still be together. You just gave up on us. Don't forget that. It wasn't that I got itchy feet, or had a midlife crisis, you left the marriage long before I did. I tried so hard to keep it going.'

She shrugged his hand off. 'I'm cold. I need to go inside.'

'Of course you're cold. Where are your shoes?' He sounded exasperated.

She looked down at her feet. 'They don't fit me anymore.'

When she moved inside and joined Aaron at the piano, he nodded to her as if he were expecting her.

'I like this beat,' she said.

'It's a sort of Brazilian/Cuban fusion I've made up. It goes down really well with the crowd in Lisbon. What do you like to sing?'

'I can't—I couldn't—'

'Which is it? "Couldn't" sounds more promising.'

She shook her head, but stayed with him, watching his long, square-tipped fingers tumbling over each other across the keys, effortlessly drawing out the sound. She was mesmerised until a voice broke in over the top of them.

'You know, honey. If you were really serious about finding yourself and standing on your own two feet, this would be a perfect way to shake off the old shackles.'

'I thought you'd gone to bed.'

'I mean it, honey. You love singing. Shake yourself a little looser. Take a risk. Sing with the man.'

'You sound like the devil on my shoulder.'

'On the contrary, I'm batting for the other side,' Ava purred. 'This is for your own good. All sorts of bad-but-good things happen when two people start to make music together.' She gave a throaty chuckle. 'Don't get me started, honey. Singing was my secret weapon.'

'I thought the smoke thing was your secret weapon.'

'I had lots of secret weapons. How do you think I was so goddamn successful? They didn't stand a chance.'

'I can't sing. I literally can't. The thought of it is terrifying. I feel like I'm choking just thinking about it.'

Jack had come back into the room. He paused when he caught her at the piano, as if the thought had occurred to him that he might retrieve her, then he frowned and crossed back over to stand by the fireplace.

'Uh uh,' Ava said, her voice registering disapproval. 'That feeling you described, does it feel like someone holding you down with their foot on your throat? Does anyone spring to mind when you feel that, honey? Anyone at all?'

Alys tried to keep her eyes on the keys so that she couldn't see Jack.

'I couldn't—'

'All I'm saying is you give it one song, honey, and you'll be a free woman. You'd like that, wouldn't you? One song.'

'One song.' Alys must have said it out loud, because Aaron had stopped playing and was looking up at her expectantly.

'One song it is. Which song would the lady care to sing?' He began to play a few notes with his left hand, as if to keep the keys warm while they waited.

Alys looked up at Jack. The light was reflecting against his glasses and she couldn't see his eyes, but his mouth looked appalled. Kate was drunk and sullen beside him, but

Lincoln, who had caught the break in the music, walked towards them smiling. He stood closest to them, and she looked between him and Jack—the one embarrassed and ashamed of her, and the other delighted for her, cheering her on. A wave of profound sadness washed over Alys and pooled at her bare feet. How would her life have been different if she had known unconditional love? If she'd been seen for who she was, and loved all the more for it? How would it have been to have parents who treasured their children, a husband who was proud of her, her own children? What sort of woman would she have become? She wrapped her arms around herself and held them there.

'Do you know any Melody Gardot songs?' Alys's voice sounded as if it were being squeezed through a muslin bag. She coughed and tried again. 'Could you play *Once I was loved* by Melody Gardot, please?'

'Give me a moment.' Aaron tried a few notes until he found the key he was looking for. 'This the one?'

The starting notes of the song were mournful, but tender, and her eyes welled up at their gentleness. Her breathing began to slow down as she settled into the music, soothing her as if it were a lullaby her mother might have sung to her if she had been some other mother, and not the one she got. She let her arms fall to her side, and all the while she kept her eyes on Lincoln's face with its beautiful smile.

The first line came out of her soft and silvery. The normal party hubbub had slowed. People were drawing closer to her and she sang into the hush. Her throat began to tighten, but she imagined that she was a Brazilian singer in one of Aaron's clubs and not Alys in her bare feet with her tired eyes.

'That's it, honey. Shake it loose,' Ava soothed.

She closed her eyes and let herself go, marvelling as her voice started to soar as if it were waking up from a long sleep and giving a lazy stretch. She heard its rich timbre that had always made Jack wince, and she recognised it as her own distinctive tone. Aaron's notes kept in perfect time with her and she lost herself in the music.

The song came to a close and Aaron played out the last of the notes into silence. She was deeply moved, and it took a moment to look at him. He took her hand and pressed it against his mouth. Then the applause exploded and Lincoln was beside them and kissing her and crowing, 'Didn't I tell you? Didn't I?' Alys looked over to the fireplace, but there was an empty space where Jack had been.

They were calling for more, and Lincoln kept treading on her toes, and she was laughing and refusing their pleas, and she felt lighter and freer than she could ever remember feeling. Ava was cheering in her ear and telling her she loved her and the world was confetti.

Then Kate appeared and pulled Lincoln roughly backwards against her. Her mouth was thin and distorted and her eyes spiteful.

'What's she got that I haven't?'

There was an embarrassed silence. Then the woman who'd bought the vineyard cut through, 'Honey, what she's got you couldn't spell - and what you've got, you used to have.' A line straight from *Barefoot Contessa.*

'Ava...?'

'I swear to God, I didn't do anything to her. How could I? I'm just a figment.'

The party broke up shortly after that as Lincoln had to carry Kate to bed. By the time Douglas's taxi arrived to collect her, he found Alys standing just inside the door, waving goodbye to the last of the guests.

'Have you forgotten your shoes?' Douglas raised an eyebrow as she climbed in beside him.

'No.' Alys slammed the door behind her and settled back to study him. 'How was your date?'

He shifted uncomfortably. 'It went very well, I think. Did something happen to your shoes?'

'And how was Dawn?'

'She was very pleasant. Very easy to talk to.'

'And will we be seeing her again?'

'Um.' Douglas frowned meaningfully at the back of the taxi driver's head. 'I must say, I'm very hungry. I didn't manage to eat my dinner. I must have been nervous.'

'Oh good, I'm starving,' Alys agreed. 'I'll make us some chilli noodles. You can tell me all about it then.'

'How was your night?'

Alys thought of Aaron's number, scrawled on a napkin, and tucked into her bag. 'Unexpected.'

Chapter 42

Reinvention

Alys was in her pyjamas, making chilli and coriander noodles.

'So what was so interesting about your evening?' Douglas, in a tartan dressing gown, had been given the job of toasting sesame seeds.

She told him about Lincoln's friends and about Aaron's music. She described Jack's girlfriend in avid detail for him. She sketched over their conversation in the garden, briefly alighted on her sudden impulse to sing, and tried to remain diplomatic when describing Kate's demise.

She kept her eyes trained on the pan in front of her as she rolled hot oil up the sides. 'You know, I think I realised tonight that my marriage is over.'

Douglas gave his pan a little shake. His eyes on the seeds that were turning brown at the edges. 'Ah. How do you feel about that?'

Alys added noodles and vegetables to the oil and a loud hissing almost drowned out her reply when it finally came. 'Relieved.'

Over steaming bowls, she interrogated Douglas. 'And will we be seeing Dawn again?'

'I don't think so, no.' Douglas hunched down over his noodles.

'Why not?'

'Oh, I don't know, really. It's a lot of effort isn't it?'

'It's not meant to be hard work, Douglas! You're meant to be having fun. What was so effortful about it?'

He set down his fork to consider his answer and began to smooth the front of his trousers. 'I don't want to have to explain myself to someone new. What should I polish? What should I leave out? I'm tired of trotting out my potted history like an old carcass for them to pick over. I understand that a relationship is a reciprocal accommodation to find the optimum fit. I accept the premise, but I think... I think it's not for me.' He smiled gravely. 'I'm an unusual man. We both know that. Who would want a man who sleeps with hundreds of dead insects in their bedroom?'

'You could move them out.'

'That's the point, Alys. I don't want to.'

Later, as she was climbing into bed, she thought about what Douglas had said about editing himself to appeal to someone else. She had been doing that her whole life. This latest bout of reinvention had brought her no closer to what she wanted. She had thought that she wanted her life to go back to how it was before, but the figments had shown her that wasn't possible. Even if Jack had wanted her back, she knew that something fundamental had shifted in her. She wouldn't fit that life as she was now. She just didn't know what else to do with herself, and facing into the void took more courage than she thought she had. Douglas had always had that instinctive sense of who he was, and always chose what he considered to be the right path even if it was the hard path. Why couldn't she be more like him? Perhaps reinvention wasn't the answer—or only part of the answer.

Aaron's number had been tucked under her pillow for safe keeping, a note for the tooth fairy. And each time she remembered it, she thought how he had kissed her hand and held it against his mouth. She was exhausted, but too wired to sleep. When Ava slid into bed alongside her, she was grateful for once for the distraction.

'That was some night, honey.' Ava's eyes sparkled with mischief.

'Can you believe we did that?'

'You did that. I'm just a figment, remember? You did it all by yourself, baby, and I couldn't have been prouder.' Ava reached out and stroked her hair. 'You've got wayward hair like me. Never does what it's told, a bit like the woman it belongs to.'

Alys tucked herself into the side of Ava, and she curved around Alys and continued to stroke her hair.

'Ava, did you ever find yourself changing parts of yourself to make someone love you more?'

'Of course, honey. I think that's how we're made.' She stopped to think. 'But some part of me always kicked in if I gave too much, you know? Call it self-preservation. I never wanted to change my identity for some man. Maybe that's why I never managed to make a success of marriage even though I loved my men to distraction. Too stubborn, I guess.'

'Did you ever worry about being alone when you were my age?'

'Oh, sure. But what can you do? We get old, our beauty fades, we're alone. That's the script.'

'When our beauty fades, who do we become?' Alys asked, stifling a yawn.

'Beats me, honey. Maybe that's what keeps me up all these nights.'

'I'm not sure I want that script, you know.'

Ava's hand was on her hair, stroking and stroking, and Alys' eyes started to close.

'Did you ever want to be a mother, Ava?'

The hand stilled for a moment. 'Now, what could I have given a child, Alys? A child needs stability. My life was always a party, always crazy. I loved every minute of it, but I couldn't have given a child what it needed.'

'Lots of people do.' Alys yawned. 'Lots of people have children they didn't really want and make a perfect mess of it.'

'I wasn't going to do that to a kid.'

Alys started to drift off.

'You'd have made a lovely mother, Ava.'

Ava kissed her on the forehead.

'Go to sleep, baby.'

Chapter 43

Bergamot

Ava was gone when Alys woke up the next morning. There was an indentation in the pillow beside her and the faintest smell of bergamot. She pushed her face into Ava's pillow and tried to inhale the last of her scent. The harder she breathed in, the more elusive it was, until there was nothing left. She knew she was being ridiculous, that Ava wasn't real, wasn't even a ghost but a wraith conjured by her own yearning. Even so, she was bereft. Ava saw through her fear and despair to the woman beneath, and because Ava believed in her, Alys did too. She thought back to the night before, and how it felt to hear her own voice pouring out of her and to have no fear in front of all those people, to just be content to be there in that moment with Aaron's music wrapped around her. She could not have done that without Ava at her side. Who would stroke her hair, and tell her she was brave and clever, and make her put on her red lipstick and sing out now?

She found Douglas in the garage, examining some specimen boxes of his father's. Soames was sitting alongside him on an old chest freezer, his eyes fixed on the back of

Douglas's head as if planning an attack. She placed the coffee she'd brought alongside the cat and swung herself up alongside him.

Douglas did not look up. He was gently rubbing the mahogany frames of the boxes with a small lint cloth.

'What are you up to?'

'Oh, I was clearing some space in here and then I got side-tracked with father's boxes. I think I'm going to move them into the bedroom—they really shouldn't be here. Too damp.'

Alys wrinkled her nose. 'Have you any space left in the bedroom?'

'I'll have to move the bed out, of course.'

'How come you're clearing some space?'

He straightened, took up his coffee, and took a cautious sip before he replied. 'I thought I might move Mother's ruby glass out of the living room, as you suggested.'

'Oh?'

'It's funny how time passes, isn't it? I hadn't really thought about it until you came to live here. It made me realise how strange it must seem for a grown man to want to preserve things just as they were when he was a boy with his parents still alive. It wasn't intentional. I suppose I felt disloyal moving their things, as if I were erasing their memory. It feels disrespectful moving on. Can't explain. Silly, really.'

'I don't think it's silly, Douglas,' Alys said. 'You had a family that you loved. It's only natural that you would want to preserve what it meant to you. I think that says a lot about what you were to each other. You have roots. You have a home here. I envy you.' She had nothing that she wanted to hold on to from her family. Unless you counted Miss Marple.

Douglas cast his eyes around the garage, his face crumpling slightly. He looked anxiously back at the boxes and took up the lint cloth again.

Alys pushed herself off the chest freezer. 'Would you like to get out of here?'

Chapter 44

Intermezzo

This time the river was the colour of green aventurine, and Alys waded in without a backward glance. When she heard Douglas behind her, she turned to face him and then fell backwards into the river, a gleeful smile on her lips. Her fall caught up the water like wings on either side of her and splashed his chest. The cold hit the back of her head and made her skin sting. Douglas howled and then launched himself after her, taking both of them underwater. She kept her eyes screwed tightly shut, and when his arms circled around her, she pulled him against her and hooked her legs around his waist. They burst to the surface, her clinging to him and crowing with laughter, and him taken aback and spluttering but holding on to her tightly all the same. She was unhinged—wild and joyful—and part of this spirit must have communicated itself to Douglas, usually so cautious and circumspect, because when they broke apart they both struck out for the deepest part of the river, and then circled each other, treading water, grinning like loons.

Reeds flickered like snakes' tongues around her feet

even at that depth, and she kicked back and floated on her back, her face screwed up against the midday sun. Douglas joined her and they lay suspended there, sculling their arms, listening to the river. A dragonfly landed on Alys's stomach and they lifted their heads to watch it drying its wings, tensing them, readying to fly again. When it took off, as lightly as it had landed, Douglas's eyes remained on the pale dome of her stomach, and Alys found that she didn't mind. She luxuriated in the attention, stretching her arms back over her head as if she were Ava. It was only skin. It was only her beautiful womanly body that she had been gifted with.

When Douglas turned and swam off upstream, Alys continued to stare at her stomach, noticing the curve where her tummy met her hip bones, and she reached down and lay an index finger to mark the spot. All these years she had felt that her body was something to be ashamed of. Now, she relaxed into the unadorned, unadulterated shape of her body, its strength, its own unique shape, its power. She stretched her legs longer, revelling in the line of her thigh muscles and her pointed toes, and the way her stomach flattened when she arched her back into the water, and she felt —horny. She rolled on to her front and there was something predatory in the way she watched Douglas striking out, his muscular shoulders pulling clear of the river. Guilt drove her to the bank, and she climbed out and scoured herself with a towel. Oblivious, Douglas climbed up on to the bank and flopped down alongside her. An innocent.

'I love these days,' he panted. 'It reminds me of when we were kids and we used to escape together and go off and have adventures. It's marvellous that we're still doing it at our age.'

'What are we escaping from this time?' she asked.

'I think...' He paused as he weighed his next words on his tongue and, sitting up, he leaned over his knees and examined where the grass had flattened in front of his feet. 'I think you and I are the same. It's not that we run, it's that we have perfected the art of hiding in plain sight, haven't we?'

She turned her back to finish drying, averting her eyes from the taunt of his lean body glistening. She scrubbed furiously at her skin. 'I wonder when we'll know it's safe to come out.'

On the way home, Alys took Douglas on a detour to meet Margo. She wasn't sure it was wise to spend any more time with a dog she couldn't keep, it would only be more painful when she disappeared to a new home, but still she couldn't help the fluttering of her heart at the sight of those brown eyes taking in Alys and the large man beside her. Alys couldn't believe that Margo was still at the shelter, and although Anna, not quite able to meet her eyes, insisted that she hadn't been hiding Margo from prospective owners, Alys thought it strange that nobody had fallen for her as she had. Douglas solemnly stroked her round tummy and regretted that Soames would not welcome any competition. They left, with Alys promising to visit again. Margo's eyes followed her as she walked backwards down the corridor.

Aaron phoned just as they had opened the front door.

'The pianist,' she mouthed to Douglas who frowned and sloped off to put the kettle on.

'I forgive you for not calling me,' Aaron said.

Surely the heat from her cheeks could be felt down the line?

'I was calling to see if you'd like to come along to the opening night of the new club? You can bring some friends, if you promise to sing with me again.'

Gurning, she thought. *I'm gurning*.

She managed a garbled acceptance and put the phone down before she made more of a fool of herself and before she could change her mind.

'How did he have your number?' Douglas said gruffly.

She saw the napkin glowing like a kryptonite beacon from under her pillow. 'Lincoln must have given it to him.' She shrugged.

Chapter 45

The Cues

She invited Candace, Mairéad and Douglas. Candace invited Tim, which confirmed Mairéad's suspicions that something funny was going on between them. To Alys's surprise, Douglas agreed to come.

The evening before Aaron's opening, her nerves began to kick in. They started as faint flutterings in her tummy, a box of butterflies whose quivering wings began to agitate and then thrash frantically, chaotically, until she had to get out of the house and walk. She wanted to ask Ava if she'd ever had stage fright, but she imagined that, if she had, her answer would have been to down a stiff gin and brave it out. She walked for an hour, listening to the dusk birdsong and eventually followed the towpath that led back to the village. She liked the village in the evening. It was quieter, there was less risk of being seen by anyone. The lights from the pub threw out an orange glow across the green, reflected in the village pond, where she and Douglas used to hunt for toads. She lingered by the pond beside a clump of bull-rushes, breathing in the marshy smell of the water, and then turned and made for The Granary. It was 7.30 pm, half an hour before closing, and Enid was at the counter going through the day's takings. She smiled when she caught sight of Alys.

'I'm not bothering you?' Alys hovered, her fingertips tiptoeing nervously over the glass counter.

'You could never bother anyone.' Enid set down a bunch of receipts and rested a stapler over them, bookmarked for later. 'To what do I owe this pleasure?'

Alys shrugged. 'I was taking a walk and I wanted to see you.'

Enid got up stiffly from her chair and locked the door, flipping the open sign over. She had just made a pot of tea and offered Alys a cup. They walked the floor, setting down their cups from time to time to straighten up, rehome discarded books back on the shelves, plump cushions. Alys knew the drill.

Enid seemed in no hurry, content to let Alys wander until she was ready to share what was on her mind. An old grandmother clock on the wall kept watch with her with its gentle ticking. Eventually, Alys perched on a chair and confessed her terror at the thought of singing to the crowd at Aaron's.

'You did it before. What's different about this?' Enid asked.

'I was drunk. It was at Lincoln's party and there weren't as many people there. The people at Aaron's club will be musicians and people who know what good music sounds like.'

'Besides making a fool of yourself, what are you afraid of?' Enid asked.

'Isn't that enough?'

'Do you want to sing at the club?'

Alys blinked. She hadn't thought about whether or not she wanted to do it.

Enid pressed her. 'Why did you say "yes"?'

'Because Aaron asked me to.'

'So because someone wanted you to do it, you said "yes", regardless of whether you wanted to do it or not?'

'He caught me off-guard,' she mumbled.

'You do know that you have a choice, don't you, Alys?' Enid said gently. 'You don't always have to do what other people want of you, if you don't want to do it. You're allowed to say "no".'

The sound of the clock was like a metronome, soothing Alys with the measured precision of each tick.

The trouble was, Alys was never sure where the line was between choosing not to do something because you didn't want to, and avoiding something because you weren't brave enough to do it. When was it ok not to make yourself do something that was probably good for you? How did you know when you were exercising free will? And when it was letting yourself off the hook?

'What are you afraid of?' Enid tried again.

'I'm afraid that I'm a coward and that if I don't go ahead and sing, I'll always be a coward,' she blurted.

'You're afraid of being afraid.'

'But I'm most afraid that I don't know what I really think or want about anything. You asked me if I wanted to sing and the honest answer is that I don't know. I'm always waiting for my cue from someone else. It's like I need other people to tell me who I am or how to be, and once I have the cue I power up and follow the instructions, go through the motions. Without the cue, I'm just—this.' She waved a hand over her body.

Enid was quiet. She looked tired and, for a moment,

Alys thought she had fallen asleep, but when she spoke her tone was slow and thoughtful.

'It's always remarkable to me how much we need to be loved. We'll do anything to earn that love. It works too. You do what people ask of you and you make them happy, they like you. Pretty soon, it becomes the only thing that matters to you. The trouble is, we become so used to listening for the cues, we become deaf to our own voice. We have to learn to hear it all over again.' Enid took Alys's hand in hers. 'Perhaps when you get to the club tomorrow, you might listen for yours, no matter how faint it is. Listen for it, and do what it says.'

Alys squeezed Enid's hand gently, trying to tell her that she loved her through her touch alone, because she didn't have the words to tell her all that she meant to her.

They sat together until the clock chimed the hour, and Enid stirred and patted Alys's back to rouse her.

'How did you get on with that Gardner biography?' she asked, gripping the chair arms to lever herself to her feet.

Alys thought of Ava. 'It was enlightening. Inspiring.'

'She was quite a broad, wasn't she?' Enid chuckled as she moved over to the biography section, her fingers playing across the spines of the books like keys on a piano. She pulled a slim volume out and gave it to Alys.

'I think you'll like this.'

'Ingrid Bergman?' Alys took the book and stared down into a photo of the actress, a beautifully lit black and white photo that set off her chiselled eyes, her fine bone structure, her natural smile.

'A great artist, but more importantly, a woman who always listened to her own voice.'

Alys took the longer way home so that she could sift through Enid's words. Alys had been listening for those cues all her life. When had that habit of hers started? She thought about her mother and that blank-faced indifference of hers. It didn't matter what Alys did, she could never pierce it. She didn't have the key to unlock her mother, and her father's distracted manner told her that she wasn't enough to hold him either. At least the rules with Jack had been clearer. He always knew what he wanted her to be. It was always clear to her how she needed to colour between the lines.

Douglas had been held up at work, so she let herself into an empty house. It was too late to eat, and the churn in her stomach—the ache in her chest—made eating impossible, anyway. She ran herself a bath and, soaking beneath the bubbles, she opened the book that Enid had given her and prepared herself to meet Ingrid Bergman.

Chapter 46

Waller

The club was tucked away at the end of a small alley in Shoreditch. They saw it just as they were about to drive past. It had done its best to remain hidden. The exterior of the club was painted a dark green, almost black. Its name, Waller, was etched in gold lettering over the door.

Alys, who was rarely in London, could not have said how to find it again had her life depended on it. Fortunately, Tim had offered to drive, so grateful was he for the invitation to join them. Candace took the front passenger seat, and Douglas squeezed into the back of the car with Mairéad and Alys. Alys sat in the uncomfortable middle, which set her even more on edge than when she first arrived. She stole a quick glance at the side of Douglas's face. London confused him, too. He had worn the same perplexed expression since he'd got in the car and caught Tim squeezing Candace's thigh.

'Isn't there a Mrs Parrish?' he whispered in Alys's ear.

'It's complicated,' Alys murmured back.

'How so?' Douglas whispered.

'Long story. Not a love match,' Alys supplied. That seemed to halt his questions, but not his confusion.

Mairéad was glued to the window, taking in the views, the lights, the people hurriedly going about their business, some only just leaving the office. Alys picked up on her excitement, wondering how she could survive in a village as quiet as theirs. She was conscious that she hadn't spent much time with Mairéad since Ava appeared, and she wanted to make it up to her that evening. Candace barely spoke. She sat with her head held high, tearful with pride. This evening was Candace and Tim's coming out and, ignoring Douglas's disapprobation, Alys found their tremulous tenderness around each other touching.

By the time they had found a suitable parking spot and walked back to the alleyway they'd driven past, they were bubbling with nervous excitement and chittering like a flock of starlings.

'We don't get out much,' Douglas apologised to the doorman's raised eyebrow. For one long moment, the doorman struggled to find Alys's name on the list and she was afraid that she had been forgotten. This club was too exclusive for someone like her. But then he went to another list—the VIP list—and there she was. It was the doorman's turn to apologise, 'I'm sorry, Miss Larsson. I ought to have checked there first. There's a note here for you, too.' He handed her a small square envelope. All eyes were on her as she read the few lines inside. 'It's from Aaron,' she explained unnecessarily. 'He says that in case he doesn't catch us when we arrive, he's reserved us a table.'

Through the double doors, they heard the music before they had got their bearings. The band was playing a Brazilian bossanova, and they checked in their coats and followed the sounds deeper into the interior and through another set of doors that led them on to a semi-circular platform raised above the main floor of the club. It took a moment to adjust to the darkness. The walls were the same dark green as the exterior of the club, but everywhere she looked Alys could see tiny, embedded golden lights that lit up the room and bathed everyone in a warm amber glow. The bar stretching along the back of the room was made of copper—a long gleaming swathe of red, pink and brown, which caught and reflected back the lights so that the first impression was one of opulent welcome.

The club was already half full. Alys was relieved to see that her dress wouldn't look out of place here. She had chosen a plain black dress with a fitted waist. It had a scoop neck that covered her shoulders, but exposed her collar bone, and its stark simplicity appealed. It was a model of understatement. Perhaps she was still hiding in plain sight, but it was all she could manage for now.

The clientele looked smart, edgy, sophisticated, and much younger than her. She watched the women. Sleek hair, red lips, an air of confidence and self-assurance, an unquestioning acceptance that they had every right to be there. How did they do it?

Mairéad sidled up to her. 'Alys, love, we're starting to look as if we're waiting for someone to announce us. Any chance we could find that table, do you think?'

Alys roused and led her friends down onto the main floor. She avoided any eye contact, focusing on the table numbers until she came to Table 4. Set close to the stage, they had a clear view of the band, and Alys's eyes went to the pianist, but he was stocky with balding, ginger hair.

A waiter appeared with a bottle of champagne and coupe glasses. 'A gift from Aaron.'

Alys glowed with pride and allowed herself to bask in the surprised expressions of her table guests.

'Please will you pass on our thanks and best wishes to him. I'm sure he's very busy tonight.'

The waiter rolled his eyes and laughed. 'This is the third club I've opened with Aaron and it's always the same. He never stops.'

When the waiter withdrew, they raised their glasses and Tim called the toast. 'To Aaron, the man-legend!' Seated between Mairéad and Candace, his arm resting along the back of Candace's chair, he looked as if he'd been let out on day release.

'May he enjoy the success he deserves,' Douglas followed, and he met Alys's eyes as they sipped their champagne.

'So, how exactly do you know this Aaron?' Everyone laughed as Mairéad voiced the question that they had on their minds.

Alys brushed off their insinuations. He was just a friend—a new friend. She admired him greatly for his talent and ambition, he was very charismatic, he had been very kind to her, but there was nothing going on. She felt as if she were explaining something fundamental to Douglas, although he was listening intently to the band.

The drinks flowed. The only sober one at the table, a flamboyant Tim, had insisted on sponsoring the champagne, until finally Candace put a hand on his arm and told him that it was 'not necessary'.

Aaron appeared half-way through the evening. Alys watched as he wove his way through the tables, greeting friends and clients as he went, waving to the boys in the band. He was smiling broadly and laughing, but there was an alertness to him, a sharpness at the same time. He was scanning the room, checking all was in order. He looked handsome in a crisp white shirt. At every table, he lingered over the women, and Alys saw how they responded to his charm. She thought of Kate. Surely she and Lincoln would be here somewhere. She couldn't see them in the throng.

When he saw Alys, his smile broadened even further and he made his way over to their table and bent over her to kiss her, catching her cheekbone. When he slowly raised his head to meet her friends, they were momentarily starstruck. Tim and Candace were wearing an identical crazed look, fixed smiles, unblinking stares. Mairéad's mouth appeared not to be working and hung open, giving her an uncharacteristically vacant expression. Only Douglas was in control of himself, and he spoke for the group when he thanked Aaron for his kindness and hospitality. Then Aaron was yanked back, and Alys hauled to her feet, and Lincoln pulled them into a clumsy bear hug that folded Alys's shoulders in like a concertina and crushed her awkwardly against Aaron. She caught the sharp citrus scent of his aftershave, and the hot breath that Lincoln squeezed out of him fanned her cheek and then she was released. He took off and introduced himself to the table and then sat down next to Douglas and hugged him.

'He's on good form tonight!' Alys laughed. She glanced around. 'No Kate?'

Aaron shook his head. 'No Kate,' he said with some finality. 'Are you going to sing with me tonight?'

'Are you playing?' She stalled, the familiar revolution of her stomach made worse by the acid of the champagne.

'I'm going to play a little later on. I'll come and find you.'

She looked across the room. It was full now and the clamour of voices was drowning out the band. Everywhere she looked were bright, shiny people all of whom belonged here, and there she was, in her borrowed dress that she would never have known to choose in a shop if Mrs W hadn't selected it first. Could she smell a faint mustiness from it? Was that her? She should have bought some perfume. A real woman would wear perfume.

Aaron was up on the stage now, greeting the band, summoning drinks from the bar. They broke off from playing, unnoticed by the crowd whose talking sounded like a cacophony of clacking geese. Alys watched the sharpness dissipate in Aaron; his easy banter with this group, a more relaxed, natural state for him.

'He seems a good sort,' Douglas spoke beside her.

'He is a man-legend, after all.'

They sat in comfortable silence, people-watching. Slumped against Douglas, Alys checked the time. It was still early. She could think of nothing she wanted more than to sink into bed, but could think of nothing else but having to sing. She wished she hadn't drunk so much. She had bypassed the tipsy stage and gone directly to feeling tired and rough at the edges. She felt off, as if she were wearing a jumper back-to-front.

After another hour, the music changed and a hush descended on the audience. The lighting changed too, and a spotlight appeared over the piano where Aaron had taken his seat and begun to play. She had recognised the fluidity of his style even before she looked up. He was warming up, letting his fingers fly, his body rocking back and forth slightly as he eased into it. She watched the rapt faces around her—lit up by the stage lighting, enthralled by him—and wished she too could enjoy the moment. She was finding it hard to breathe properly, and her heart had taken up residence in her ears. As if he had heard its frantic beat,

Douglas drew her closer to him. She took strength from the solid mass of him, and buried her nose into the side of his neck. She breathed the sweet smell of his skin and cedar wood like an oxygen mask. From there, she drowned out the music and it came as a shock when Douglas nudged her upright. Aaron was ready for her.

'It's wonderful to have you all here tonight to celebrate the opening of Waller. Most of you have been on the journey with me and know what goes into pulling something like this off. And so, my friends, I thank you for your patience and I promise to be a better, more present friend from here on out.' There was some laughter and heckling in the crowd, and he waved them down. 'Ok, ok, until the next time. Now. I have a surprise for you. I heard this lady sing a week or so ago and I think she's very special. She's very kindly agreed to sing a number for us tonight. Ladies and gentlemen—Alys Larsson.'

There was cheering and clapping as Alys got unsteadily to her feet. Her skirt caught in the nap of the tablecloth and an empty glass tipped over. She had been sitting too long and her hips ached when she stepped away from her friends, her heart pumping in her ears even louder now. She made her way stiffly to the stage and reached for Aaron's outstretched hand. Her own was clammy.

'You ok?' he asked. She nodded mutely. 'What do you want to sing tonight? Do you want to do the same number?' She nodded again. She couldn't seem to let go of his hand. When she faced out to the audience, she could see the faces of the people at the front tables, but not those that stretched all the way back to the bar and out wide to the wings. There was a hush as people craned their necks to take her in. A blankness came down over her like a heavy velvet curtain. She couldn't think of the first line of the song. Aaron began to play the introduction softly, tentatively, feathering the keys. Nothing came to her. She looked out to find Douglas, but her eyes caught on her own seat. There was a woman sitting in it, taking off some white gloves, one finger at a time, neatly and efficiently, her eyes trained on Alys. It was Ingrid Bergman, the planes of her beautiful face highlighted in the light thrown off by the stage, in sharp contrast to Mairéad next to her whose face was made even plainer by a pained expression.

When Ingrid Bergman had finished removing her gloves, she laid them down in front of her and sat a little straighter. There was an expectant expression on her face, as if to say. 'Well? You've brought me all this way. What have you got to show me?' Alys looked across at Douglas, who was oblivious to the figment alongside him and was looking with concern back at her, his hands on the table as if he were planning to rescue her. She looked back at Ingrid, the introduction meandering to the point where she knew she should start if only she knew the words.

The hubbub had abated, and faces were turned to the stage. She had their attention. Someone coughed in the second row. She skimmed across the eyes that were trained on her. A man who looked like Hitchcock turned a lazy head towards his partner and made a comment, his eyes on her. The woman alongside him laughed, revealing pink gums and teeth so small she might have stolen them from a child.

What was wrong with her? A thought came to her. She had been barefoot when she sung before. She slipped her shoes off and straightened up. Ingrid raised an eyebrow. The introduction started again. Over at the bar, someone heckled, a whistle, and a thunder clap of laughter ricocheted across the room. Her heart was in her ears, her stomach was in her throat. Everything seemed to be moving north. It made no difference being barefoot. She was just the usual outsider in a roomful of shiny, clean people who belonged. Laughable, in spite of her borrowed dress, trying to be something she wasn't. Who did she think she was? The difference when she sang at Lincoln's was that she had Ava on her side. Ava made her forget all about Alys Larsson. Now, here, she was firmly back to earth and she wasn't enough. She could see people starting to shift in their seats, glancing around at each other. They looked awkward, embarrassed for her. At her own table, she read pity.

Ingrid looked inquiringly at Alys and then gave a gentle shake of the head. She picked up her gloves and slowly and carefully began to draw them back on. The spotlight was so harsh on Alys. How pale and old she must look to them all. If only it wasn't so hot.

Aaron began to sing the first line, prompting her to join him, to sit with him. Alys mumbled an apology. She had to get off the stage. She kept her head down all the way until she reached the table. She couldn't look at her friends, or Aaron. She felt the weight of the collective stares of 150 people at her back. Douglas pulled her into him and kissed the top of her head.

'It's ok,' he whispered. 'I'm here. It's ok.'

They left after the next song. Aaron saw them get to their feet and blew Alys a kiss. Forgiven.

Alys kept her eyes on the exit and tried not to see the faces turned up at her. Without a word, her friends formed a loose circle around her where they could, but it made it hard to cut a path through the tables. She looked steadily ahead as if she had planned to leave at this time after all. Tim had gone on ahead to fetch the car. They waited in silence outside. A couple came out after them, gave a nod of acknowledgement to Alys who did her best to smile. When the car appeared at the end of the street, they walked swiftly as one and bundled Alys into the back as if she were a star incognito.

Alys sank her head back on the head rest, her stomach still churning. Her ears ringing in the aftermath of hours of loud music. The dashboard was lit up, but it was comfortingly dark in the back, and she was relieved that they wouldn't be able to see her face.

Tim pulled out and picked up speed, as if anxious to leave Waller behind them. He focussed on the road ahead, his driving manoeuvres so studied, he might have been sitting his driving test. No one spoke. Alys watched as London passed by them, a vast conveyer belt of shops, and street corners, and alleyways, the shabby and rundown alongside the grandiose. At times, a little architectural gem from times past, set back in between taller, starker facades, like a wonky tooth that made for an endearing smile. And everywhere she looked people, laughing, gabbling, smart-stepping out with their friends, unseeing others asleep in grubby sleeping bags in doorways. Her tired brain tried to grapple with the vagaries of life and then let the thought go.

'That was fun! So lovely to come into Town once in a while,' Candace said brightly. Tim braced himself.

Alys winced. 'I'm so sorry I ruined it for you.'

'Nonsense,' Douglas replied.

Candace agreed. 'We'd never have set foot in Waller if it hadn't been for you. People like us don't get to go to places like that.'

People like us. That was her problem—she had never learned where the lines lay for people like her. They'd only been invited because she had agreed to sing. She wondered if she should offer to reimburse Aaron in the morning.

'Besides,' Candace sniffed. 'I don't know what you're apologising for. I've never been prouder of you. You carried yourself with such dignity.'

'Except when she had to go back for the shoes. That was unfortunate,' Tim observed. Candace swivelled a level stare at him.

'I agree with Candace,' Mairéad spoke up.

'Why?' Alys said. 'Tim's right. I made a complete fool of myself. Such humiliation. I don't know what I was thinking. I—I completely lost my nerve. I just couldn't go through with it.' Tears made her voice thick.

'So, you didn't feel like singing tonight.' Mairéad brushed it off. 'You got your glad rags on, you showed up. Those folks will forget all about you by next week, believe me. Look it, we weren't looking for the perfect performance tonight. We were going after courage. It takes courage to do something different at our age, Alys. Harder still after all those years of playing it safe. That's what gets my applause.' Tears trickled out of the corner of Alys's eyes and pooled underneath her ears. She settled back into Douglas's side and kept watch as London slowly peeled away to darker stretches of motorway, then leafier suburbs, then a string of small villages where the houses were dark—the occupants already in their beds, amber street lights keeping watch.

It was after midnight when Tim finally slowed to a stop outside Douglas's front gate. Douglas let them in and they made straight for the stairs, without turning any lights on, their feet dragging on the steps. Alys slipped her dress off and left it where it lay. She pulled her nightie over her head, then brushed her teeth, washed her face clean of the grime of London air and got into bed. She lay for a moment, reliving the evening's events, searching for the point at which it had turned a corner. It had been wrong long before she'd reached Waller. She thought of Ingrid Bergman and how straightforward she had appeared, as if she were looking directly at Alys and seeing her for herself. She had not been unkind, just matter of fact. Alys thought about courage and all the ways that one could be brave in life, and she got out of bed and walked across the corridor into Douglas's room. It was dark, made darker by the frames on the walls. Douglas stirred, then froze when he saw her silhouetted in the doorframe. She closed the door quietly behind her and, carefully lifting the corner of the bedclothes, she climbed in beside him and closed them over her again, her head on the pillow, her eyes on his profile in the dark. He settled back down and she could feel the tension in his body against the expanse of sheets. His bedclothes smelled of him—his woody cologne, the sweet masculine scent of skin. She closed her eyes and slept.

Chapter 47

First Night

The first thing that swam into focus when she woke was a Giant Blue Morpho, its iridescent wings shimmering in the early morning light; alongside it, a tiny orange butterfly with brown tipped wings she didn't recognise. Douglas's side of the bed was empty, so she lay and stretched her legs and continued her perusal of the butterflies. Rather than being macabre, it was beautiful to wake up surrounded by them, as if she had lain all night under a multicoloured canopy that only came into view when the light shone through it. When Douglas finally appeared in the doorway, he hesitated as if awaiting permission to enter his own bedroom. Alys sat up, and her earlier ease gave way to shyness.

'I brought you a coffee.' Douglas, awkward in his pyjamas, proffered her a cup and then stepped back, unsure of where to go. He decided against climbing back in beside her, and instead perched on the corner of the bed and attempted to cross his legs.

Alys was going to apologise for her presence, but couldn't think of an explanation of why she had decided to sleep there. It had just felt the natural thing to do at the end of a trying day. Instead, she turned their attention to the butterflies.

'I've been lying here playing the Butterfly Game.' The Butterfly Game had been a favourite of theirs. Whenever Mr Weatherley allowed them to look at his specimen cases, Douglas and Alys would spend hours covering the labels and trying to memorise the Latin names of the butterflies. If you got all the specimens in a case first time, you got a lick of a Sherbet Fountain. Alys loved those Saturday mornings, walking down to Balfour's newsagents, pooling their pocket money, then sitting with a butterfly book, trying to match the pictures to the actual butterflies in the cases.

Douglas grinned. 'How did you do?'

'Must try harder.' She grimaced. Awkwardness crept back in.

'Douglas, I'm sorry if I...'

'What are you up to today?' He stood up, cutting off whatever she was going to say.

She took his cue. 'I thought I'd watch some Ingrid Bergman movies, and then I promised I'd see Enid. She'll want to know about last night.' She grimaced again. 'You?'

'It's my Saturday on. Busy today. I'll not be back until after six.'

'I'll make us something nice for dinner.'

'I'd like that.'

'You'll need to get changed.' Alys threw back the covers and sprung out of bed. Douglas averted his gaze.

'We're like a couple of 1950s newlyweds after our first night together,' Alys laughed and was relieved to hear a slow chuckle from Douglas, but he wouldn't turn to face her, and she knew that he was blushing.

Chapter 48

The Thing with Feathers

She started with *Casablanca*, of course. She'd seen it before, but this time she focused on Ingrid Bergman, whose tremulous vulnerability had made her the star of the film and a screen icon. Alys had never liked *Casablanca*. She always felt sorry for Ilsa Lund, having to sacrifice her true love for a lukewarm version with Victor Laszlo and his cause. She had always wanted Ilsa to tell Rick that she had changed her mind. She didn't want him to do the thinking for them both after all, that she was perfectly capable of making her own decisions and had decided to stay. She despised Victor for his hypocrisy—accepting all that admiration for being so noble, when really he was just as selfish as the next man—so willing to accept Rick's lie, knowing all the time that he was keeping Ilsa from what she really wanted.

She chose *Indiscreet* as an antidote. Colour, glamour, sparkling wit and the elegant Cary Grant—who knows a good thing when he sees it and keeps the woman. Ingrid Bergman was beautiful and radiant and honest and funny and tender all at once.

A bowl of hot soup, and Alys watched another, *The Inn of the Sixth Happiness*. This time Ingrid Bergman played a missionary who ventured out to China, took the name Jen-Ai and, against all the odds, made a life for herself in a war-torn province, saving orphaned children as she went. Alys replayed the film in her head as she later made her way to The Granary. It was her favourite of the films, but still she couldn't grasp the essence of Ingrid Bergman. For all her talent and natural style, Alys couldn't see the woman. She told Enid as much when she saw her.

'Did you read the book I gave you?' Enid asked.

'Yes, I devoured it in one sitting.'

'Well then, there's the woman. I wasn't talking about her films being inspiring. I was talking about her life story. You should read over it again a bit more slowly.'

Alys followed Enid into the old stables area. An adjunct to the main barn, the shape of its sloping ceilings made it lower than the high ceilings of the main store, but it had beautiful stable doors that opened on to a courtyard garden that Enid never had time for. She used the area for additional storage. 'Give me a hand with these boxes,' she called over her shoulder. 'I'm having a clear out.'

Enid threw open the stable doors. 'Put them there for the time being. Someone's going to collect them in the morning.' They worked slowly and purposefully. Enid the brains, and Alys the brawn of the operation. Even so, it seemed to tire Enid and, before too long, Alys pulled up some chairs and fetched Enid a glass of water.

'What are you doing with all this clearing out anyway?' Alys asked.

Enid ignored her. 'I want to hear how last night went.' She listened carefully as Alys explained in detail the disaster that was to be her debut.

'So that was your answer? You didn't want to sing after all.' Enid hooted.

'No, I suppose I didn't.' Alys pondered this. 'I don't want to sing in front of big crowds. It feels like a private thing to me. I wish I'd known that before I went up on the stage.'

'What about this Aaron fellow? Any good?'

'A very talented pianist.' Alys answered primly.

Enid tutted. 'You know what I mean.'

'You look like one of those old women who sits outside brothels.' Alys sniffed. 'I like him. He's a very kind, gracious man and he is extremely sexy. But he's not for me. For one thing, I couldn't compete with all the other women who fling their knickers at him and he's never around—his work is his life. Besides, I'm not ready for a relationship. I'm not sure I'll ever be ready for another relationship. I am still married, after all. And even if I weren't, I think I would want someone I could count on, someone I could trust. I wouldn't want another man I'd have to try to keep up with. I'd want someone I could just be myself with.'

Enid buried her smile in her glass.

'So what's all this? Why the spring clean?' Alys changed the subject. 'Are you going to do something with this garden? It could be so beautiful.' They both looked out uncertainly over the courtyard. A stack of broken garden furniture took centre stage. A small, dying tree languished in the corner with old circulars caught up by the wind and wrapped around its base. Weeds poked up between the uneven stone slabs that made up the floor of the garden.

'It obviously needs a good sweep up,' Alys began.

'I'm going to retire, Alys. It's time for me to think about the next stage in my life.'

'You can't retire!' Alys started.

'I can't go on,' Enid retorted. 'Oh, my mind's alright, I reckon I could go on for decades, but my buggering body has let me down. You see how hard it's getting for me to move the stock around. Some nights I can't even get up the stairs to bed. It's only a matter of time before I have another fall. I'm tired, Alys. It'll break my heart to do it, but I have to make a sound decision whilst I still can. Sit down, dear. It's hurting my neck to look up at you.'

'But where will you go?' Alys sank back into her chair, deflated.

'I have my sister. She lives close by in a very nice bungalow. She's been asking me to live with her for years. I've been putting it off because of her bloody cats, but I think she and I will be good company for each other now.'

'But what about this place? You can't sell it.'

Enid shook her head. 'No, I won't sell it. I want you to take it over.'

Alys stilled. 'Me? Run this place. Are you joking?'

Enid looked grave. 'I'm deadly serious.'

'But I couldn't do what you do here.'

'Of course you could,' Enid said. 'You've been doing it alongside me for years. It was always in my mind to pass it on to you. You are passionate about books, excellent with the customers—far more patient than I am, I think we can both acknowledge that—and it's time the place had some fresh thinking in it. It needs to develop and evolve and you will bring that.'

'Enid, I—I don't know what you think you know about my circumstances, but I really don't have any money to my name. I don't want Jack's money. I am living at Douglas's for a reason. Even if I could do the job, I couldn't afford to give you what this place is worth.'

Enid hushed her. 'I know all that. Here's my proposition: I will be moving to Sheila's in two weeks' time, at which point you are welcome to stay with your Douglas or move in upstairs and have your own place to yourself. I'll come and work a handover period and we'll split the profits. When you're comfortable, I'll become a sleeping partner. We'll agree a fair split of the revenue—I won't need much—and you can run it and make alterations as you see fit. When I die, my will stipulates that The Granary transfers to you outright.

'Mine?' Alys still couldn't take in that Enid was leaving. Everything that came after was a blur.

'Yours, child.' Enid smiled gently.

'I couldn't. I—I'd mess it up. I'd break it.'

'Alys, you once asked me how you become someone. You do it by committing to something that you love and think is important, by working hard for it. That thing can be a person, but it can also be a place or an ideal. Do you understand what I'm saying? If you want to find yourself, there's the map. Think about it.'

She took the long way back, stopping off to buy some aubergines and herbs, rolling Enid's proposal around as she walked. No one had ever done anything like this for her before and the consideration of it, Enid's careful planning, made her cry. There was something else there as well. A fluttering of excitement? Could she run it by herself? She saw now how stealthily Enid had prepared her over the years. There was very little that Alys didn't know about the business. It would mean a lot of work, but she'd have Enid to help at first and then perhaps she could persuade Candace or Mairéad to join her. She vacillated between wild imaginings and outright terror, and all the while the thing with feathers sat preening on her shoulder.

Home again, she began to prepare dinner, slicing the aubergine and gently frying it until it was golden, blending fenugreek, cumin and nigella seeds, and dry roasting them so that the kitchen was filled with their aroma.

The responsibility was daunting. Enid had worked so hard to build up The Granary. What if Alys ruined her life's work? When had Alys ever made a success of anything? Enid had told her to think about it, that there would be no hard feelings if Alys decided it wasn't for her. The shop would come to her anyway, and she could always sell it and do something else with the money. She thought about Enid's beautiful apartment and how it could be hers—small, cosy, with her favourite things around her. She imagined the linen bedding she'd always coveted, the handmade crockery she had collected over the years stretched out over the shelves along the kitchen. She pictured Douglas, Mairéad and Candace, and maybe even Tim, coming for dinner, their knees pressed up around the tiny dining table, their laughing faces candlelit. She thought how it would feel to have a home that felt all her own, with the work she so loved waiting for her below. When Douglas came home, she pressed a glass into his hand and told him her news.

'Well, of course, it makes perfect sense,' he reflected. 'That sly old fox.'

'Don't you think it's the most ridiculous idea? I mean, imagine me running The Granary. We'd be bankrupt in a week.' She attempted to pass it off with a laugh that petered out halfway through.

'You're doing that thing again when you apologise for

yourself, Alys. It's like getting the first punch in before someone can hurt you.'

'But why would she do something like this for me? She must be losing her marbles.'

'On the contrary, Enid is the most clear-sighted person I know. I wouldn't argue with her judgement, Alys. In fact, I think you'd make a perfect proprietor. You've breathed books since you were a child and Enid knows that. She sees you for who you are.'

Tears sprang to her eyes.

'So you really think I could do it?'

'I really think you could do it,' he said solemnly.

'Thank you, Douglas.' Her eyes met his, her smile tremulous.

The phone rang—a shrill and strident note—and they both jumped.

Alys checked the screen. 'It's Jack,' she said quizzically. She hadn't heard from him since Lincoln's party.

'Hey...' Her face changed from polite surprise to solemnity.

'Oh Jack, I'm so sorry. Is there anything I... Ok, I'll be over as soon as I can.' She ended the call, her eyes on Douglas. 'Tom died. I need to go to Jack.'

'I'll call you a taxi.'

Chapter 49

Compassion

She let herself in with her key. She found him in the study, a bottle of whisky at his side, his eyes red-rimmed. She sank down to the floor and hugged his knees. He reached down, put both his arms around her, and began to sob. Incoherent ramblings spilled over her, Jack's wet face against her hair. She was speechless in the face of such loss. The desk lamp held them in its orbit, and she rocked back and forth, bring him with her movement, soothing him all the time, her own tears falling silently. When his sobbing subsided, she put the whisky away and fixed him some supper, coaxing him to eat as if a small child. He ate, crying, struggling to swallow.

Tom had died, not on the golf course as Linus had predicted, but in his chair, Hannah busy in the next room.

'He was always so distant, wasn't he? I mean, it didn't matter what you did, it was never enough to earn his approval. I'd have had to have been Elon fucking Musk and it still wouldn't have been enough.'

She thought back to Hannah's party. Did he know he

was going to die? Is that why he had shared so much with her?

'Oh, I think he loved you deeply, Jack. I think he struggled to find the words to tell you.' She told him of their last conversation, bringing another bout of sobbing from Jack.

'I loved him so much.' He quietened. 'I always knew he loved you. That was the one thing I did that did please him—marrying you. I got that right.'

She hushed him. It felt wrong to talk about their marriage now.

Silently she led him upstairs, drew him a bath. He was passive, accepting of her direction, letting her undress him, her hands running over the familiar terrain of his skin dispassionately, as if she were a nurse and he her patient. She eased him into the water and he pulled her in after him, kissing her as she slipped against him. It was a sweet kiss, and her mouth opened as if responding to an old call, him cradling the back of her head, holding her to him. She allowed herself this, and when she felt his chest begin to heave again, she gently disengaged and pulled back. Her sleeves and top soaked through.

She left him to clear up the kitchen. The house was stark and cold, and she moved through it as a stranger would. Afterwards, she towelled him dry, found him some pyjamas and changed into one of his sweatshirts herself. When she tucked him into bed, his eyes were already drooping.

'Don't leave me,' he mumbled. She sat on the edge of the bed and stroked his hair, slowly and methodically, as Ava had done for her. Her eyes on his face until she saw him sink into sleep, his breath slowing, deepening. She rose quietly and, turning the lights out on passing, called for a taxi from the kitchen, breathing deeply in the night air as she went out to meet it.

Douglas had left her dinner on a plate, covered. It was late and her appetite waned long before. She climbed the stairs wearily. He had left his bedroom door open slightly. She hesitated for a moment, suspended in indecision, before moving on to her own room.

Ingrid Bergman was sitting at the foot of her bed, eating an ice cream.

'Hello, Ingrid Bergman,' Alys said, as if it were perfectly natural that she would be there.

'Good evening, Alys,' Ingrid Bergman said.

'I hope you don't mind, but I don't think I can face a conversation just now,' Alys said.

When she woke, the diffuse morning light made everything slightly blurry. She lay for a moment, adjusting to wakefulness. Ingrid Bergman was sitting at the foot of her bed, eating an ice-cream.

'Is that the same ice cream?' Alys asked.

'No, a different one,' Ingrid Bergman replied.

Chapter 50

The Lion Inside

'I was the shyest human ever invented, but I had a lion inside me that wouldn't shut up.'

Ingrid Bergman

'It's funny how you figments always visit me when I'm in bed,' Alys mused.

'Nonsense,' Ingrid Bergman said. 'I came to see you at that club.'

'You didn't stay very long.'

'You didn't sing very long.'

'I didn't sing at all,' Alys said ruefully.

'You were out of your depth, my dear.' Ingrid Bergman matter-of-factly finished her ice-cream.

'Could you not have told me before I went up on the stage?'

'I thought you knew! Besides, where would the fun have been in that?'

'I'm not sure I experienced fun.'

'Ah, but didn't you feel alive? You are never more alive than when facing down a challenge! You must always have challenges in your life. You can't regret these things, Alys. You have to take what you have learned and move on.'

'I learned that I'm not Ava Gardner,' Alys mused.

'There you are, then. It was worth it, after all. Of course you're not Ava Gardner. You are Alys Larsson. You are just making a pretty bad job of being Alys Larsson.'

Alys sat upright. 'Why are you here, Ingrid Bergman?' She felt it only right to address her by her full name.

'I'm here at your invitation, Alys. I imagine you need my help to sort out the tangled web of your life.'

Alys wrinkled her nose. 'I'm not sure I'd call it a tangled web exactly...'

'What would you call it?' Ingrid Bergman's blue eyes unblinking.

Alys thought back over the weekend—her humiliation at Waller, her passing attraction to Aaron, sleeping with Douglas, Enid's proposal, the news of Tom's passing, Jack's kiss that still lingered with her.

'A bit complicated,' she conceded.

'So you see, you do need my help. Oh, I may be an international screen icon, but first and foremost I am a very practical, down-to-earth Swede, honest to a fault, and I know what it is to live a complicated life. I'm also hungry and I always think better when I eat. How about you rustle up a little breakfast and we can hatch a plan?'

Alys sighed and threw back the covers.

'I'm not sure I did invite you, you know,' she said grudgingly, as Ingrid Bergman beamed at her.

Douglas had risen early. The aubergine curry had been replaced by a fruit salad and a note reminding her that he was with his rambling club, and would be home late afternoon.

She made scrambled eggs on toast and watched as Ingrid Bergman cleared her plate, drank two coffees and lit a Gauloise.

'So,' she said, her tone turning businesslike. 'Tell me about Jack. I know the backstory—no need to go over old ground—I want to know what he is to you now.'

'You don't mess around, do you?'

'I don't have time to waste, and neither do you. Who is this Jack to you?'

Alys began to pick at the fruit salad, weighing her answer carefully. She didn't know who he was to her, or how she felt about him. She had to work through the heartbreak of him not loving her anymore and, as painful as that had been, she had moved on. It surprised her how quickly. That part of her, the part that had adored Jack, had been cauterised. There was no feeling in the scar tissue that had formed over the wound.

Then there was his kiss last night, and she had to admit that she could still respond to him on some level. His need for her was a new, strange development. He had sounded regretful, as if he missed her, but she put that down to his grief.

'He's still my husband,' she offered.

Ingrid Bergman tutted. 'So?'

'When you're married to someone for so many years, of course they are significant to you.'

There was a loud sigh.

She thought back to Lincoln's party and how liberating it was to realise that she no longer needed to try to please Jack, that she no longer had to worry what Jack thought of her. She hadn't felt that anxiety in months now. Since she'd left, in fact. Had Jack not made the decision to end their marriage, she would still be there, scrabbling around, trying to make him happy. She thought about how relaxed he had looked before he'd seen her.

'Actually, I don't think I was a very good wife,' Alys mumbled. 'I don't think I ever really understood Jack. Of course, I'm not sure he ever took the time to understand me, either. We were strangers, really. Trying to make each other something we needed.'

'You're a stranger to yourself,' Ingrid Bergman pointed out helpfully.

'I think I realised that after he left me. I've been trying to find myself ever since, but I'm starting to think that I'm going about it the wrong way. I'm just going through the same old pattern that I always do. Wait for someone else to tell me what to do, how to think. I just seem to let events steer me.'

'Ahh, that's why you invited me!' Ingrid Bergman slapped her thighs gleefully. 'I've got to tell you, I'm sort of relieved because I'm not sure I've got the patience for your love life. But if there is one thing I was always very good at, that was listening to my own voice. I trusted it and it never let me down. This is what you must find, Alys. You must learn to listen to your intuition, even if it's buried deep, even if you can only hear the faintest murmur.'

Alys was silent for a moment. 'I don't think I have an intuition.'

'Of course you do,' Ingrid Bergman scoffed. 'You're a woman, aren't you? Oh, you can't hear it because of all the noise in your head—all that shame, and duty, and anxiety about what other people think of you. Do you imagine it was any less noisy for me? The American public had me down as some saint, a farm girl bursting with rude health, a madonna. Always they need some stereotype, some box with a label to put us in so that they can understand us. I was so high up on that blasted pedestal, they couldn't see the real woman. Then when I left my respectable husband and little girl for Rossellini—well, I fell off that pedestal so hard, it took them seven years to get over it. But here's the thing, I heard my own voice loud and clear over their clamour and I followed it. I have never regretted anything I did because it was my voice that drove me. I never was content to stay in the box.

'Of course, if you haven't been listening to your voice, it gives up. "What is the point," it cries, "when she doesn't want to hear what I have to say?" You have to coax it out, Alys, you have to show it that you're ready to hear beyond the tin whistles and the drums.

'Let's try again. Think about something that you need to make a decision on. What about your friend Enid's offer? What does your intuition tell you about that?'

Alys closed her eyes and concentrated. At first, she heard the clamour, the voices telling her that she was too flaky to take on such a huge undertaking, that she would make a mess of it as she had so many times before, that people would laugh at her—another Faulkener in a village shop—that she should stick to what she knew. Beyond that was a worry that she was only considering it to please Enid, because she didn't want to hurt her feelings. Was she letting events steer her as she always did? Doing whatever was asked of her, with very little thought as to whether she wanted to do it or not? Was she doing the same with Enid's proposal?

But then a warm feeling flared deep in her gut, like a small ginger cat curled up, purring.

'I think my intuition might be a ginger tom.'

'Very good.' Ingrid Bergman seemed unsurprised. 'What does the cat say?'

'It says that I should say yes.'

Ingrid Bergman laughed. 'There you are, Alys.' She jumped to her feet. 'Let's go swimming. I always think better when I swim.'

Alys took Ingrid Bergman to the swimming spot. She looked every inch the screen goddess and the healthy farm girl as she stripped down to her underwear and strode in. She was a strong swimmer and swam upstream for a while before drifting back to Alys.

'What does the cat say about Jack?' she asked as she windmilled her arms over her head in a lazy back-stroke.

Alys listened, but the ginger tom was nowhere to be found.

'The jury's out.'

'Let me ask you this question—When have you been yourself with a man, Alys, not hiding, not trying to be someone else?'

Alys floated on her back. The night before had been the first time that she could remember being herself with Jack, without trying to be something other or appease him, she had just stepped in and taken over without thinking. All those years of marriage and she couldn't think of another example of when she could just be herself, the way she always was with Douglas. She never thought about it when she was with him. She was too caught up in their conversation or one of their little adventures. She thought again about how natural it had felt to climb into bed with him. Whoever she was with him, that was her. She detected a faint purring.

'What about you?' Alys asked. 'When were you yourself with a man?'

Ingrid Bergman sculled around a little. 'Well, I didn't always get it right. I gave up too much control sometimes. My first husband, Petter, was a little like your Jack.' She tipped her head further back in the water. 'A relationship is a fluid thing. Sometimes the boundaries blur between you and the other, you know? I think if you have a strong intuition, you always know when you've gone too far and what you need to take back.' She rolled over on to her stomach. 'I loved each of my husbands. If the marriage didn't work, it was as much my fault as theirs. I was always so driven, you see. Work meant everything to me. Still, I have no regrets and we remained good friends. I think that matters most to us and to our children. I may not have been the perfect wife and mother, but I never pretended to be. That was for others to think of me and they didn't know me so well. No, I wasn't perfect, but I came to the conclusion that you can be good enough at a lot of things, and that will carry you through with your head above the water.'

Later, as they sat under blankets, drinking hot coffee from the flask, Ingrid Bergman turned to Alys. 'Why did you not have any children?'

Alys choked back her coffee. 'Are you always this direct?'

'Yes, I think so. Why not? Could you not have any? I imagine someone like you with a big brood of unruly mop heads around your hips. Did you not want any?'

Alys tightened her blanket around her.

'Oh, no, I wanted them alright. I wanted nothing more than to have a big family. My brother and I had a sparse sort of upbringing, chaotic in many ways. I always dreamed that I'd give my children a very different sort of experience—all the stability and unconditional love we didn't have growing up. For the first years of our marriage, I had to accept that Jack was busy establishing himself. I told myself that there would be time for children, and that he was an ideal father, making sure that our children would be born into a safe and secure foundation. I was very grateful for his commitment.' Her mouth twisted downward. 'But, when a few years after that he still didn't seem interested, I began to worry. I was never one of those people who took for granted that you wanted a baby and it happened effortlessly. I didn't want to leave it until the last minute. I pressed him as far as I could. In fact, it was all I could think and talk about and eventually, he gave in and said we could try.

'A year went by and nothing happened, and I arranged for us to see someone about it. The consultant was lovely, insisted there was nothing we needed to worry about, it just took time. I became obsessed, I suppose, and then one night Jack lost his temper. He told me that he didn't want children, had never wanted children in spite of everything he had told me before we were married. It turned out that for the whole year we had been trying, and he had watched me turn myself inside out, sat and comforted me as I cried, reassured me, in the background he'd been doing everything he could to make himself impotent. I'd noticed how rarely we made love, and how much more he'd been drinking, but I put it down to the pressures of his work. It turned out that he'd even taken himself off to hot tubs and saunas, sitting on heated seats, taking prescription drugs, anything he thought might limit our chances. He had expected me to give up sooner. He hadn't realised how badly I'd wanted a family.'

She was silent for a moment. 'He really didn't know me at all.'

A moorhen dashed out over the water ahead of them, emitting a plaintive cry as it went.

'You asked me what Jack is to me. Whatever it is, it changed from then on. I could never quite forgive him for such cruelty, such selfishness. He should have been clear from the outset. He should have at least given me the choice about something so important, and to watch me suffer all that time without compunction, without remorse. I don't think I've ever forgiven him for it.' She lapsed into silence again.

Ingrid Bergman took her hand and kissed it hard, but Alys's frozen fingers felt nothing.

Chapter 51

Old Wound

She was silent on the way home and was so lost in her thoughts she couldn't have said when Ingrid Bergman left her. She was just suddenly aware that she was alone, and she was grateful for the figment's tact.

It had a been a long while since she had picked at that old wound of hers. Of course, she had been furious when she first discovered what he had done, but her anger was nothing to the devastation she felt. She could have left him, she was still a relatively young woman, but she had loved him still, in spite of his deceitfulness. Besides, she had told herself, even if she had left him, there was no guarantee that she would have found a suitable partner with whom she'd want to have children. Single men of their age were not plentiful. There was nothing to say that she would have been able to have a child, anyway. She had all the arguments stacked up in favour of staying. The simple truth was that she was too scared to start again. She had only herself to blame for giving up on her dream.

With each year that passed, she grew a little sadder, fighting a flicker of desperation, hoping that Jack would change his mind, but he never did. He was content to assume that his wife had come to her senses at last. It didn't occur to him that the 'flakiness' that had started to grate on him was really an attrition, a stealthy unravelling of all that she had believed of herself and their life together. She became a ghost to herself. She had never once asked, until he'd left her, whether he was worth the price she had paid.

She thought about Ingrid Bergman as her eyelids slipped down that night. She had said that you couldn't regret anything. You had to learn from the experience and move on. You had always to listen to your voice, she had counselled. Whose voice had she been listening to when she decided to marry Jack, and then when she decided to stay with him? She thought of all the little turning points throughout her life to date, all those seemingly inconsequential decisions she had made that had brought her to this point. How many of them had been shaped by her voice? She lay as quietly as she could and in the stillness she listened for the cat.

Chapter 52

Finding Joy

Alys had taken Mairéad for breakfast the following morning, and told her of Enid's proposal and her decision to resign. To her surprise, Mairéad blinked furiously.

'You're turning soft,' Alys told her.

'Never.' Mairéad wiped her eyes staunchly. 'You know, Alys, I am very proud of you for getting out from under the duvet and squaring your shoulders. You've created a life of your own. I know you berated yourself for not singing that night at Waller, but I think your voice is a quieter one, isn't it? No less powerful. I hope you always listen for it, and I hope I get to hear more of it.' She sniffed. 'It is also hugely satisfying to see that my bullying has paid off.'

Alys reached across the table and grasped Mairéad's fingers. Her own eyes welling with tears.

'Thank you for bullying me, Mairéad. I couldn't have done it without your relentless invasion of my privacy. You made me see that another life was possible.'

Mairéad waved her off to dab at her eyes. 'Of course,

you'll need some help with the business. Someone good at finances and the like,' her brisk tone changing the subject.

'I will.' Alys smiled and at last she felt a release of excitement, bubbling up into her throat, making her light-headed. 'Mairéad, I think this is what joy feels like.'

Tim was looking harassed and exhausted, and her resignation did nothing to improve his mood.

'But why, Alys? What have we done? Aren't you happy here?'

She paused for thought. 'I'm not unhappy here. But that's the point, Tim, I'm just languishing.'

'Are you bored? You've outgrown your role, that's it. God knows, I've offered you a promotion every year for decades now. What else could I have done? I hate managing people—I'm just not cut out for it. Do you need more money?'

'It's not you, Tim. It's me. I need a change. Have you ever had the feeling that you just wanted to shuck off everything and start again?'

To her alarm, Tim's face crumpled and his chest sagged. He knew exactly what she meant, he said. He was in love with Candace and had been trying to leave Fiona for over a year, only he was a coward and couldn't pluck up the courage to tell her how he really felt. He didn't deserve her—Candace, that is—although he didn't really deserve his wife either. The only thing he was sure he deserved was a good thrashing. The news of her resignation was lost in the all-consuming angst of his self-loathing. He agreed to a month's notice if she promised to continue some proofreading from The Granary to fill the gap until he could find her replacement. Distraught, he might as well have been agreeing to sign over the deeds to one of his kidneys for all the notice he took. She celebrated what felt like progress with a fresh cup of coffee. Ingrid Bergman was sitting on the edge of her desk, eating an ice-cream.

'What are you doing here?' Alys hissed.

'You said you were tired of people always showing up in your bedroom. I simply wished to see where you worked. Besides, I can't sit around all day. If I'm not working. I go crazy.'

Alys sat alongside her, cradling her coffee. 'I did it. I am officially off the books.'

'How does it feel to heed your own voice and take the first step?'

'Very strange,' Alys conceded. 'I'm getting to be me. That's a very hard concept to get my head around. Just the idea that I have a choice about what I want. I don't know what to think about that. If I think too hard about it, the realisation that I always had a choice could crush me.'

'We never look back, Alys,' Ingrid Bergman said briskly. 'We keep our eyes firmly on the horizon. This is what it feels like to be courageous. Can't you feel the vitality in the action?'

'Who are you talking to?' Mairéad asked curiously, balancing a stack of printer paper in her arms.

'Ingrid Bergman.' Alys waved a hand at her guest, who was engaged in gnawing the chocolate off the wooden choc-ice stick.

Mairéad looked around. 'Is she here? Can you see—dead people?' Mairéad whispered.

'No, of course not. I'd never have had you pegged as superstitious. She's a figment.'

Mairéad looked blankly at her.

'Of my imagination,' Alys added for clarification.

'Oh well, then.' Mairéad sounded unconvinced.

Douglas had been subdued when she told him of her decision to move out. 'You're leaving?'

'I can't ponce off you forever, can I?' she joked.

'Can't you?' He looked crestfallen.

'Douglas, you don't want me hanging around you all the time, like a bad guest who doesn't know when to go home. I'm cramping your style.' There was a brief moment of thoughtful silence as they both pondered Douglas's particular style, and whether or not Alys's presence cramped it.

'I am so grateful for you swooping in and rescuing me as you did. I don't know what I'd have done without you, but this time I think I need to learn how to be on my own.'

Douglas twirled his wine around his glass. 'I'll miss you.'

'I'll be a stone's throw away.'

'Not the same.'

He stirred himself and raised his glass. 'To you, Alys Larsson. It has been my privilege to be your best friend all these years and I wish you every happiness in your new venture.'

She reached over and kissed him lightly on his cheek, just as he moved away and her mouth brushed the side of his mouth. She lingered, close to him. 'Thank you, Douglas. For everything.'

Chapter 53

Life Well Lived

Tom's funeral was held on the same day as Enid finally left her home of 30 years. There was no room for the larger furniture at her sister's house, so they arranged that Enid would bring her bed, but leave the rest for Alys as her 'starter kit'. Mairéad and Candace stepped forward to accompany Enid to her sister's, and a red-faced Tim, commandeered into dismantling the bed, was glad to see Douglas when he appeared to lend a hand. Douglas had offered to accompany Alys to the funeral, but it had been something she wanted to do alone. As it happened, she wasn't alone. Ingrid Bergman came with her.

It began as a crisp spring day, and Alys thought how pleased Tom would have been to have a clear day for it. He had always hated the rain. Ingrid Bergman came as far as the church door, and then sloped off to read her book in the graveyard. She was engrossed within moments, tendrils of smoke from her Gauloise around her face, oblivious to the throng that was gathering. Flanked by her boys, Hannah looked every part the formidable mafia widow with a wide-brimmed black hat, like a large crow with its wings outstretched.

Jack had been looking for Alys, and he jumped a little when he saw her and beckoned her to join them in the family aisle, but Alys, giving a little wave to the boys, shook her head. Lincoln had saved a space for her towards the back. Hannah registered her arrival, but turned back to the front without acknowledgement. Alys had no intention of returning to the house afterwards, and it occurred to her that the back of her mother-in-law's head would likely be her lasting memory of her, and she was at peace with that. When Jack had called with the funeral details, he assured her that the family had been told of their split. She hadn't asked for their reactions. She had belonged to the Larsson family only in name. They would reform over the hole that she left, a shiny lacquered veneer, as if she had never existed.

Listening to the gentle undulations of the vicar's eulogy, she reflected on the richness of Tom's life, the young athlete he started out as, the scientist who took his skill into the corporate world, his adored wife and successful boys. He hadn't got it all right, but he had made something of value of his life, and she listened for the turning points that had created it. How much was simply down to good fortune and how much was due to decisiveness? Jack followed Linus's recitation of Psalm 23, stumbling over the Derek Walcott poem *Love After Love*, his voice hesitant and strained. Alys let the words land inside her as they told her to find herself, the stranger she had ignored for another, urging her to feast on all the little details that went to make up a life well-lived. Was he speaking for Tom or for them?

Jack came to find her after the burial. She was standing under a small tree the shape of an umbrella, which was covered in blush-coloured blossom. A light breeze coaxed a few of the flowers to drift to the ground.

'It was a lovely service. So many people here. You must be very proud.' She smiled.

'I am,' he agreed. 'I was hoping to persuade you to change your mind about coming back. We'd love to have you there.'

She shook her head. 'Thanks, Jack, but I think it's best I don't. It's easier for everyone, don't you think?

'He left you some money, you know? He changed his will after I told them about us. He said, knowing you, you'd walk away empty-handed, and he wanted to take care of "his daughter".'

Alys was aghast. First, Enid, now Tom. What had she done to deserve their love? She thought about the disdainful look that Hannah had cast at her in the church.

'I didn't know. I don't know what to say. He was full of surprises, wasn't he?'

Jack's eyes reddened, and she pulled him back against the tree and held him close to her, waiting until the rise and fall of his shoulders settled.

'I made a mistake, Alys,' his voice hoarse against her neck. 'Things are just not the same without you. I miss you.'

'Sssh,' she soothed.

'No, I need to tell you some things. Things I should have said a long time ago.'

He struggled to find his words, this man so articulate in normal times.

'I'm so sorry I ruined things. I blamed you for giving up on our marriage and being so distant. It made me feel so rejected. I knew it was my fault. I just didn't want to admit that I'd made a mistake.'

In the darkness of those days after he had left, she'd have given anything to have heard him say these words.

'Come back to me, Alys. I'll be better. I'll be a proper husband. I'll be whatever you want.'

She winced and then paused to consider the difference between what we want and what we need and how so often they aren't the same. He took her silence for hesitation.

'Think about it, ok? Just think about it for me? I'm not pressing you for an answer now. Just think about it.'

'Jack, I—'

He shut her off with a swift kiss. 'I have to go. Our car is leaving. Think about how good things could be between us. You owe us that at least, Alys.'

He straightened up when he stepped out from under the canopy, brushing off the blossom from his shoulders. She watched as he strode over to his family, the familiar jauntiness back in his stride. The boys blew kisses to her, and she gave them a wave back. She wondered what he had told them. She hadn't even had a chance to tell him that she was taking over The Granary.

Ingrid Bergman was sitting on a low stone wall, smoking a cigarette. They set off up the lane towards the bus stop. They'd be in time for the 4.30 if they hurried.

'Thanks for coming, Ingrid Bergman.'

'Did you hear your voice? You heard it, didn't you?'

'Yes, I did. My own voice. It wasn't the ginger tom, after all. I think that was just hunger.'

'You know, I'm curious, why do you keep calling me by my full name?'

Alys slowed. 'I read somewhere that when you went to Hollywood, they wanted to do a studio makeover, to change the way you looked, your name. The way they always did in those days. You were only a young woman, you must have been 24 or so, but you told them, "I am Ingrid Bergman. That is my name. I'm going to keep it."'

Ingrid Bergman nodded. 'It's a good name. I like it.'

'You knew who you were,' Alys said.

Chapter 54

Bader and Fairbanks

She let herself into Douglas' house, poured a glass of Chablis to toast Tom with, and then made her way upstairs to the bathroom. As the bath was running, she went back down for the bottle. She stayed in the bath until the water went cool, thinking about Tom and what he had done for her, trying to remember his little kindnesses over the years, but coming up with very little. If he had ever thought of her as his daughter, he had kept his cards very close to his chest. Perhaps it was only later on in his life that he came to see her as such. People were capable of change, after all. Her thoughts drifted to Jack and his unhappiness, and how he was on a journey of his own, whether he knew it or not.

When she heard the front door close and Douglas call up to her, she stirred and lifted herself out of the water. She wrapped her dressing gown around her and went to her room. Her small things were stretched out across the dressing table where she had begun to pack them. She took down Cinderella Mouse and gently wrapped her in gauze. Her hands rested on Douglas Fairbanks, Douglas Bader and his sardine tin aeroplane, and slipped them into her pockets.

Douglas was making a pasta sauce when she joined him. He and Tim had successfully reassembled Enid's bed for her at Sheila's, and they had all gone to the pub afterwards to celebrate the move. Alys wished she'd been there. He was trying to curb his good spirits out of consideration for the day she'd had, but she loved his excitement and wanted to hear what he thought of Enid's apartment, her new home.

'You'll be very happy there, Alys. It's very "you",' he said.

He was right. If one's identity could be a place, The Granary would be hers.

She told him about Tom's gift, but held back from talking about Jack and his offer, partly out of respect for Jack and partly because... well, she couldn't have said.

After dinner, she gave him the two Douglases and the sardine tin aeroplane.

'I made these for your birthday, but I thought you might as well have them now since I'm moving out. A small thank you.'

He marvelled at their shiny eyes, the expressions on their faces, the tiny leather flying jacket, the pipe.

'Which one did I grow up to be?' he wondered.

'Both, of course!'

He set the Douglases up on the kitchen shelf, amidst the cookery books where they gazed benignly down at them as they cleared up in companionable silence. When Douglas went up for a shower, Alys stayed behind to turn the lights off and lock up. In the living room, she started when she saw that the ruby glass cabinet had finally been exorcised, replaced by a small walnut cabinet which housed Douglas's vinyl collection. Running her finger along the colourful spines, she permitted herself a slight smile, barely noticeable in case Mrs Weatherley had decided to linger. Soames appeared from the seat of Douglas's armchair and carved a line around her shins. She caught a faint purr.

'I'm going to miss you two when I go,' she whispered. She turned slowly about the room, taking in the little details that made it Douglas's, so that when she turned the light out, the imprint of its tranquillity and comfort stayed with her.

She took the stairs to bed. His bedroom door had been left slightly ajar. She pushed it slightly with her finger. It opened a crack to show the room in shadows, the edge of the bed, before it gently returned to its resting place. A moment's breath, then she pushed it further and slipped inside, closing the door behind her. Roused by the door closing, Douglas half-rose, waiting to see what Alys wanted. He was bare-chested and Alys took in the lines of his body, its strong contours uplit by the orange glow of the street lamp through the curtains. When she took off her dressing gown, he reached across and pulled the covers back for her, settling them over her when she lay down with him. Their heads on the pillows, their faces close, stock still, butterflies overhead. In the dim light, she caught the intensity of his expression, the way his eyes darkened. She reached out a finger and traced along his cheek bone, grazing the side of his mouth, along his jawline and down to rest in the hollow of his throat. He leaned forward so slightly that, if she hadn't been watching for it she would have missed it, and she met his mouth with hers. For a second they held the beat, offering the other the chance to change their mind and retreat, then her eyes closed as her mouth opened and he was kissing her. When her head rolled back, she brought him with her as if locked on and the kiss deepened. Her fingertips tentatively sought out his skin. His hand stroked the line of her hip to pull her against him, then moved up to graze the underside of her breast.

Everything he did was exquisitely slow and methodical, and she caught a memory of the boy he had been, his earnestness when holding in his palm something of infinite worth to him. When he rolled on top of her, he held his weight in check, and paused, looking down at her, as if he needed to say something but then couldn't summon the words.

'What's wrong?' She tried to keep the tremor from her voice.

'Is this ok for you?' he stuttered.

'Is it ok for you?' she countered.

He hesitated.

'Actually.' She put her hand against his chest and pushed him back. 'You're right. I'm sorry, it's been an emotional day. I'm not myself. This is too weird.'

He sat up, watchful. 'Of course. Forgive me.'

'I'm worn out, and I should leave you to get some rest too.'

She levered herself up from the bed and quickly reached for her robe. She didn't trust herself to say more.

Closing over this door, she scuttled into her own bedroom and crawled into her own cold bed. It felt damp underneath her. Holding herself in check, she went through the motions of climbing back out of bed and finding some pyjamas, and still she couldn't warm up, although her cheeks were burning. Her chest felt as if someone had dropped an anvil on it, and then weighed it down with a full set of Encyclopaedia Britannica, and then sat on the top of the pile, and for a while she focused on taking one ragged, aching breath after another. There were no tears, as if her body had dried up and shrivelled at this latest sting of humiliation.

That was what listening to her voice got her. '*Ah, but didn't you feel alive!*'

What had she been thinking? She hadn't been thinking rationally. Her guard was down. It had been an emotional day with the funeral, Tom's gift, Jack's declaration, Enid moving on, layer the Chablis on top, and she could see how her thinking had become confused, distorted. She had listened to her body and it wanted Douglas, whose body had clearly wanted hers up until the point when it didn't. What had she done to make him change his mind? Even her best friend, who loved her more than anyone, had sensed her wrongness and pulled back.

That was the problem. She should never have tried to make their relationship something more than best friends. She might have ruined everything. What if they couldn't go back to the way they were before? She was struggling to marry up the pieces of what Douglas meant to her. It had become complicated. Something had changed for her and as soon as she acknowledged that, the figure sitting on the Encyclopaedias hopped off, taking the books with him. The anvil on her chest toppled sideways and with her first full breath she understood what had happened. She was surprised to find her cheeks were wet.

Chapter 55

A Singular Set of Circumstances

She was dreaming, but her dream was a memory. She was the age she was the summer her parents took her to the village fair for the first time. The fair people arrived every summer, the leaflets strewn through the streets the days before their advent, stirring up a maelstrom of excitement in the otherwise humdrum existence of the villagers. The grown-ups complained of the litter, the shopkeepers kept a watchful eye of the fair folk when they appeared in town. The children were starry-eyed with longing and their excitement seeped into the stalwart, stodgy bastions of everyday life in the village. Some sort of summer madness caught them all up when the fair came to town. Every front room sported a new globe fish tank with two identical goldfish in them, one of which was always destined to die within the first week.

Alys was beside herself with excitement at the thought of earning a goldfish from her own endeavours, and bringing it home in a plastic bag. Her brother was too small still to understand the enormity of their adventure. He had outgrown the pram that their parents pushed him in, and his head banged uncomfortably against its metal frame. There was the darkness of the night, and the novelty of being taken out after tea when really it was bedtime. There was the sound of carousel music in the air, and as she got closer, she heard the farting sound that the generators made behind the rides, and caught the smell of popcorn and candy floss. Her hand lay loose in her mother's hand in the dark. They could have been going anywhere at all, and little Alys wouldn't have cared because they were going together, and the excitement caught her up, making her speak in tongues to release the energy in her. She was skipping and jumping lopsidedly, trying to lever herself into the jumps using her mother's limp hold on her, and all the time her eyes shining with possibility and hope. They reached the perimeter of the fairground, delineated by the harsh light that lit up the grass on the common, turning something familiar into a luminous other.

She woke before they stepped into the orbit of the fairground. In that semi-lucid, drowsy state, she reached back for the memory of that small child so gleeful, so hopeful of what was to come. Her instinct was to reach out and take the child's other hand and swing her high into the night sky and lower her down until her soles slapped on the pavement.

Love rose up in her for that child, for herself, so fierce that it made her eyes sting with tears. She reached her hands around her shoulders and rocked herself gently, wishing that her love could reach back along those long years to tell the child who didn't know what was ahead of her, what would become of her, what she needed her to hear. If the figments had taught her anything, it was that this was all she had. Underneath it all, the essence of her had been waiting in all its wonky strangeness so patiently for her to recognise and claim it. She thought of the Derek Walcott poem. She thought of Mairéad and her doggedness. She knew then, with some certainty, that things would be alright, and there was nothing left for her to fear. She had already been through the worst of it.

She met Douglas on the stairs. He was in the process of precariously juggling two over-filled cups of coffee, and his tongue was firmly stuck to the left side of his mouth as a counterbalance.

'I was coming up to find you.'

'I was coming down to find you.'

There was a tricky moment when she tried to rescue her cup from him, but his scorched fingers had locked on to the handle. Then the awkward thought bumped against them that, if they continued upstairs, they would have to sit on a bed somewhere, so he reversed and they regrouped in the living room.

She took a sip of coffee and burnt her lips. 'I see you got rid of the cabinet.'

'I gifted the glass to Mairéad's mum. Apparently, she cried when she opened the box.' He shook his head in amazement.

'It feels more you in here.'

'Well, it was time.'

'About last night, I'm so sorry, I...' she started.

'Please, Alys.' Alarm suffused his face. 'It was my fault entirely.'

'Your fault?'

'Entirely. I should have respected how emotionally wrought you were.'

'It was me who got into your bed,' she added wryly.

'Because, as you said, you weren't thinking straight. Why else would you have?'

Why, indeed? Alys imagined Ava raising an eyebrow.

'With your permission, Alys, perhaps we could draw a line under an unfortunate night, a singular set of circumstances.'

It's only his circumstances, it's not the man himself.

'Of course.' She nodded. 'Of course, that makes sense.'

'Now, I know that you have taken the day off to move, and I'm afraid I also arranged to take today off to help you. Obviously, that was before we—before last night—and I would absolutely understand if you would rather not. I see now that I should have checked with you first. Please, be honest. I can arrange to go into work and mill around for a bit instead...'

'I would very much like your help, Douglas, thank you, but there's something I need to do first.'

Chapter 56

The Sixth Happiness

Jack took a while to come to his door. As she suspected, the brothers Larsson had seen their father off as any good Viking would and had not gone to bed. Jack hadn't been home long. The pallor of his skin showed up the dark smudges under his eyes like stripes of war paint.

'You look terrible.' She handed him his sweatshirt.

'I feel worse.' He moved aside to let her in.

She told him of her plans to move to The Granary when his back was turned to her. She didn't think she would get the words out if she had to look at his haunted eyes. He was methodically counting scoops of coffee into a jug and he froze for a second before continuing—a slight tremor in his hand.

'I should have given you children,' he replied.

'It wouldn't have made a difference, Jack. It would have just made things more complicated now.'

He turned back to her.

'Ah, but it would have made all the difference, Alys. You see, you would have been happy. I know that. Having a family was everything to you. If I'd given you that, you would still love me and I wouldn't have had to see that hurt in your eyes every time I looked at you.'

'I did still love you,' she protested, but he shook his head.

'Not the way you did before. You did that thing you always do when you're stressed. You went away in your head and you didn't come back to me—not wholly, not as my Alys.'

'So you're saying it was my fault?' An edge to her voice.

'No,' he said emphatically. 'All mine. I was just terrified of not making a success of myself. Kids didn't fit in. Pure chaos. They'd have just been a distraction. I started climbing the greasy pole and every time I stopped, I knew, I knew it was all pointless, but I kept buying all this shit to make it worthwhile, to justify myself. You saw it. You were always smarter than me. You saw it for what it was. As time went by, the more I bought, the less you cared, and I had to work even harder to keep the emptiness at bay.' He was crying now, wiping his sleeve across his cheeks to stem the flow. 'The truth is, I was terrified of the thought of you having a baby. What if I'd been no good? I couldn't take the risk of ending up like my dad.' He sat down at the table, his head bowed low. 'I'm sorry, Alys. We should have been a family. I'm sorry I did that to you.'

'I'm sorry that I can't try again,' she said and, reaching forward, she took his hands in hers and steepled their fingers.

'I'll tell you something, Jack Larsson. I don't regret us for one minute. You are family to me. You always will be.'

He pulled her into him and she folded herself into his chest, arms reaching around him, and there they stayed, their coffee cooling beside them.

Finally, she extricated herself to smooth his hair back from his face and kiss his cheek, her lips pressing into him with her blessing.

'You know, you should watch *The Inn of the Sixth Happiness*. It's an Ingrid Bergman film. She's in China with a missionary she's just met and the old woman lists the happinesses—wealth, longevity, good health, virtue and peaceful death in old age.'

'That only makes five.'

'Ah,' Alys said. 'The sixth you have to find for yourself. You know in your heart when you find it.'

'Have you found yours?'

'I think I'm getting there.' She rose to her feet.

'Is there anything you want from here for your new place?' He cast a doubtful look around.

'No, you're alright.' She followed his gaze. 'I'm looking for a clean slate.'

He began to follow her to the door.

'Oh, wait a second.' He disappeared into the study and returned holding something in his hand.

'I should return this.'

'Yellowstone Bear!' Alys crooned. 'That's where you got to!'

'I took him. I'm not sure why,' Jack admitted.

She curled Jack's fingers around the tiny bear with his hopeful smile. 'He belongs with you, I think.' She smiled.

Chapter 57

Alys Alone

'A kiss is a lovely trick designed by nature to stop speech when words become superfluous.'
Ingrid Bergman

Douglas was waiting outside The Granary with a box of cleaning equipment.

'Everything ok?' His tone was casual.

'Never better,' she said brightly, letting them into the bookshop. They stood inside the door, like trespassers, listening for footfall. Streams of golden sunlight festooned the shop, and Alys breathed in the familiar smell of the books.

She took her time walking through the ground floor, marvelling at how high the ceilings were, how expansive a space it was when empty. She had never been there without Enid, and the old woman's absence was palpable. Douglas was still hovering just inside the door, giving her time to take it in. When she returned to him, her eyes were shining, as if one of the shards of sunlight had beamed down into the top of her head and lit her up from within.

'I can't believe she gave it to me. I can't believe all this is mine.'

He shrugged. 'It was always the plan.'

'So you did know!'

He shrugged again, uncomfortably.

'Why didn't you say?'

'That would have been highly inappropriate. Not my place at all.'

She took the stairs to the apartment two at a time, running her hands along the empty wall where Enid's photos used to hang.

'I'm afraid you'll want to give it a bit of a clean,' Douglas called up to her.

She tiptoed into the kitchen where the doors of the empty cupboards lay ajar. She trailed a finger along the side of the little kitchen table, perfect for one, and spun on her feet, her excitement rising as she walked through the living room. Enid's mid-century furniture without Enid's clutter was strikingly beautiful. The old rug that had covered the floor had been rolled to one side, revealing wide wooden boards, dusty with a fine coating of sand. The walls sported pale patches where her paintings used to hang, as if plasters had been ripped off.

She could hear Douglas on the stairs, taking his time so that she could stake a claim for herself. When she got to the bedroom, instead of the empty room she was expecting, she found a large wooden bed. 'Douglas!' she shouted.

'Do you like it?' he said nervously. 'I wasn't sure. We can take it down again if it's not what you'd like. It's made of cherry wood. The mattress is new.'

'Where did you find it?' She gasped.

'It's a funny thing, but Tim came up with it. His wife bought it in France, had it shipped over, all without checking the measurements first, and it didn't fit in their bedroom. It's been languishing in their garage. A bit of a sore point between them, to be honest, so they were glad to see the back of it. Tim told me to tell you not to expect a leaving present.'

She threw the windows wide to let fresh air flow through as she dusted, fits of sneezing interrupting her efforts from time to time. She filled buckets of hot soapy water to wipe down surfaces and got on her knees to tackle the floor. Housekeeping had not been one of Enid's strengths and, judging by the grime in her living quarters, it had been beyond her capability at the end. Alys was in her element, singing as she moved through the tiny apartment, tipping bucket after bucket of grey water down the sink. She had tied her hair back with a polka dot scarf, and her face and clothes got dirtier with every room she cleaned.

Douglas came back and forth with her belongings. He had affixed a small cart to the back of his bike, which only allowed him to bring a few boxes at a time. With each journey, he stopped to make them coffee and marvel at her progress. When he brought the last of her clothes up, he found her sitting in a newly inherited armchair, streaked with grime and grinning from ear to ear.

Late afternoon, they pushed open the side doors and tackled the courtyard together as the sun tipped over its apex and started its descent. The boxes had already been cleared by Enid's handyman, so all that remained was for them to sweep the old cobblestones and drag out a table and some chairs out into the centre. When Alys went up to shower, Douglas set out again and returned with platters of Parma ham, crusty bread, marinated tomatoes and olives, and a selection of cheeses. Alys spread an old tablecloth on the table in the courtyard, found the stump of an old candle, and arranged their supper while he opened a bottle of champagne. There were no champagne glasses, so they made do with a brandy glass and a mug with 'World's Best Dad' on the side.

'To you, Alys. To your beautiful new home and this exciting new chapter. May it bring you your heart's desires.'

'To us,' she added solemnly and felt her cheeks flush. *What had become of 'us'?*

'It's so lovely out here. I never understood why Enid didn't make something of it. Some big pots, some garden furniture, a few fairy lights. It could be magical.'

She had forgotten to bring down plates and cutlery, and both were too tired to venture upstairs, so they ate with their fingers. Picking at the cheese, they watched the sun sit on the top of the wall before sliding rapidly behind it and leaving them in the dusk.

Alys wedged the candle stub in the top of the champagne bottle and lit it. 'You know, my favourite film of all time?' she asked. '*Calamity Jane*. Doris Day is this whip-cracking, sharp shooting stagecoach messenger in Deadwood, Dakota Territory. She's always swiggin' likker, and shooting off her gun, and starting fights you know she can finish better than any man there. She doesn't act like a woman of the times, because no one ever taught her how to be. She's this feral, wild spirit and then a lady's maid, Katie Brown, pretending to be a famous singer, comes to town to entertain the men and they both like the same man.

Calamity is ashamed of herself and her coarse ways and, after a few false starts, Katie teaches her how to be a lady. It's like Pygmalion in the Wild West.

'When I was young, I loved that they made her what passed for pretty and feminine in those times. I still remember Doris's blue, blue eyes and that yellow dress she wore. But what I loved most of all was the home she made for herself. She and Katie transformed her rundown, filthy old wooden cabin into a place that was clean and homely with gingham curtains in the window, a painted front door, and it was so cosy and so safe and they sang this song together about how a woman's touch can make all the difference. I think really that's all I ever wanted when I was growing up. To have a tiny cabin like she had all of my own.'

'And now you do.' Douglas smiled.

'And now I do. I couldn't stop thinking about that film today when I was shaking my dusters out of the window and tipping the dirty water away—how I was like Calamity Jane making a home for myself. Now when I think about that film, though, it makes me angry. They tamed her so that she could be lovable. She'd finally learned to behave, and her reward was a strapping Howard Keel as a husband. That storyline sticks in my craw.'

'What would you have for her now, then?' Douglas asked, amused.

'Oh, rend the yellow dress from seam to seam, I say! Have her ride bareback with the wind in her tatted hair, and give me the bone-gnawing, earth-eating wildness of her!'

Douglas took his wallet out of his pocket and fished a slightly crumpled photo out of it. 'I've been carrying this around. You should have it—as a reminder.' It was the picture he took of her when they first went swimming. She looked like a water sprite, wild and natural, grinning up at him. 'And with that, I'll take my leave of you and let you get some rest. Are you sure you're going to be alright here on your own?' He looked doubtfully up at the barn as it rose over them, watchful in the darkening sky.

'Of course!' Alys blinked. 'If Enid could do it, why not me?'

'Why not indeed?'

They brought in the remnants of their feast, and Douglas made a show of locking all the patio doors. He took an age to reach the front door, tacking off to turn the lights out here and there. She too found reasons of her own to call him back to see a treasure she'd discovered, to help with one last job. Finally, when their procrastination was becoming an embarrassment, she saw him to the door. She reached up to hug him and memories of the night before flooded back into her body as it curved to fit against his, liking this new formation of them. He held her tightly for a while, his hands fanning out across her back, and then she felt his lips rest momentarily on her cheek before he released her.

'Thank you so much—for everything, Douglas. I don't know where I'd be without you.'

He shrugged. 'You'd be busy being Wild Alys, that's where you'd be.'

'And where would you be?' she murmured, her eyes on his.

'Ah, where indeed? Stultifying in my mausoleum of women's clothing, I imagine.'

'You could join me on the wild side?'

Douglas looked pained. He took a moment before replying and when he spoke, his voice had a finality about it. He released the hand he'd been holding.

'It's not as easy as that, Alys. Some of us weren't meant

to be wild. We're not all as brave as you. Best left at that.' His parting smile was kind, his eyebrows raised regretfully.

She nodded, thanked him again, closed the door quickly before he saw her eyes fill, and she rested her weary body against the back of the door, all bravado seeping out of her. She was Alys alone, and it didn't feel as exhilarating as she'd imagined it would. She told herself that she was tired. It had been a long day, yet she couldn't face going to bed. Slowly she drifted around the bookshop, its floor floodlit by street-lights, the bookcases looming over her like avuncular guardians smiling at her foolishness. She couldn't believe that she had tried to seduce Douglas a second time. What was wrong with her? She was so needy. Was there no end to the humiliation she was prepared to expose herself to? Had the figments taught her nothing?

Garbo would never tell Douglas that her feelings for him had changed. She would keep that locked down tightly and carry on as before. Ava would lock herself away to suffer the loss of hope and then spring back as ebullient as ever. Ingrid Bergman would accept the end of the affair with equanimity and settle for friendship. A small patch of light lay in the central aisle and she stepped into it and examined her bare feet for a while. They looked ghostly in the diffuse light, and she wriggled her toes and listened for her voice. It told her to tell Douglas the truth—that the real Alys, wild or not, had fallen in love with him, no matter what he felt for her. Real, lasting love for no other reason than because he was Douglas Weatherley, who knew what a hummingbird moth looked like and who took her swimming, who could be so absorbed in a crime thriller that he wouldn't hear pan lids banged together behind him (she knew, she'd tried), who often laughed without making a sound, and who made the best tea, and who was the best friend and, bizarrely, the best kisser and who smelled like cedar wood, and whose constancy and kindness made her feel safe and enough as she was. Something like a deep calmness descended on her then, warm honey running down the sides of her, pooling at her feet. 'Now I feel alive,' she told the books. 'This is what it feels like.'

Across the room, she heard someone try the front door. The handle creaked a warning before the door flew open, banging the wall behind.

'I thought I told you to lock up behind you. I could have been anyone!' Douglas cried in exasperation.

She gazed at him beatifically from her pool of light.

'What's wrong?' He reached her in seconds and pulled her towards him, trying to read her expression.

She shook her head, smiling, and his eyes became very still and darker than ever. He kissed her then. Her fingers came up to his jaw and fumbled to the back of his head, and she held him to her, her eyes squeezed tightly shut with all her emotion and love channelled into her kiss as they rocked backwards and forwards slightly in the light. When they pulled apart, they were drowsy with languor.

Douglas tilted his head back to look at her. 'I love you, Alys Larsson. I have always loved you. I don't just mean as a best friend, I hasten to add, but properly.' He cleared his throat. 'As a man loves a woman. I have waited a very long time to tell you that. I need you to know that no matter what happens, no matter what you choose to do in life, I will go on loving you. I have no doubt that I will love you until my dying day. Possibly beyond. Who can say?' A little frown appeared as he was momentarily distracted by thoughts of the afterlife.

Alys kissed him back to her, tiny, swift kisses fluttering over his face like the brush of butterfly wings, whispering over and over how much she loved him. Then she threaded her fingers between his and led him upstairs. She took the stairs slowly. 'What made you come back?' she called over her shoulder.

'I asked myself, What would Douglas Fairbanks do?'

Chapter 58

Opening Night

Late Summer

'When I'm old and gray, I want to have a house by the sea. And paint. With a lot of wonderful chums, good music and booze around. And a damn good kitchen to cook in.'
Ava

The doors to The Granary lay wide open to the balmy summer evening. Inside, tiny fairy lights lined the bookcases and, to the newcomers, it looked like a library in a doll's house. Music tinkled out over the floor, mingled with the chattering guests, and wafted out into the side courtyard where Candace was milling in between them, a tray of canapés held high over her narrow shoulders. She turned back inside and followed the music to its source—a far corner where a cluster of old armchairs had made way for a glossy piano. Aaron, getting into his stride, opened his mouth obligingly for a chilli prawn from her as she went past. She snatched up his empty glass from the top of the piano and signalled to Tim for another rum coco, passing out the last of the canapés to those hovering around the piano before returning to her new office—the latest addition to The Granary; Tom's Cafe. Alys had renovated the side stable to incorporate a small coffee bar where Candace ministered to the caffeine-deprived Saturday morning fathers and on weekdays, other regulars who would vie for the outdoor tables in the side garden. On Fridays, Candace took care of Mairéad, who had negotiated part-time hours with a bewildered Tim so that she could write crime fiction. Every Friday morning, Mairéad would set herself up at a small table under a skylight and tap away furiously, her face twisted into a scowl as she wrestled with her plot, stopping only occasionally to snarl, 'Are you going to buy that?'

This was the official opening of Tom's Cafe. Earlier, before the guests had arrived, Alys took her two friends up to her apartment for a glass of champagne, leading them past her newly assembled gallery of photos—picnics at the swimming hole, dinner parties with their faces glowing in the candlelight, a sleepy photo of Douglas and her, another of Enid and her on their first day as business partners. She presented each of them with their own tiny thing. To Candace she gifted a tiny bird of paradise, exquisitely crafted with sequins, silk and sparse tufts of coloured feathers. To Mairéad she awarded a miniature Boudicca, her face fierce under a knitted brow, her body strong and resolute.

Now, as Candace oversaw the catering, Mairéad and Enid hunkered down into armchairs, waving an imperious arm for refills and cackling like witches. At their feet, a small brown dachshund with a round tummy dozed, oblivious to the noise around her. From time to time, Mairéad would lean down to rub her ears, drawing a little sigh of contentment from her.

The flock of Alys's small things had been dispersed throughout the shop. Some peered out at customers from the haberdasher's case, but the remainder peeked out from high shelves, and observant children could often be heard squeaking with delight at a sighting of a squirrel or a badger between the books.

Douglas was in the courtyard, deep in conversation with Jack and his new girlfriend, a keen hiker he'd met on the trail, a single mother to four-year-old twins.

Alys and Lincoln were behind the bar, mixing jugs of their signature cocktail. Alys was wearing a red dress that showed off the rich colour of her hair, the red lipstick Candace had applied earlier now staining her lips. Her cheeks were glowing in the heat, her eyes shining, and she was laughing. Someone called at the bar to tell her that Aaron was asking for her and she caught the opening bars of *Feeling Good* by Nina Simone—her cue. She quickly washed her hands, wiping them on the sides of her dress, and pushed her curls out of her face. She stepped out from behind the bar and moved across the shop floor in her bare feet to join Aaron.

As she went, her face broke into a broad smile and she could have been Grusinskaya from *Grand Hotel*, or Maxine Faulk from *The Night of the Iguana*, or Jen-Ai from *The Inn of the Sixth Happiness*. Or just plain old Alys Larsson.

The End

Acknowledgements

I first met Alys in the bath. That is, the image of a woman with her toe in a bath tap came to visit me and took up residence in my head. For several years, we co-habited. My friend, Manuela, would regularly ask after her. I wrote a few half-hearted bits of novels but my thoughts always circled back to the woman in the bath. What was she doing there? Was she stuck? Waiting for something or someone? Or was she... languishing?

I was journaling in a café one day, wondering what it meant to be a woman in middle age. When so many of our roles and the things we've based our identity on have shifted, I pondered, how do we find ourselves again? It struck me that there were very few role models for women in midlife. Off the top of my head, I could only come up with that sexy genius, Helen Mirren.

The woman in the bath gave a splash. I'd caught her attention. She'd been languishing after all. From that point on, I started to flesh out a woman who had reached middle age with no clear sense of who she was; someone always on the margins of female friendship and life in general. What if this woman had resigned herself to a half-life but then something happened to force her to reinvent herself. Without contemporary role models, who would she turn to for inspiration? Who else but the goddesses of the silver screen! Not their idolised, sexualised personas but the real women beneath who, despite the studios, had managed to preserve a quiet power. These women had something to teach her about what it was to be a real woman. They helped her draw on the parts of her that were always there, just lying dormant.

The seeds of *Alys Larsson* were in the palm of my hand. The trouble was, I'd spent thirty years scribbling and journaling but never managed to get anything over the line. I knew that something had to be different in the way I went about things so I signed up to the Bestseller Academy with Mark Desvaux and Mark Stay. Their podcast, The Bestseller Experiment, had kept cheerful company with me on my lockdown ramblings. I am so grateful for Mark D's faith in me and his encouragement, Mark S's skilful mentoring and generous support and the wider community at the Academy. It really is a special place and I'd highly recommend it if you're one of those people who is waiting not writing.

In addition to my mentors, I'd like to plant a kiss on the cheek of the writer Tara Marakat who was Alys's first reader and an invaluable font of wisdom and love–thank you, Dear Heart!

Thank you, Monday Night Club fellow writers, Jac Harmon, Mark Hood, Robyn Sarty and Nicole Stillwater for helping me keep my foot on the pedal.

I'd also like to thank my special friends in Belfast who read and reviewed Alys Larsson for me. Thank you, Cathy Johnston, Jenny Lowry, Julia Mascery, Debbie Park, Sharon Ramsey, Gill Riley, Nicola Stinson and Zoe Wilcox, for your love and kindness. Thank you, Nic, for your maverick PR moves and for hosting a magical book club party in Alys's honour. (I knew I'd made it as a real writer when you all talked about the book for five minutes and then hit the fizz.)

Lastly, and mostly, I'd like to thank my beautiful family for the encouragement and freedom they give me. If I were Alys, I'd have made you each a tiny thing but alas, my love and deep gratitude will have to suffice.

About the Author

'Denise McGahan lives in an old stone farmhouse in the hills above Belfast with her family and a clattering of animals. Alys Larsson is her first novel.

www.denisemcgahan.com

twitter.com/Denise_McGahan

instagram.com/DeniseMcGahanBooks

Printed in Great Britain
by Amazon

18455279R00196